Past Echoes

Michael Harmon

Copyright © 2024 by [Author or Pen Name]

All rights reserved.

No portion of this book may be reproduced in any form without written permission from the publisher or author, except as permitted by U.S. copyright law.

Contents

1. Chapter 1 — 1
2. Chapter 2 — 7
3. Chapter 3 — 14
4. Chapter 4 — 20
5. Chapter 5 — 25
6. Chapter 6 — 30
7. Chapter 7 — 35
8. Chapter 8 — 41
9. Chapter 9 — 49
10. Chapter 10 — 56
11. Chapter 11 — 61
12. Chapter 12 — 67
13. Chapter 13 — 78
14. Chapter 14 — 86
15. Chapter 15 — 97

16. Chapter 16 — 104
17. Chapter 17 — 113
18. Chapter 18 — 118
19. Chapter 19 — 126
20. Chapter 20 — 137
21. Chapter 21 — 142
22. Chapter 22 — 154
23. Chapter 23 — 161
24. Chapter 24 — 174
25. Chapter 25 — 179
26. Chapter 26 — 187
27. Chapter 27 — 194
28. Chapter 28 — 199
29. Chapter 29 — 206
30. Chapter 30 — 216
31. Chapter 31 — 224
32. Chapter 32 — 231
33. Chapter 33 — 237
34. Chapter 34 — 243
35. Chapter 35 — 249
36. Chapter 36 — 257
37. Chapter 37 — 266
38. Chapter 38 — 274

39. Chapter 39 280

40. Epilogue 286

Chapter 1

"Sunshine."

"Wake up." Rough hands jolted her from a deep sleep, and her eyes snapped open, heart racing in a moment of mild panic. As her vision cleared, she found her little sister's face staring back at her.

"We're here," Ben announced from the driver's seat.

Sunshine blinked, her gaze drifting from her sister to their new home. She stared as It loomed against the pale sky, its brick walls weathered by time.

The family climbed out of the vehicle, each of them pausing for a moment to take in the grandeur before them. Ben and Vivien wasted no time heading toward the front door.

Violet perched herself on a nearby stone wall while Sunshine remained frozen by the car, her feet rooted to the ground as though the earth itself refused to let her go any closer.

Sunshine could feel the air grow colder the longer she watched. There was a weight to the place, a sense that it was watching her just as she was watching it.

Ben strode up to the door with a grin, ringing the doorbell. He turned quickly, wrapping an arm around Vivien, pulling her close. "I love it. Don't you love it, hon?" he asked, his voice eager. "I mean, it looks even better than it did online."

Vivien nodded, though her grip tightened around Hallie, cradling the dog to her chest as her eyes swept over her surroundings. "Yeah, it's—it's interesting," she added, her voice trailing off.

Sunshine hesitated a few feet behind, her feet dragging as she walked up to stand beside her sister.

"Great," Violet muttered dryly, tilting her head toward Sunshine with a smirk. "We're the Addams family now."

Sunshine shot a glance at the house, then at Violet. "Yeah, except they liked their creepy mansion,"

Ben turned toward his daughters, waving them over with exaggerated exuberance. "Hey, buzz kills, get over here!"

Reluctantly, the sisters trudged toward him, stepping into the reach of his outstretched arm.

"Isn't this place amazing?" Ben asked, desperate for at least one positive comment.

Violet pressed her lips into a thin, unimpressed line. "Hmm."

"Having a splendid time here in jolly old Hill House," Sunshine's voice dripped with sarcasm as she recited the familiar line from Shirley Jackson.

"It's a classic L.A. Victorian, built around 1920 by the doctor to the stars at the time. Just fabulous," Marcy, the realtor, announced as she led the family through the halls. Her voice was thick with sales pitch enthusiasm, though her words were directed mostly at Vivien. "These are real Tiffany fixtures, original to the house. As you can see, the previous owners cherished this place like their own child. They restored everything."

"Gay?" Vivien asked.

Marcy raised an eyebrow and gave a knowing smirk. "What do you think?"

"Tiffany. Wow." Ben mimicked, sidling up between his daughters as his eyes scanned the vintage light fixtures. Sunshine let out a quiet snicker.

Their footsteps echoed across the checkerboard floors as Marcy guided them into the kitchen. "Do you cook?" she asked Vivien with a practiced smile.

"Viv is a great cook," Ben cut in, quick to praise his wife. "I got her cooking lessons a few years ago, and she ended up teaching the teacher a few things."

Sunshine locked eyes with her sister, mouthing, "Kiss ass," prompting Violet to suppress a laugh.

"Cooking lessons. How romantic," Marcy remarked, her tone half-amused, half-unimpressed. She shifted her gaze to Ben. "Aren't you a psychologist?"

"Psychiatrist."

That was Sunshine's cue to make her escape. While her family continued to engage in conversation, she slipped away to explore the corners of the house on her own.

Sunshine wandered through the halls, her footsteps soft as she traversed the old wooden floors. Her fingers grazed the smooth mahogany walls, feeling the cool, polished surface beneath her touch. The home was undeniably beautiful—elegant, with a timeless charm. For a fleeting moment, she thought to herself, Maybe living here wouldn't be so bad.

A sudden breeze brushed against the back of her neck. Sunshine froze mid-step and a strange heaviness settled in the air around her. The feeling was unmistakable—someone, or something, was behind her.

Heart pounding, she slowly turned, her eyes scanning the hallway. But to her dismay, there was nothing. No shadow, no movement—only stillness.

Sunshine shook off the unsettling sensation, forcing a breath before stepping into the next room. Hallie's barking echoed off the walls but she barely registered the noise. She snaked her arms around herself, her movements slow as she let her eyes drift over the small details of the room. The faint scent of dust and age lingered despite the cleanliness.

"When I saw the pictures of this room online, I thought maybe you could use it as your music room," Ben suggested as he, Vivien, and Marcy stepped into the room where Sunshine had been quietly standing.

Sunshine glanced over her shoulder, a small, almost shy smile tugging at the corners of her mouth.

"Are you a musician?" Marcy asked, her eyes narrowing with curiosity.

"Pianist. A very good one, in fact," Ben chimed in proudly before Sunshine could respond.

Sunshine nodded. "I'm hoping to get into Juilliard next year."

"If you're as good as your father says, I'm sure you'll have no problem getting in," Marcy encouraged with a warm smile.

Ben wrapped an arm around Sunshine's shoulders, giving her a gentle, reassuring squeeze. "She gets the musical talent from Viv. She plays the cello."

"Used to," Vivien corrected without much emotion, her attention seemingly elsewhere. She walked over to the peeling wallpaper, her fingers brushing against the delicate, crumbling edges as if lost in thought.

"Why'd you quit?" Marcy asked, shifting her focus to Vivien.

"This wallpaper's peeling over here," Vivien said aloud, ignoring the question as she tugged gently on a loose corner, revealing a glimpse of something beneath. "Looks like there's a mural underneath it."

Marcy's eyes widened with sudden realization. "The last owners must've covered it up. They were modernists," she said, almost apologetically. "Speaking of the last owners... full disclosure requires that I tell you about what happened to them."

"Oh, God... they didn't die in here or anything, did they?" Vivien asked, half-joking, as she joined the group while Violet, cradling Hallie in her arms, strolled into the room.

Marcy didn't miss a beat. "Yes, actually, both of them. Murder-suicide," she replied matter-of-factly. "I sold them the house, too. They were just the sweetest couple. You never know, I guess."

Vivien and Ben exchanged wide-eyed, stunned looks, while Sunshine's mouth fell open in disbelief.

"Well, that explains why it's half the price of every other house in the neighborhood," Ben murmured, his voice trailing off as he processed the information.

Sensing the tension, Marcy quickly offered an alternative. "I do have a very nice mid-century ranch, but it's in the Valley, and you're going to get a third of the house for twice the price."

Ben nodded slowly. "Right."

"Where did it happen?" Violet asked, her interest piqued.

"The basement,"
Violet's lips curled into a smirk. "We'll take it."

Chapter 2

Sunshine absentmindedly twirled the pencil between her fingers, her gaze flicking between the whiteboard and her AP Calculus teacher, who was deep in the intricacies of equations. Every so often, she jotted down key points in her notebook, her handwriting neat and precise. As she leaned forward, her tongue grazed her bottom lip in quiet concentration, absorbing the information.

It was her senior year—the year—and the pressure was beginning to mount. If she wanted to impress Juilliard, she had to be flawless. There wasn't room for distractions. Her thoughts briefly wandered to the house, hoping that by the time she got home, her piano would be settled in, along with the rest of her family's belongings. Once it was in place, she could finally lose herself in hours of practice, refining every note for the audition that could shape her future.

Her gaze drifted to the side, drawn to a hushed conversation just beyond her desk. She subtly observed as the boy next to her leaned in, speaking low and steady to the person beside him. Their exchange was smooth, almost rehearsed, and as she watched, he coolly slipped a small plastic bag into the customer's waiting hand. In return, crisp bills were passed back with barely a word spoken.

The corner of Sunshine's mouth tugged upward in faint amusement. Drugs weren't really her thing—she had learned that the hard way. After getting caught stealing her father's prescription pads to score Adderall, she had made a conscious effort to rely on her own energy and focus to push through. But now, as her senior year loomed large and Juilliard was on the line, she felt the familiar temptation gnaw at her resolve. She wasn't taking any chances.

As soon as the bell rang, Sunshine wasted no time. She quickly shoved her notebook into her backpack, slinging it over her shoulder, and darted out of the classroom. Her eyes locked on the boy from earlier—the one with what she needed. She weaved through the bustling hallway, dodging clusters of teenagers until she was close enough to reach out and tap his shoulder.

"Hey," she called, her voice just loud enough to catch his attention over the chatter and slamming lockers.

The boy glanced back, his eyes trailing lazily over her before finally meeting her gaze. "Hey," he replied, his tone casual, yet detached.

"I'm Sunshine," she introduced herself, extending a hand with a confident smile.

He gave her a half-hearted smile, "And I have a girlfriend." With that, he turned to walk away, clearly expecting the conversation to end there.

Sunshine stepped in front of him, her laugh a little too forced. "No—no, it's not like that," she said, waving off the misunderstanding. "I wanted to buy from you."

His face immediately shifted, a guarded expression slipping into place. "I don't know what you're talking about," he said with a shrug, his eyes darting over his shoulder like he expected someone to be listening.

"Oh, please." Sunshine rolled her eyes, lowering her voice as she leaned in slightly. "I saw you earlier."

He stood there for a moment, jaw clenched in thought, weighing his options. Then, with a resigned sigh, he nodded. "Alright," he muttered. "Walk with me."

Sunshine walked alongside him, their steps falling into sync as they made their way toward the quad.

"What are you looking for?" he asked, his voice low, barely audible over the din of the crowded hallway.

"Addies," Sunshine replied, her tone cool and steady. "I've got cash."

He paused just outside the door, glancing over his shoulder to make sure no one was watching too closely. "I'm fresh out," he stated. "But I'll let you know when I re-up. All I've got right now are oxy's."

Sunshine let out a soft sigh, her eyes scanning the crowd nervously. She hesitated for a moment, weighing her options. It wasn't what she came for, but she didn't want to walk away empty-handed. Finally, with a resigned breath, she looked back at him. "How much?"

"Five a pop."

Sunshine nodded, reaching discreetly into her bra and pulling out a crisp fifty-dollar bill. "I'll take ten,"

Sunshine's fingers glided effortlessly across the piano keys, each note resonating with practiced precision. Her movements were fluid, second nature, the product of years of dedication and late nights. The sheet music rested before her, though she barely needed it—her eyes only flickered to it occasionally as her hands knew the melody by heart.

The rich, harmonious sound filled the room, wrapping around the scattered boxes that remained unpacked. Sunshine let herself be absorbed in the music, the notes carrying her away from the chaos of the move.

Lost in the melody, Sunshine's fingers danced across the keys with a steady rhythm, until her finger slipped, pressing the wrong key. The jarring note echoed, breaking the spell. She huffed in frustration, her hands hovering over the piano before she angrily jabbed at the keys again. Rubbing her tired eyes, she leaned back, exhaling sharply.

But the silence didn't last long. A blood-curdling scream ripped through the air, coming from upstairs.

Sunshine's heart leapt in her chest as she rushed up the stairs, her pulse quickening with each step. She could hear muffled voices, coming from above, and her eyes darted to the ladder leading to the attic. Without hesitating, she climbed it, her hands gripping the rungs tightly as she pulled herself up. When she reached the top, her parents were standing still, their eyes fixed on something hanging from the ceiling—a black rubber suit.

Ben broke the tension with a chuckle, his hand slipping around Vivien's waist. "I guess these guys were into some kinky stuff, huh?" he quipped, his grin playful. "Should I try it on?"

Vivien didn't share his humor. She shook her head, her voice stern. "That's not funny, Ben."

"Ew," Sunshine muttered, announcing her presence as she stepped further into the attic. Both her parents glanced back at her, their expressions unreadable.

Just then, Violet climbed up beside her sister, her eyes scanning the attic before landing on the suit. "What happened?" she asked, but the question died in her throat when she saw what everyone was staring at. "Holy shit."

"Let's get rid of it," Vivien, clearly unnerved, gently pushed past Ben, moving towards her daughters. "Come on." she ordered, her voice soft but urgent.

Sunshine nodded, following her mother and sister back toward the ladder. But just as she reached the top of the stairs, her eyes flicked back to the rubber suit, lingering a moment longer.

Sunshine slid her earbuds into place, the familiar, haunting notes of Beethoven's Moonlight Sonata flooding her senses. She reached into the drawer of her bedside table, her fingers brushing against a small, crinkled baggy filled with white pills. Without hesitation, she plucked one from the bag and popped it into her mouth, chasing it down with a quick sip of water from the glass by her bed.

With a sigh, she settled back onto her pillow, pulling the blankets up to her chin as the sonata swelled in her ears. Her eyes fluttered shut, the weight of the day melting away. In her mind, she wasn't just listening—she was there, seated at a grand piano, her fingers gliding effortlessly across the keys, playing alongside Beethoven himself. The music filled her, consumed her, until it was the only thing left.

After a while, the edges of the physical world around her began to blur as the pill took effect, casting everything in a dreamlike fog. Sunshine felt the weight of drowsiness wash over her, her limbs growing heavy as if she were sinking into a soft, endless cloud. The music from her earbuds grew distant, echoing through her mind like a lullaby. Her worries, her stresses, all the sharp edges of reality, dulled and faded, dissolving into the haze along with her drifting thoughts.

It felt as though she were drifting in a dream—perhaps she had already fallen asleep. A sudden weight pressed down on the bed, the mattress sinking slightly under the pressure. She shivered as a cold draft brushed over her skin, her blanket slipping down without warning.

She felt gentle tugs around her hips, followed by the unsettling sensation of rubber-clad hands gliding slowly down her legs. Her heart raced as fear coursed through her drowsy mind.

A sharp, unexpected pain flared between her legs, but just as quickly, the sensation twisted into something strange, almost pleasurable, sending a confused jolt through her. Her mind tried to grasp what was happening, but it felt like she was swimming through fog. Slowly, in the haze of her dream, she forced her eyes open.

And then she saw him.

A man loomed over her, his face obscured by the glossy black suit from the attic that clung to his body. His eyes, dark and soulless, stared into hers. There was a cruel, haunting stillness to his gaze, and in that instant, a wave of terror gripped her.

This had to be a nightmare — a twisted reflection of her fear from earlier. Yet everything felt so real, too real. Her chest tightened, fear coiling inside her like a spring wound too tight, but she couldn't move. Couldn't scream. She was trapped in the nightmare.

Chapter 3

The persistent ringing of the doorbell pierced through Sunshine's restless sleep, jolting her from the depths of her dreams. Agitation quickly replaced the drowsiness as she tossed off her blanket with a frustrated groan. "Is anybody going to get that?" she shouted into the empty house, but the bell rang again.

With a grumble, she stumbled out of bed, her bare feet hitting the cold floor as she stomped down the stairs. She yanked the front door open, already bracing herself for whoever had dared to disturb her.

Her bleary eyes met a boy about her age, his blonde shaggy hair framing his face. He was dressed in a green and black striped sweater, his hands shoved deep into his jean pockets.

"Can I help you?" Sunshine asked, her voice laced with irritation and lingering sleepiness.

The boy studied her for a moment before responding. "I have an appointment with Dr. Harmon."

Sunshine's shoulders relaxed, and she nodded toward the interior of the house. "His office is that way."

The boy nodded in acknowledgment and stepped inside, a heavy silence between them as she led him to her father's office. As they approached, Sunshine could hear her father speaking on the phone.

"Dad," she called out, announcing their arrival. Ben turned to face them, his expression shifting as he saw his patient. "Your patient is here."

"Oh, Tate," Ben recalled. "You're early."

Sunshine glanced once more at Tate before turning and making her way back up the stairs, the quiet thud of her footsteps echoing in the hallway as she left them to their session.

Sunshine entered the bathroom, rubbing the remnants of sleep from her eyes. She glanced over to see her sister standing by the sink, diligently brushing her teeth.

"Morning," Violet said around a mouthful of toothpaste, her voice muffled and frothy.

Sunshine mumbled a sleepy response as she headed for the toilet. She pulled down her bottoms and sat, letting out a groan as she noticed the telltale sign of blood in her underwear.

Violet finished rinsing her mouth and spat into the sink before she turned to her sister. "Want me to grab you a tampon?"

Sunshine shook her head. "No. I think I'm just spotting. I shouldn't start for another couple of weeks."

"Suit yourself," Violet shrugged, turning back to the mirror. Sunshine finished up and walked over to the sink to wash her hands, the cool water refreshing against her skin.

"Is that girl still messing with you?" Sunshine asked as she dried her hands with a nearby towel.

"Leah?" Violet's tone was dismissive, her eyes narrowing slightly. "I'm not scared of that bitch."

Sunshine smirked, leaning casually against the counter. "You're not scared of anything."

Violet shot her a playful glare through the mirror. "Then you don't need to worry."

Sunshine huffed through her nose, a small, weary smile curling at the corners of her mouth as she pushed herself away from the counter. The remnants of sleep still clung to her, making her movements sluggish.

She assumed it was just the lingering effects of the pill she had taken, making her feel unusually groggy and disoriented. With a final glance at Violet, who was now preoccupied with her own morning routine, Sunshine turned and shuffled back toward her room to get ready for school.

Sunshine settled onto her bed, her laptop propped open in front of her as she furiously typed away on her English essay. Her brow furrowed in concentration, she bit down on her lower lip, her focus entirely consumed by the screen.

As she paused to consider her next sentence, she noticed a movement outside her door. She looked up to see Violet walking past, followed closely by Tate, her father's patient. The sight made her eyebrows knit together.

"Vi!" Sunshine called out. Violet halted in her tracks and stepped back to the doorframe, Tate following closely behind her.

"Yeah?" Violet replied.

Sunshine's gaze shifted to Tate, meeting his eyes briefly before turning her attention back to Violet. "What are you doing?"

"Hanging out," Violet shrugged, her eyes flickering back to Tate. "You said I needed to make friends here."

"I didn't mean friends with one of Dad's patients," Sunshine said, her voice carrying a hint of exasperation.

"I'm not crazy," Tate interjected, a touch of annoyance in his voice.

"Sane people don't come to my dad for help," Sunshine shot back with a passive-aggressive smile.

Violet's expression hardened as she crossed her arms. "Just mind your business, okay?"

Sunshine rolled her eyes, a sigh escaping her lips as she turned her attention back to her laptop. "Whatever," she muttered as she refocused on her essay.

Her gaze fixed on the blank screen of her laptop. The essay she had been working on now felt like a distant concern as her thoughts wandered. Despite her usual kindness towards strangers, she couldn't shake the uneasy feeling Tate stirred within her. There was something about him—an intangible sense of discomfort—that set her on edge.

She tried to rationalize her unease. Maybe it was just a feeling, an instinct telling her something was off. Sunshine wanted nothing more than for Violet to fit in, but the anxiety lingered. Even though she knew Violet wasn't interested in Tate romantically—he was, after all, the complete opposite of her sister's usual type—Sunshine couldn't help but worry.

Sunshine waited in line in the bustling cafeteria, her gaze fixed on the lunch lady as she ladled a dubious-looking mystery dish onto her tray. Sunshine couldn't suppress a wince at the sight of the unidentifiable slop, and she moved down the line with a resigned sigh.

After collecting her food, she made her way to her usual table, the chatter and clatter of the cafeteria blending into a background hum. She slid into her seat, setting her tray down with a soft thud.

In a practiced, discreet motion, Sunshine reached into her bag and pulled out a small, orange pill. With a swift glance around to ensure no one was watching, she tossed the Adderall into her mouth. She quickly chased it down with a few gulps from her water bottle.

As Sunshine poked at her unappetizing lunch, her gaze drifted around the cafeteria, searching for Violet. It was unusual for them not to sit together, and Sunshine felt a pang of concern. Her eyes roamed the room until they were drawn to a cluster of students gathered in the far corner.

There, amidst a crowd of whispering onlookers, she spotted Violet in the thick of a heated argument. Her sister was surrounded by a group of girls, their faces animated and tense.

Sunshine's brow furrowed as she tried to make out the details of the confrontation. Violet's posture was firm, her arms crossed defensively, while the other girls seemed to be pressing in on her.

Leah, the ringleader and Violet's relentless tormentor, swung her hand with a sharp slap, landing it hard across Violet's face. The sound echoed through the cafeteria, and Sunshine's eyes widened in horror. Without a second thought, she sprang to her feet.

Violet, her face flushed with anger and pain, grabbed Leah by the collar of her shirt. With a powerful shove, she slammed Leah into the lockers with a loud bang. "I'm not scared of you!" Violet's voice was fierce and defiant as Leah squirmed and struggled to break free.

"You should be!" Leah shot back. Meanwhile, Leah's two accomplices lunged at Violet, pulling her away from Leah and tossing her roughly into the side of a lunch table. The impact knocked Violet to the ground, her body crumpling against the hard surface.

Sunshine reached the scene just as the two girls managed to pin Violet down. In a surge of adrenaline, she seized the closest girl by the hair, yanking it back forcefully. The girl yelped and toppled backward, hitting the floor with a thud.

"Get off of her!" Sunshine's voice was a harsh, urgent command, but before she could react further, the second girl grabbed her and knocked her to the ground. Sunshine grunted as she landed hard on her side.

The surrounding crowd of students formed a tight circle around the brawl, chanting "Fight! Fight!"

Leah's friend was on top of her, delivering a series of punches. One blow struck Sunshine's lip, splitting it open and sending a trickle of blood down her chin. Pain and fury ignited within her, and she retaliated by grabbing the girl's face. With a grimace, Sunshine slammed her forehead against the girl's, the impact sending a sharp, reverberating pain through her skull.

The girl fell back, clutching her head and moaning in pain. Sunshine scrambled to her feet, her vision clearing just in time to see Violet searing a cigarette on Leah's hand. Leah let out a scream of pain.

Violet quickly stood up and helped Sunshine up. The two of them dashed out of the lunchroom, fleeing the chaotic scene behind them.

"Ow, she freaking burned me!" Leah's enraged shout followed them as they escaped, the echo of her anger fading behind them.

Chapter 4

"Here's the plan," Sunshine said in a hushed tone as they approached their house, trying to ignore the throb in her head. "We sneak in through the kitchen door, and clean up as much as we can before Mom sees."

Violet nodded, her forehead still oozing from where Leah had clawed at her. They circled around to the back of the house, slipping up to the kitchen door as quietly as possible. Sunshine carefully pushed it open, wincing when it creaked.

"Shit," Sunshine hissed under her breath. There, standing at the island, was their mother.

"Hey," Vivien greeted, looking up at them with soft smile.

Sunshine's pulse quickened. "Hey, Mom," she replied, trying to keep her voice calm while subtly nudging Violet toward the hallway.

"Whoa," Vivien's tone shifted and Sunshine's attempts to rush out of the kitchen came to an abrupt halt. "Come here."

Vivien's eyes roamed over their bruised and battered appearances. "What happened?"

Sunshine instinctively touched her swollen lip, her fingers coming away with dry blood. She opened her mouth to speak, but Violet beat her to it.

"Fell down," Violet lied smoothly, her expression deadpan.

Vivien didn't seem convinced. Her gaze flickered between the two of them, the maternal instinct kicking in full force as she tried to assess the damage.

"Both of you fell down?" Vivien repeated, her skepticism obvious as she met each of her daughters' eyes.

Violet and Sunshine exchanged a glance, their silent communication confirming they were busted.

A slow sigh escaped Vivien's lips as the pieces fell into place. "Come here. Sit, sit, sit," she instructed, waving them over to the island.

The two sisters complied, sliding onto the stools, Violet removing her hat to reveal the extent of the wound on her forehead.

"Boys or girls?" Vivien's voice softened as she crossed the kitchen to retrieve the first-aid kit from a cabinet.

"Girls," Sunshine replied, her voice flat as she stared at the countertop.

"Three of them," Violet added.

Vivien let out a low breath, turning back with the kit in hand. "Hope they look worse than you guys do."

Sunshine gave a small, bitter smile. "Safe to say we did some damage."

Vivien's mouth twitched, pride mingling with concern as she returned to the girls. "Do you know their names?" she asked, opening the first-aid kit.

"We're not narcing," Violet replied bluntly.

Vivien sighed. "You know, we can easily move you two to a different school. There are a lot of really good private schools in this neighborhood."

Violet shook her head. "Sunny was just defending me. It's not fair to change schools because of me and I'm not running away. I'm not scared of them."

Vivien's lips curled into a faint smile as she dabbed a peroxide-soaked cloth on Violet's forehead, removing the blood with gentle care. "Not afraid of anything." she murmured fondly, her eyes softening. "It's like that time in kindergarten when you insisted I bring you home from the slumber party because all the other girls were sleeping with the light on."

Violet gave a small, knowing smile as Vivien stood, moving in front of her eldest daughter with the same gentleness. "Alright, your turn," she said quietly, cupping Sunshine's chin to tilt her head up. She dabbed at the split lip, and Sunshine winced at the sting, but there was something soothing about her mother's care.

"I know you two have had the short end of the stick lately," Vivien continued, her voice quieter now. "This move, the school, and… your dad and I haven't exactly been great to be around." She paused, eyes searching Sunshine's face as she brushed a lock of hair from her cheek.

"It's okay, Mom," Sunshine said, her voice gentle.

But Violet wasn't one to leave things unsaid. "Why don't you guys get divorced if you're so miserable?" she asked bluntly.

Vivien glanced at her, wiping the last bit of blood from Sunshine's face before moving to put away the first-aid kit. "We still love each other," she said simply.

Violet scoffed lightly. "You could've fooled me. I thought you hated each other. Well, at least you hated him. I don't blame you. He was a shithead." Vivien shot her a look, eyebrow raised at the language. "Sorry," Violet muttered, not really meaning it.

"It's okay." Vivien chuckled, surprising them both. "He was a shithead." Her smile was brief, fading as quickly as it had appeared. "You know, we've got a lot of history. Your dad's been through a lot. I've been through a lot. I guess we just need each other."

There was a pause, the kind where words hovered in the air, waiting to be spoken.

"What are you scared of?" Violet's voice was quieter now, a rare softness to it.

Vivien froze for a second, the weight of the question catching her off guard.

"You said I wasn't scared of anything, so... what scares you?" Violet pressed.

Vivien's lips parted. "Lately?" she repeated, her eyes flickering between her daughters, both of them waiting for her answer. "Everything. Life will do that to you."

Violet stormed back and forth across her room, her fists clenched at her sides, eyes burning with fury. "I hate her! I just want to kill her!"

Tate lounged in the corner, casually draped across a worn armchair, watching Violet with an almost amused expression. "Then do it," he said coolly. "One less high school bitch making the lives of the less fortunate more tolerable is, in my opinion, a public service."

Sunshine, sitting cross-legged on Violet's bed, glanced up from her laptop. "That's a bit extreme," she remarked.

Tate's eyes flicked over to her. "Maybe," he conceded, but there was no real apology in his tone. He returned his attention to Violet, who had stopped pacing. "Look, you want her to leave you alone, right? Stop making your life a living hell? Short of killing her, there's only one real solution." He paused. "Scare her. Make her afraid of you. That's the only thing bullies react to."

Violet halted, her breath catching as she met his intense gaze. "How?" she asked.

"I've seen her buy coke from someone in my class," Sunshine said casually. "Tell her you have coke."

"I don't have coke," Violet muttered, throwing her hands up as if the whole plan had already collapsed.

"You won't need any," Tate said, his voice steady. "It's just an excuse to get her here. After that, she'll leave empty-handed... and terrified. And I promise you, she'll never bother you again."

Violet's brow furrowed as she considered it, glancing between her sister and Tate, weighing the options in her mind. The idea lingered in the air, tempting her, offering a way out from the relentless bullying. "How am I going to terrify her?"

Tate's unsettling grin widened as he leaned forward slightly. "That's where I come in."

Chapter 5

Sunshine's fingers hovered nervously over the light switch as they waited for Violet. She cast a glance at Tate, who was seated in the rocking chair, his calm, almost predatory demeanor unsettling her further.

"You're not gonna hurt her, are you?" Sunshine whispered, her voice barely audible.

Tate didn't even look at her as he replied, his tone steady, almost too calm. "I'm just gonna scare her." He rocked forward, the creak of the chair echoing in the stillness. "Turn off the lights."

With a hesitant glance toward the stairs, Sunshine obeyed, flipping the switch. Darkness swallowed the room, leaving them in silence. The sound of the basement door creaking open above them made her flinch slightly. Footsteps thudded down the stairs as Violet led Leah into the trap, their voices growing louder.

"It's showtime," Tate murmured just loud enough for Sunshine to hear.

"What's down there?" Leah asked, her tone sharp and suspicious.

"My stash," Violet replied coolly. "Parents toss my room every week."

Leah's footsteps grew more purposeful as they went deeper into the basement. "If you're screwing with me..." her voice trailed off in a warning.

"It's just the basement," Violet shot back. "I found the best hiding place. This is great shit, too. All the coke coming to the U.S. from Central America smuggled in on lobster boats in Gloucester. I used to show my boobs to the lobstermen in return for a key or two before they cut it."

"So where is it?" "Right around the corner. To the right."

As the two girls neared, Sunshine could hear Leah's disdainful mutter. "This place is a dump."

"Then keep going," Violet pressed, guiding her forward.

Sunshine waited, her hand hovering over the light switch. When Leah finally entered the room, she flicked on the lights.

The sudden brightness revealed Tate, sitting ominously in the rocking chair, his expression cold, almost amused. "So," he began slowly, his voice dripping with mockery, "this is the coke whore."

Leah blinked in surprise, quickly recovering, her voice snapping with bravado as she tried to hide her unease. "Who the hell are you?"

Violet moved to stand beside Sunshine, a smirk curling on her lips.

Tate remained calm, his eyes never leaving Leah's face. "Get the lights," he commanded, his voice low.

Sunshine's fingers hand flicked the switch, and the room was swallowed by darkness once again. Instantly, the flickering of lights began—sharp, sporadic flashes that disoriented her senses. Tate's maniacal laughter echoed through the room.

"What is going on?!" Leah's voice rose in panic, cracking under the weight of her fear. "What is going on?!"

In the strobe, Tate's figure began to warp—his body bending and twisting unnaturally, his limbs jerking in ways that made him seem almost inhuman. Sunshine's breath hitched as she backed up against the cold wall, her heart hammering wildly. Each flash painted a new nightmare: a monster—large, grotesque, with razor-sharp teeth—flickering in and out of Tate's place, its eyes gleaming with a sick hunger.

"Come on, whore! Come on! Coke whore!" Tate's voice shouted through the chaos, his words vicious and taunting.

Leah screamed as Tate launched himself onto her, pinning her to the ground. "Get off me! Get off me!" Her desperate pleas were drowned by the echoes of her own terror. Each flicker of light revealed the monster's terrifying form looming over her—claws sharp, its grotesque mouth opening wide as if ready to consume her.

From across the room, Sunshine stood paralyzed, her chest heaving, unable to tear her wide eyes from the horror unfolding in front of her. The monster's misshapen form became clearer with each flash of the lights, its clawed fingers reaching for Leah's face.

Violet, tears streaming down her face, was sobbing uncontrollably, her voice desperate. "Stop! Stop! Please, stop!" Her screams echoed through the basement, cutting through the madness, but they did nothing to quell the horror.

The monster's claws moved closer to Leah's face, each flicker revealing more of its grotesque form. Leah whimpered, her voice barely a whisper now. "Mommy..." she cried out, her eyes filled with fear as the monster's claws slashed across her face.

Violet spun to Sunshine, desperation etched into her features. "Do something!" she screamed.

Finally snapping out of her frozen state, her fingers fumbled as she forced herself to flip the lights back on.

Suddenly, the room was bathed in steady light, the terrifying flickering ceasing. The monster was gone. Tate sat calmly in the rocking chair, grinning like nothing had happened, his eyes gleaming with sadistic satisfaction. Leah lay crumpled on the floor, sobbing uncontrollably, her body trembling.

Sunshine's heart pounded in her chest, her body frozen against the wall as she watched Leah scramble to her feet and bolt up the stairs.

"Leah, wait!" Violet started to chase after her but stopped abruptly, standing just outside the archway between the two sections of the basement.

Sunshine's breaths came in short, sharp gasps. Her fingers dug into the cold surface of the wall behind her, seeking some kind of stability in the chaos. Her mind raced, struggling to process what she had seen.

Tate stood from his chair, moving casually. He glanced over at her, his dark eyes meeting hers briefly, his expression unreadable before he turned to lean against the concrete wall, addressing Violet.

"I don't think she'll be bothering you anymore," Tate said, his voice carrying a sick sense of pride.

Violet's voice trembled, her whole body tense. "What was that?!"

"What? She kneed me in the balls and got away. She must have run into a wall or something," he explained, brushing it off as if it were nothing.

"No, I saw something!" Violet's voice cracked with disbelief.

Sunshine remained glued to the wall, listening to the conversation with hot tears silently streaking down her cheeks. She had seen it too. Whatever had been in that basement wasn't just a trick of the light or a figment of her imagination. It had been real. Terrifyingly real.

"What are you talk- Violet. You're acting crazy. This is cool. We showed that bitch."

"Get out!" Violet's scream cut through the basement. "I never want to see you again!"

Sunshine heard the sound of her shoving him before she stormed up the stairs.

Tate's voice shouted after her. "I thought you weren't afraid of anything!"

Sunshine wiped at her cheeks hastily, trying to erase the evidence of her fear. Her breathing was uneven as she tried to calm herself. She pushed herself off the wall, her legs shaky as she stepped into the open area where Tate stood.

He didn't say anything, just watched her with glossy eyes. Sunshine's lips parted as if she wanted to speak, but no words came. She felt the weight of everything she'd seen—everything that had just happened—press down on her, too heavy to put into words.

She shut her mouth, casting her gaze to the floor as she turned toward the stairs. With one last, fleeting glance at Tate, she climbed the steps slowly, leaving him alone in the basement.

Chapter 6

Sunshine tossed and turned in her bed, her sleep restless and plagued by the same nightmare that had haunted her for what felt like an eternity. The dream always started the same way: the room cold, bathed in darkness, and the subtle creak of the door opening slowly. Her breath hitched as she felt his presence before she even saw him—the Rubber Man. His silhouette stood in the doorway, his featureless mask gleaming in the moonlight.

She wanted to move, to scream, to run, but as always, her body betrayed her. Paralyzed, frozen in place, she could only watch as he moved closer. Her heart pounded against her ribs, her chest tight with fear. The sound of the latex suit stretched as he climbed onto the bed, each movement unnervingly slow.

Sunshine's mind screamed, but no sound left her lips. The Rubber Man hovered over her, his cold, gloved hands pinning her down. Her limbs were heavy, like she was sinking into quicksand, unable to escape the inevitable. He had his way with her, again and again, just as he always did in these dreams, the sense of helplessness overwhelming her. No matter how hard she fought, no matter how much she struggled, the outcome was always the same.

Sunshine shot up in her bed, her skin drenched in sweat, breathing ragged as she struggled to shake off the remnants of the nightmare. She pressed her hand to her chest, feeling the erratic thudding of her heart.

Her eyes darted around the room, desperate to reassure herself that she was safe. But then, her heart nearly stopped when she saw a figure standing still, outlined in the shadows near the corner. She held her breath, her muscles locking up in terror.

She slowly reached for the lamp on her bedside table, her fingers trembling as she switched it on. The warm light flooded the room, chasing away the darkness, and in an instant, the figure was gone. There was nothing there—just empty space where she swore someone had been standing only a second ago.

Sunshine let out a shaky breath as she pressed her palms against her face, trying to steady herself.

She lifted her head and stared blankly at the room, the silence now deafening. The events in the basement earlier flashed through her mind—Leah's terrified screams and the monster that had taken Tate's place. That hadn't been a dream.

Sunshine wiped at her face, trying to pull herself together, but her hands were still shaking. She felt like she was slowly unraveling, her grip on reality slipping away piece by piece. What was happening to her? What was real, and what was just a figment of her mind?

Finally giving in to the restlessness, she slid out of bed. The cool air of the house hit her skin, and she shivered as her bare feet padded quietly across the cold wooden floor of the hallway. She focused on the slightly cracked door to Violet's room just down the hall.

She hesitated for a moment, her hand hovering near the doorknob, before gently pushing the door open. Inside, Violet lay in bed, facing the wall, but Sunshine could tell from the tension in her body that she wasn't asleep.

"Can't sleep?" Sunshine whispered, her voice soft as she moved toward her sister's bed.

Violet stirred but didn't turn around. "No," she replied, her voice quiet and distant, her hands tucked under her cheek.

Sunshine slipped under the covers beside her, the warmth of Violet's body a small comfort against the lingering chill of the night. Instinctively, she wrapped her arms around Violet, pulling her close.

"Me neither," she admitted softly.

There was a long pause before Violet finally spoke again, her voice barely above a whisper. "Did you see it, too?"

"I don't know what I saw," Sunshine admitted, the words tasting bitter on her tongue. "I saw Tate and then... something that wasn't Tate."

Violet shifted slightly in her arms, her body tense. She was quiet for a moment before she spoke. "It had to have been a mask, right? It couldn't have been real."

Sunshine's chest tightened as she felt her sister's desperation. She wished she could give Violet the comforting answer she wanted, but she couldn't. "I don't know," she whispered, her voice cracking. "But whatever it was... I don't think you should hang out with him anymore."

Violet didn't say anything for a moment, but Sunshine could feel her nod. "I don't plan on it,"

The piercing shrill of the house alarm filled the room, yanking both Sunshine and Violet out of their momentary peace. The sound echoed off the walls, bouncing through the house like a siren in the night. Sunshine shot up in bed, heart hammering as adrenaline surged through her veins.

"What the hell?" Violet muttered, rubbing her eyes as she sat up.

Sunshine was already moving, her bare feet hitting floor. "Stay here," she instructed firmly, glancing back at her sister before cautiously walking to the door.

Her hand hovered over the doorknob for a brief second, her pulse quickening as she wondered what could have set off the alarm. Slowly, she twisted the knob and cracked the door open just enough to peek into the hallway.

Her eyes caught movement at the far end of the hall. Her body froze until the figure came into focus. It was her mother moving quickly but quietly. When Vivien spotted Sunshine, she frantically motioned for her to go back inside, her eyes wide with urgency.

Sunshine's stomach knotted in fear as she stepped back and let her mother slip into the room, shutting the door firmly behind her.

"Someone use their phone, call the police," Vivien whispered urgently.

"What? What's going on?" Sunshine asked, panic rising in her throat. Her voice felt too loud against the sudden silence as the alarm abruptly cut off, leaving a heavy, unsettling quiet in its wake.

"Someone's in the house. Just do what I say," Vivien ordered, her voice sharp as she glanced toward the door, listening for any sound outside. Without explanation, she hurried out of the room.

Sunshine's head spun as she turned to Violet, who was already reaching for her phone. Violet's fingers dialed 911, her eyes wide as she relayed their situation to the operator.

After what felt like an eternity of sitting in tense silence, Sunshine and Violet were huddled on the bed, their nerves stretched thin. Every passing second seemed to drag out, the faint creaks of the house only heightening their anxiety as they waited for any sign that it was safe.

The door suddenly creaked open, and both sisters jumped as Vivien stepped back into the room. Her face looked calmer now, the fear and urgency replaced with something more like exasperation.

"It's just Addy," Vivien sighed, running a hand through her hair. "She snuck into the house again."

Sunshine and Violet exchanged a look, both visibly relieved. The tension in the air began to dissipate as they absorbed their mother's words, but the adrenaline still lingered, buzzing beneath their skin.

Vivien nodded, clearly frustrated. "I'm going to have a talk with Constance tomorrow. This has to stop."

Chapter 7

Sunshine stood at the sink, her hands moving methodically as she scrubbed each dish. She rinsed off the last plate, the suds swirling down the drain as she placed it into the dishwasher with a soft clink. The repetitive motions brought a fleeting sense of calm, but her mind remained restless. It had been a couple of weeks since the events in the basement, and the unsettling images still lingered in her mind.

Violet hadn't kept her promise to stay away from Tate, a fact that gnawed at Sunshine. She understood there wasn't much she could do about it, but that didn't mean she had to forgive or forget what had happened. The air between them had grown colder, and whenever Tate was mentioned, a bitter tension surfaced within her.

Sunshine dried her hands on a towel, letting out a quiet sigh before reaching for a water bottle from the counter. With the hum of the dishwasher now filling the quiet kitchen, she turned and headed down the hallway.

As she passed her father's office, she halted mid-step. Tate's voice drifted through the barely cracked door. She stood there for a moment, debating whether to keep walking or indulge the curiosity tugging at her. Despite the warnings in the back of her mind, she took a quiet step closer to the door.

Sunshine leaned against the wall, peering through the crack, her breath held as she tried to make out the conversation.

"Do you think about sex a lot?"

"I think about one girl in particular. Your daughter. I jerk off thinking about her. A lot." As soon as the words left his mouth, she saw it—the flicker of satisfaction lighting up his face.

"I'm not comfortable with you talking about Violet, Tate."

"I'm not talking about Violet."

Sunshine's eyes widened, a flicker of surprise crossing her face as the room fell into a sudden, uncomfortable silence. He had been talking about her. The weight of that revelation left her momentarily speechless. It didn't make sense; they had hardly spoken to one another, and truth be told, she preferred it that way.

"Don't you want to know what I'd do to her? How I lay her on the bed and I caress her soft skin, make her purr like a little kitten. She's a virgin. They get wet so easily."

And with that, Tate's gaze shifted, honing in on the small sliver of Sunshine visible through the door. His eyes locked onto hers with unnerving intensity, as if piercing straight into her soul. For a moment, she felt utterly exposed. Panic surged within her, and she tore her gaze away, heart pounding as she spun on her heel, darting up the stairs.

Sunshine descended the steps with a casual, lighthearted stride, her mind set on the simple pleasure of something sweet from the kitchen. But as she entered, the sight that greeted her made her slow her pace—her parents were gathered around the island, along with Moira and the woman from next door, Constance.

"Your sense of humor was, and continues to be, a delight," Moira remarked, lacking any real warmth.

An awkward silence hung between them. Vivien's eyes flicked toward the two chocolate cupcakes sitting on the counter—one artfully topped with a candied violet, the other adorned with a sunflower made of delicate frosting petals.

"Constance brought you a cupcake," she finally said, gesturing to the treats, desperate to break the tension.

Sunshine's eyes lit up with excitement, her mouth already watering at the sight. She walked over eagerly, hand outstretched, ready to claim the sunflower-topped cupcake. But just as her fingers brushed the edge of the plate, Constance's hand shot out, gripping her wrist tightly.

Startled, Sunshine looked up, meeting Constance's intense gaze. The older woman's eyes seemed to bore into her, as though she were studying her, searching for something hidden beneath the surface.

"Don't eat that," Constance commanded, her voice low and firm in her southern accent.

Sunshine blinked in confusion. "But I thought—"

"Don't." The word came out sharp, cutting her off before she could finish. Without hesitation, Constance snatched the cupcake from the plate and tossed it into the trash with a careless flick of her wrist.

The room filled with confusion, the silence thickening as everyone exchanged uneasy glances. Constance dusted her hands together, brushing away invisible crumbs, her eyes darting between Sunshine and Vivien.

"Is there anything more wonderful than the promise of a new child?" she said suddenly, her voice softer, almost wistful. "Or more heartbreaking when that promise is broken?" Without waiting for a reply, Constance turned on her heel and swept out of the kitchen, leaving an uncomfortable stillness in her wake.

"I'll bring this to the car," Moira interjected, breaking the silence as she picked up Ben's suitcase. Sunshine noticed her father's gaze linger on Moira for just a moment too long, his attention drawn to her in a way that made her stomach twist.

"Thank you," Vivien murmured, glancing back as Moira left the room.

Sunshine's eyes shifted to her mother, catching the subtle guilt etched on Vivien's face. "You're pregnant?" she asked, her voice filled with quiet surprise. This was news to her; her mother hadn't breathed a word about it.

Vivien hesitated, worry flickering across her features. "I was planning on telling you," she began, her voice soft and careful, gauging her daughter's reaction.

Sunshine forced a smile, swallowing her mixed feelings. "That's great, Mom."

Though part of her felt uneasy—memories of what happened last time still fresh in her mind—she truly wanted to be happy for her mother. The timing seemed off, especially with her parents' relationship on shaky ground, but it was hard not to feel a small glimmer of hope.

Sunshine padded into the living room, the aroma of buttery popcorn wafting through the air as she carried a large bowl. She settled onto the couch beside her mother, who was lounging with an air of tired resignation. The absence of her father had paved the way for a rare mother-daughter night.

"Is Violet not coming?" Sunshine asked, glancing around the room for any sign of her sister.

Vivien exhaled a long, weary sigh, her head resting on her propped-up arm, which draped casually over the back of the couch. Her gaze was distant, her posture heavy with unspoken frustration. "She's mad at me."

"What? Why?" Sunshine's brows knitted together in confusion as she grabbed a handful of popcorn and tossed a piece into her mouth.

Vivien rolled her eyes, a gesture of exasperation, and shifted slightly to face Sunshine more directly. "Because I'm pregnant... and apparently, old."

Sunshine shook her head. "She's just worried about you."

Vivien's breath was a soft, almost defeated sigh. "It doesn't feel like it."

Sunshine offered a reassuring smile, hoping to lighten the mood. "She's just going through a lot right now. Don't take it personally."

Before Vivien could respond, the sharp chime of the doorbell sliced through the quiet, startling them both. Sunshine's eyes flicked toward the door.

"Who's that?" Sunshine asked, a note of surprise in her voice.

Vivien looked equally puzzled. She slowly rose from the couch. Her steps were soft on the wood as she approached the front door. She leaned closer to the peephole, peering through it with a furrowed brow, her fingers lightly resting on the door frame as if bracing for whatever—or whoever—was on the other side.

"Who is it?" Vivien called through the door.

"Excuse me, ma'am. I don't want to bother you, but I'm hurt and needing some help."

Chapter 8

"What happened to you?" Vivien called through the door, her voice tense as she took in the sight of the woman on the other side, disheveled and clearly injured.

"Mom?" Sunshine stood up from the couch and moving to her mother's side, curiosity turning to concern.

The woman outside spoke, her voice strained and desperate. "I'm hurt and need help. Open the door."

Vivien glanced at Sunshine, a flicker of uncertainty in her eyes. Sunshine, however, shook her head firmly, instinctively sensing that something was wrong. There was something off about this whole situation, a feeling that tugged at her gut.

Vivien turned back to the peephole, hesitating. "You said you're hurt," she called out cautiously. "Can you tell me what happened? How did you get injured?"

"Can't you see the blood on my face? He's out here! Let me in, please!"

Vivien's hand wavered above the door handle. Sunshine's unease was palpable now, a tight knot of dread building in her chest.

Vivien, sensing the same disquiet, reached up and quietly slid the lock into place.

The sound of the lock must have reached the woman outside, because her voice shifted, becoming more urgent, almost accusing. "What kind of woman are you? He's coming! He's gonna stab me!"

The woman's voice erupted into a desperate frenzy, her fists pounding against the door with increasing intensity. The thud of each hit reverberated through the house, filling the space with a menacing rhythm.

"II'm going to get help. I'm calling 911." Vivien motioned quickly toward her daughter, urging her to go call the police.

Sunshine nodded before she bolted up the stairs. Her mind spun as she reached her room, frantically searching for her phone. But it wasn't there. Panic swelled in her chest—she must have left it in her locker at school.

She dashed down the hall, bursting into Violet's room, where her sister sat engrossed in homework. "Where's your phone?" Sunshine demanded, her voice tinged with urgency.

Violet looked up, confused by her sister's panicked tone. "What?"

"Your phone!" Sunshine repeated, her voice rising in desperation.

"Jeez, give me a second!" Violet huffed, climbing off the bed and grabbing her backpack. She dumped its contents onto the bed, rummaging through books and papers. Sunshine's impatience grew with every passing second.

Suddenly, Violet froze, her face draining of color as her gaze lifted, staring in terror over Sunshine's shoulder. Sunshine turned just in time to see a masked man lunging at her.

"I have money. Please, take anything you want," Vivien pleaded, her voice shaky but steady, hoping to appeal to their greed.

"We're not here to rob you," the woman from outside replied coldly. "Masks off."

With a swift gesture, the three intruders pulled off their masks, revealing their faces—two women and the man who had forced them down here.

The leader, the same woman who had begged for help at the door, now stood in full control, her eyes gleaming with twisted anticipation. "The transcript was very clear. The nurses saw R. Franklin; he had nothing to hide," she said, glancing down at her watch with chilling precision. "Twelve minutes."

"And then the fun begins," the blonde woman chimed in, a wide grin spreading across her face, her excitement barely contained.

"I have a surprise for you all," the ringleader announced, moving to a nearby table. She picked up an object draped in a white cloth, slowly peeling it away to reveal a battered, broken bowl.

"No way," the man whispered in awe, leaning over her shoulder.

"I got it on eBay. Authenticated," the ringleader said, her voice filled with genuine admiration. "It's the one he used to bash Maria." The admiration in her tone for a brutal murderer made Sunshine and Violet share a horrified glance.

"Let me see that," the man said, snatching the bowl from her. He turned it over in his hands, his face lighting up. "Holy shit. You can feel the energy in this. This is bitchin'!"

The blonde woman scanned the room. "So, who goes first?" she asked, her gaze predatory. "Which one is Gladys?"

The ringleader's knife swung toward Violet, pointing directly at her, marking her as their chosen victim. With a twisted grin, the blonde tossed a worn, vintage nurse's uniform toward Violet.

"Screw you, psycho!" Violet spat, shoving the uniform back at her. "I'm not putting that on."

"You have to," the blonde replied flatly, her voice void of emotion. "Everything has to be perfect."

"Take your clothes off!" the man yelled suddenly, his hand darting forward to grab at Violet's shirt. Chaos erupted as both Vivien and Sunshine screamed, their voices rising in panic.

"Mom!" Violet's voice cracked as she backed away, her breath coming in ragged gasps.

"No! Put it on me!" Vivien cried, desperation in her eyes as she tried to shield her daughter.

The ringleader sneered, her knife glinting in the light. "The roles have already been cast, Mama bear." Her grin widened as she took a step closer. "R. Franklin hated nurses. A broken thermometer, mercury poisoning—that's what made him snap. That's why he took Gladys upstairs and drowned her in the tub."

Then she turned toward Sunshine. Standing just inches from her, the ringleader used the tip of her knife to gently brush a stray hair from Sunshine's face. "And you, Maria—he saved you for last. R. Franklin was the first. Before Manson. He changed the culture. We're paying tribute to him tonight."

Vivien's voice trembled with defiance. "My daughter's aren't going to be a part of your sick reenactment."

The ringleader glanced at her, a smirk playing at the edges of her lips. With a lazy flick of her wrist, she tossed two nurse uniforms at the sisters. "Put these on. You won't like it if I have to make you."

Violet and Sunshine hesitated but they stood, fear and defiance battling within them.

Violet's eyes flicked between the uniform in her hands and the intruders, her jaw tightening with resolve. In a flash, she lunged forward, slamming her forehead into the ringleader's, sending her stumbling backward with a grunt of pain. Seizing the moment, Violet bolted down the hall.

The man sprang into action, rushing after her. But just as the man moved past Vivien, she stuck out her foot, tripping him. He crashed to the floor with a heavy thud, giving Sunshine a split second to act.

As the ringleader chased after Violet, Sunshine bolted for the stairs, her legs pumping with adrenaline. She could hear the rapid thuds of footsteps behind her, the sound of the blonde woman closing in.

Just as she reached the bottom of the staircase, she felt a sharp yank as fingers clawed into her hair, yanking her back violently. She let out a gasp of pain as she was dragged down. In an instant, cold steel pressed against her throat , the sharp edge of the knife biting into her skin. Sunshine winced, freezing in place as a thin trickle of blood slid down her neck.

"You crazy bitch, let go of me!" she spat, her voice cracking under the weight of fear and fury. She writhed in the woman's grip, but the pressure of the blade digging into her flesh stopped her from fighting back too hard.

"I've been waiting for this for far too long for you to ruin it, sweetie," the blonde woman hissed in her ear, her voice sickeningly sweet. She tugged Sunshine back toward the room where they had been held captive, the knife never wavering from its place against her throat. "Hand me the uniform, will you?" she called out to her accomplice.

"What are you doing with her?" Vivien's panicked voice filled the room, her words trembling with desperation. She struggled against the ropes binding her to the chair, her body tipped over awkwardly on the ground. "Don't hurt her, please!"

The man, still looming near, grabbed the crumpled nurse's uniform and shoved it into the blonde's free hand. Without a word, the woman dragged Sunshine into the living room—the same room where Maria had been murdered all those years ago.

With a forceful shove, the woman threw Sunshine down onto the couch, her body hitting the cushions with a dull thud. The knife hovered inches from her face, gleaming menacingly as the blonde tossed the uniform at her. "Now, please. Just put the clothes on."

Sunshine's chest heaved with fear. Her bottom lip trembled as she looked up at the woman towering over her, hot tears pricking at the corners of her eyes, but she fought to hold them back.

Sunshine slowly lifted herself off the couch, just enough to tug her dress up over her head. Her skin prickled with cold air as the dress fell to the floor, leaving her standing in just her underwear.

Her hands shook as she reached for the white tights, the fabric soft between her fingers, yet each pull of the material felt heavy with dread. She stood up, sliding the tights up her legs, her movements slow and cautious, every second stretched taut with tension.

Sunshine swallowed hard as she picked up the uniform, the fabric scratchy against her skin. She slipped her arms into the sleeves, being swallowed by the role they were forcing her to play.

As she buttoned the front, her hands shook more with every second, her breath unsteady as the dress fit snugly against her body.

Sunshine's heart pounded in her chest as she finished, standing still in the stiff uniform. She could feel the eyes of the blonde on her, watching her every move like a predator savoring the moment before the kill.

"Good," the blonde woman purred. Her eyes gleamed with excitement as she reached into her back pocket, pulling out a bundle of coarse rope. The woman toyed with it for a moment, letting the rope dangle in front of her like a taunt before stepping closer.

"Let's get you tied up,"

Sunshine lay face down on the couch, her body twisted painfully in the tight confines of the hogtie. Her wrists and ankles were cruelly bound together, pulling her legs back in a way that made her muscles ache with each passing second. She could feel the rough rope digging into her skin, its relentless grip a constant reminder of her helplessness.

Tears streamed silently from her eyes, falling off her cheeks and soaking into the fabric beneath her. Her breath came out in ragged gasps as she tried to calm the rising panic inside her.

Her captor had left moments ago, mentioning getting something to eat and checking on the ringleader, leaving Sunshine alone in the living room, bound and unable to move. The absence of their immediate presence was only a small relief—her mind raced with thoughts of what would happen to her when she came back.

A blurry figure stepped into view, and Sunshine's heart skipped a beat. As her vision cleared, her eyes went wide — it was Tate. Despite everything, she felt an unexpected surge of hope, something she hadn't allowed herself to feel since the nightmare began.

"Tate," she whispered, her voice shaky but laced with an unusual sense of gratitude, relief flooding through her at the sight of him.

Tate knelt beside her, bringing his face close to hers, his expression calm and reassuring. His dark eyes locked onto hers, as though trying to anchor her in the chaos. "Hey," he murmured softly, his voice a soothing balm against the terror, "everything's gonna be okay."

"Tate, th-there's p-people trying to kill us," Sunshine stammered, her voice breaking as the tears spilled freely again.

"I know," he whispered back, his tone so gentle it almost felt out of place in the horrifying reality they were in. He reached out, brushing a tear away from her cheek with his thumb. His touch was surprisingly soft, and for a fleeting moment, it made her feel less alone. "I've got it taken care of, just stay here."

Sunshine let out a breathy laugh, sarcastic despite the tears. "No problem,"

Tate gave a small smile, glancing over her tied-up form. "Right," he acknowledged, standing up straight. He gave her one last reassuring look before turning away.

Chapter 9

Sunshine stood just beyond the doorway, her back pressed against the wall, listening intently to the murmur of voices in the dining room. Ever since they'd moved into the house, her life felt like it was spiraling—everything escalating out of control. The lack of rest, the anxiety gnawing at her mind, and the constant sense of dread had seeped into every corner of her existence. Her grades had plummeted, she could barely focus, and a persistent exhaustion clung to her, dragging her down.

She peered around the corner, catching a glimpse of her parents sitting at the table with the two detectives. The soft rustling of papers as one of the detectives pushed a photo across the table reached her ears.

"This is the female you say you saw on Wednesday morning?" the detective asked, his voice steady, professional.

Sunshine leaned in slightly, straining to hear her father's response.

"Yes. Yes, that's her," Ben replied, his voice tight with unease. "She must have been casing the house. I'd... I'd never seen her before."

Just then, Sunshine flinched at the sudden appearance of her sister. "What are you doing?" Violet whispered, her eyebrows raised.

Sunshine quickly brought a finger to her lips, her eyes wide. "Shh. Listen," she whispered back, motioning for Violet to join her. They both stood just out of sight, eavesdropping on the conversation.

The detective's next words had Sunshine's blood run cold. "And you won't see her again. We found her six blocks from here, practically cut in half. Looks like maybe she couldn't go through with it. Ran off. Her friends went after her, tried to do a Black Dahlia on her."

Sunshine gasped, her wide eyes locked with Violet's.

"Seems your attackers were obsessed with famous LA murders," the second detective added, his tone unnervingly casual. "Had a little club going. Planned to re-create more than a few. We're still looking. Don't worry."

"Even in a town this big, people don't just disappear," the detective muttered, rising from his seat. He gestured to the kitchen. "I'm gonna check for more prints."

As the detectives walked out past them, Sunshine and Violet exchanged a glance, then cautiously stepped into the room. Ben stood up, his face tight with stress and concern as he approached his daughters.

"Your mom said that Tate helped you escape?" Ben asked, his gaze shifting between them.

Violet nodded. "Yeah. Thanks for not dragging him into all that."

Ben's face hardened. "What was he doing in the house?"

Violet's irritation flared as she met his gaze head-on. "How should I know?"

"Violet..."

"You think I let him in? I don't know why Tate was here, but I'm glad he was. You weren't." Her words were sharp, biting, leaving no room for argument.

Sunshine stayed quiet, watching the tension unfold between them.

Violet turned to leave, but not before glancing back at Vivien, who sat quietly at the table, her hands clasped tightly on the table. "You were really brave, Mom," Violet said softly, the anger in her voice momentarily replaced with something close to admiration.

Then she was gone, leaving Sunshine, Vivien, and Ben alone in the quiet aftermath. Ben looked over at Sunshine, then back to Vivien, regret heavy in his voice. "I'm sorry I wasn't here."

Vivien sighed, her gaze still focused downward, her fingers fidgeting nervously. "Me too. But you're here now."

Ben nodded, stepping closer. "That's right. I'm home."

Vivien shook her head, her eyes finally lifting to meet him. "No, you're not. We're selling this house."

Sunshine's heart dropped. "What? Mom, what about school?" Her voice cracked with desperation. Her grades were already slipping, and the thought of moving schools, especially when the year had barely started, felt like too much. Everything in her life was already unraveling, and this would only make it worse.

Vivien stood, not wanting to engage in the argument. "I don't want to hear it, Sunshine. We'll figure it out later."

"They're selling the house," Sunshine muttered, her voice low as she shut her locker with a soft clang. She had pulled out the textbook she needed, glancing briefly at her sister who stood leaning against the row of lockers with a growing look of frustration.

"What?" Violet's voice came out in a breath, her irritation clear as her brow furrowed.

Sunshine nodded. "I didn't know if I should mention it or not. I'm sure they would've told you, but... yeah. I'm not happy about it either."

Violet pushed herself off the locker, crossing her arms tightly. "I love our house. I don't get it."

Sunshine let out a sigh, leaning her back against the lockers. "Bad shit has been happening in that house since we moved in."

Violet scoffed, rolling her eyes. "Please. It was shit even before we moved in, and you know it."

"I know..." Sunshine pursed her lips, contemplating for a moment. "I don't think we need to move. At most, we just need to get the house exorcised by a priest or something."

Violet let out a short laugh, but before their conversation could go any further, Leah approached. Sunshine immediately noticed the oversized sun hat Leah was wearing, almost like she was trying to hide behind it. Beneath the hat, a bandage was taped to her cheek. As soon as Sunshine saw it, flashes of that night invaded her thoughts, but she quickly shook them off.

Leah gave Sunshine a forced smile before turning to Violet. "Since my Halloween plans are canceled because I refuse to go out like this," she said, gesturing vaguely to her bandaged face, "did you wanna come over?"

Sunshine's jaw dropped. What? A few weeks ago, Leah and Violet couldn't stand each other, and now they were acting like best friends? It was surreal.

"Uh... yeah," Violet nodded, a little hesitant but sincere. "I'd like that."

Sunshine blinked, her eyes darting between the two girls. Was she missing something?

"Cool." Leah nodded before striding away, leaving the sisters in an awkward silence.

Sunshine couldn't hold it in. "Did hell freeze over?" she muttered, still watching Leah walk off in disbelief.

Violet rolled her eyes, shouldering her bag. "I gotta get to class."

"Yeah, okay." Sunshine nodded her head dramatically, unable to shake the absurdity of what just happened.

Violet backed away, tossing up a peace sign with a smirk. "Bye."

Sunshine moved around her room, earbuds in, half-heartedly cleaning while her playlist shuffled through song after song. She was searching for that perfect track for her audition, but the music couldn't hold her focus for long. The extra pills she had taken were making it impossible for her to stay still. The need to keep busy took over, so she folded clothes, tossed old notes into the trash, and straightened her bookshelf.

As she leaned down to pick up a stray hoodie, movement caught her eye just beyond the door. She stilled, glancing toward it. Through the slight gap, she saw a figure slipping out of Violet's room. Tate. He was sneaking down the hallway like a shadow, about to descend the stairs.

Without thinking, Sunshine pulled out her headphones and stepped into her doorway, her voice a barely-there whisper. "Tate?" He froze mid-step, turning his head to look at her. For a split second, his face was unreadable, caught in the act. "Can we talk?"

Tate quickly moved toward her, stepping into the soft glow of her room. Sunshine quietly shut the door behind him, locking them inside so no one would catch him if her parents woke up.

"What's up?" Tate asked casually, though his eyes flickered curiously around her room.

Sunshine hesitated, trying to find the words. "I, uh... I just wanted to thank you." She paused, fidgeting with the hem of her sleeve. "I know I haven't been the best towards you, and I'm really sorry."

Tate's eyes softened slightly. "Don't worry about it."

Sunshine's tongue glided along her dry bottom lip, hesitating before she suddenly stepped forward and wrapped her arms around Tate. Her cheek pressed against his chest, and she held him tightly, surprising both of them.

Tate froze, caught off guard by the unexpected affection. He stood stiffly for a moment, unsure how to respond, but after a second, his arms tentatively came up around her, holding her gently in return.

Her tears came without warning, welling up and spilling over as the weight of everything hit her all at once. She buried her face against him, overwhelmed by how grateful she felt. She realized that without Tate, she and her family might not have made it through that terrifying night. He had saved them, and in that moment, everything she had thought about him shifted.

Maybe he wasn't as bad as she had always assumed.

Sunshine sniffled, tears cascading down her cheeks, soaking into Tate's shirt. He felt the shudder in her breath, and his hand moved instinctively to rub her back in soothing circles.

"Hey, it's okay," Tate whispered, his voice soft and surprisingly gentle. He continued to rub her back, trying to comfort her. "Don't cry."

Sunshine pulled back, embarrassed by her tears, and quickly wiped at her face with the sleeve of her sweater. "I'm sorry," she mumbled, her voice thick with emotion. "I've been so emotional lately."

"It's alright," Tate reassured, his tone understanding. "You've been through a lot. You don't need to apologize."

Sunshine nodded, sniffling again as she wiped the last of her tears.

The two stood in a quiet, lingering moment, their eyes locked. Sunshine could still feel the warmth of his embrace clinging to her, a strange sense of calm settling in the room. Tate broke the silence first, his gaze shifting toward the door as he stepped back slightly.

"I should go," he murmured, his voice soft but with a tinge of hesitation.

"Yeah," Sunshine replied, her voice barely above a whisper.

Tate gave her one last glance, an unreadable expression flickering in his eyes before he turned toward the door. As he reached for the handle, Sunshine stood frozen in place, watching him leave, unsure of what to say or do to keep the moment from slipping away entirely. With a soft click, the door closed behind him, leaving her alone.

Chapter 10

The leasing agent stood in the middle of the sparsely furnished apartment, her tone detached. "So as I mentioned on the phone, the carpet will be steam cleaned before move-in," she explained, gesturing to a nearby outlet. "And there's a dock there for your iPod or iWhatever."

Vivien glanced around the space, her eyes scanning the drab beige walls and the lackluster decor. "Uh, well, I'll tell you what I do like," she said, her voice heavy with fatigue. "I like that security guy at the door..."

"Excuse me. Can we have a moment? Alone?" Violet interrupted, her voice sharp.

The agent blinked, slightly taken aback, but quickly recovered. "Sure," she replied, with a forced smile, already heading for the door. "I'll be in the rental office. Got someone else coming in twenty minutes." She disappeared, the door closing behind her with a faint click, leaving an awkward silence in her wake.

Violet wasted no time, her frustration bubbling to the surface. "Glad we moved all the way to California since we could be literally anywhere."

"I think it has a certain..."

"You and Dad, both of you—" Violet cut her off, her words laced with accusation. "You don't deal with anything. The affair, the miscarriage. For most people, that's just life and they deal. But you guys had to uproot everything—drag everyone across the country to start over..."

Sunshine stood nearby, her arms crossed tightly across her chest, forcing her lips into an awkward, thin line. Here we go again. Violet had never been one to shy away from confrontation, especially with their parents. She seemed to thrive on calling them out, exposing every flaw like a surgeon wielding a scalpel. Sunshine admired that fierce spirit in her sister, but it also meant being stuck in the crossfire of endless arguments.

Vivien tried to reason with her, but there was a weariness in her voice. "Honey, I don't think you've quite processed what happened to us in that house. That was devastating. That was a nightmare."

Violet scoffed, her frustration only growing. "This place is the nightmare. I love our house, it's got soul. It's where we kicked some ass, Mom. You say we were victims of something bad there. I say that's the place where we survived."

Vivien took a deep breath, her gaze softening at her daughter's defiance. "I love that you see it that way. I really do. But I'm pregnant. I can't stay there." She turned to Sunshine, her voice almost pleading for some support. "Sunshine?"

Sunshine stood there quietly, her eyes roaming the small, impersonal apartment. "I don't know, Mom," she finally sighed, looking down at her feet. "I left my friends and my whole life behind for that house. Vi did too... I vote no."

Vivien's face fell, her shoulders slumping as she absorbed her daughters' words. She let out a heavy sigh. "This is the decision that your father and I have made for our family together."

"Yeah, whatever." Violet rolled her eyes, her expression hardening. "But I'm telling you, you go ahead with this whacked-out plan, and I'm out of here. I'll run away. And believe me, I know how to leave so you'll never find me."

Sunshine lay in bed, the covers twisted around her legs from all the tossing and turning. No matter how hard she tried, she couldn't shake the persistent thoughts of Tate. She had always found him attractive in a way she tried to ignore, but now, those feelings had grown into something else, something she couldn't easily dismiss.

Her feelings had crept in unexpectedly, and now, they refused to leave. She wanted to be near him, to touch him, to feel his arms around her again like when he'd comforted her. That simple moment, so innocent yet so intense, had her head spinning. It was like a switch had flipped inside her.

Sunshine groaned and rolled over, burying her face in the pillow as if that could smother the thoughts flooding her brain. A crush? Really? She wanted to bang her head against the nearest wall. This was so messed up. Tate was her sister's best friend—and, above all, there was something about him that still left her uneasy. She couldn't forget how unsettling he'd been in the basement, how there was this dark, dangerous edge to him that scared her.

But then he had saved them. Her family. Her sister. And that had changed everything. Sunshine now saw him in a new light—maybe too much of a new light.

Sunshine's bottom lip caught between her teeth as her thoughts drifted back to Tate's session with her father, the words he'd said about her still lingering in her mind. He had talked about her, in a way no one ever had. The things he had said he wanted to do to her... Her cheeks flushed, warmth spreading through her body as she felt a smile tug at the corners of her mouth.

He had been right—she was a virgin. But not because of any lofty ideals about purity or waiting for marriage. It was a choice, one tied to her ambition, her drive to chase her dreams. Sunshine never had the time or interest in relationships, in anything that could distract her from her goals.

She couldn't afford to let something, or someone, hold her back. The idea of ⊠⊠giving that part of herself away always felt like it might derail her plans, like it could change her, tie her down in a way she wasn't ready for.

But Tate made her wonder, made her question that resolve. And now, she couldn't stop thinking about him. About what it would feel like to let go, just for a moment, and let someone get close.

Sunshine rolled onto her back, her breath coming in short, uneven bursts. The room felt warmer, her body responding to the flood of thoughts she couldn't push away. Her eyes fluttered shut, and in the darkness of her mind, she could see Tate—his intense gaze, the way he spoke so confidently, so unapologetically about the things he would do to her.

Her bottom lip glistened under her tongue, a soft sigh escaping her as her hand, which had been resting idly on her stomach, began to move. Slowly, almost hesitantly, her fingers traced a path downward. Her body stirred with each inch of progress, the heat pooling low as she imagined his hands instead of hers, imagined his voice whispering in her ear.

As she rubbed tight circles on her heat, the image of Tate held her focus, his presence guiding her every sensation. Each thought of him stirred something deeper within, sending waves of pleasure coursing through her body. The higher she climbed, the more vivid her imagination became.

But as the images of Tate became more intense, another figure began to emerge—darker, faceless. The Rubber Man. His sleek, black form loomed in her mind, hovering over her, taking Tate's place. The shift was jarring, confusing her as the two figures began to blur together.

She hesitated, her mind reeling, unsure of why the faceless figure had appeared in her fantasy. Yet, something about the rubber man intrigued her in ways she didn't expect. He and Tate alternated in her thoughts, flashes of one bleeding into the other, both figures commanding her attention.

A part of her wanted to pull away, to regain control, but another part—one she hadn't realized existed—was drawn to the dark, forbidden energy the rubber man brought.

Sunshine surrendered fully to the fantasy, allowing herself to be swept away. Her mouth fell open, a soft gasp escaping her lips as her body arched into the sensation. The warmth that had been slowly building now surged through her like a tidal wave, her skin tingling with electric heat. She could almost feel Tate's hands ghosting over her, his whispered promises echoing in her mind.

Chapter 11

Sunshine tugged at the uncomfortably tight fabric of the Tiffany costume as she stepped out of the dressing room, her face twisted in frustration. The leather jacket felt stiff, and the lace on the skirt itched against her skin. She let out a long, exasperated sigh, catching Violet's bored gaze.

"I like it," Violet said flatly, leaning against the wall, clearly not interested in the whole ordeal. She had no intention of dressing up this year—her plans with Leah didn't exactly involve Halloween spirit, and honestly, she wasn't in the mood for anything.

Sunshine raised an eyebrow, her annoyance deepening. "You said that about the last two costumes I tried on," she shot back, folding her arms.

"I liked those too," Violet shrugged, still glued to her phone.

"You're useless," Sunshine grumbled, rolling her eyes as she turned back toward the dressing room. She knew Violet didn't care, but her lack of enthusiasm was just adding to Sunshine's frustration. Nothing was going right today, and finding a decent costume was becoming more of a chore than a fun distraction.

Sunshine stared at herself in the mirror, letting out a slow breath. She tugged at the edges of the costume again, but it wasn't the outfit that was the real problem.

After a moment, she sighed. Between the move, school, and everything that had happened in the house, she hadn't paid attention to the subtle ways her figure had filled out more than before.

"Maybe I just need to size up," she mumbled to herself, running her hands down the sides of her body.

Sunshine slipped back into her regular clothes, carefully folding the costume and placing it back in the bag. Stepping out of the dressing room, she noticed Violet was nowhere to be found. Typical. She wandered further into the store and soon spotted her father browsing through the costume racks. He caught sight of her and waved her over.

"Sunny, vampire or doctor?" Ben asked, holding up two costumes with a playful smile as she approached.

"Hmm." Sunshine tilted her head, pretending to consider the options. "Vampire."

"I was thinking that too," Ben grinned, lowering the doctor costume. His eyes flicked to the bag in her hand. "Oh, Bride of Chucky."

Sunshine held up the costume slightly, shrugging. "It's the best I could find."

Ben chuckled softly. "Well, you'll make it work. You always do."

Sunshine gave a half-hearted smile, but her eyes betrayed the stress she was carrying. Ben noticed and tilted his head slightly, lowering the vampire costume to his side.

"What's up? You seem off." His voice softened with genuine concern.

Sunshine shrugged, trying to brush it off. "I'm fine, Dad."

It wasn't that she didn't trust her dad. She did. But being a therapist's daughter often made things complicated. Every conversation felt like it had the potential to turn into a therapy session, and sometimes that was the last thing she wanted. She could feel the gentle probing coming before he even said anything, the subtle attempt to get her to open up.

Ben noticed her hesitation, his smile soft but understanding. He placed a hand on her shoulder, a comforting presence that grounded her even though it sometimes made her want to pull away. "Hey," he began, his voice warm with sincerity, "if you need to talk to someone, we can always get you some help."

He gave her shoulder a gentle squeeze, and she could feel the concern in his touch. But she'd heard this spiel so many times before. It was the standard line. The therapist line. He meant well, but it made her feel like a patient, not a daughter. Sunshine rolled her eyes, not out of anger but out of sheer exhaustion from hearing the same thing on repeat.

"Yeah, just not you," she teased, letting a small smirk tug at her lips as she looked back up at him. "You're way too expensive."

"Well, I am the best in the business," he joked, nudging her gently.

"Yeah, yeah." Sunshine nudged him back, her mock annoyance hiding the fact that his attempt to lighten the mood had worked.

Sunshine's fingers glided over the keys of her keyboard, the soft hum of the music filling her headphones. She was lost in the melody, the notes flowing effortlessly as she imagined herself at her audition, dazzling the admissions panel with her skill and passion. The house was busy with people visiting to spruce it up for selling, but the headphones allowed her to shut it all out.

Just as she hit a smooth chord, a sudden gust of wind blew through the room. Sunshine paused, her fingers hovering over the next note, her instincts kicking in. Something felt... off. Slowly, she slipped her headphones down as she turned to look behind her. The room was still, undisturbed, but the feeling lingered.

She stood, eyes scanning her surroundings when a soft giggle came from under her bed. Sunshine's heart leapt into her throat as her eyes widened. Slowly, she approached the bed, every muscle tense with anticipation. She bent down, ready to look, when something cold grabbed her ankle.

She screamed, stumbling back in shock.

"Trick or treat, smell my feet, give me something good to eat," a familiar voice sang from under the bed.

Sunshine gasped, her hand clutching her chest as her heartbeat raced. "Jesus Christ, Addy!" She exhaled, trying to steady her breath. "You can't keep sneaking in here like that!"

Addy, her head poking out from under the bed, crawled out with a wide grin. "I want to be a pretty girl for Halloween."

Sunshine blinked, trying to process what she said. "What?"

"Make me a pretty girl like you, Sunshine."

A small smile tugged at the corner of Sunshine's lips, the initial shock fading. "Alright, come on." She motioned for Addy to sit on the bed, and the girl eagerly climbed up.

Sunshine moved to her dresser, grabbing her makeup bag and tossing it onto the bed. Sitting down in front of Addy, she opened the bag and pulled out an eyeshadow palette. "What color are you thinking?" she asked, holding it up for Addy to see.

Addy's eyes sparkled as she examined the colors, eventually pointing to a light blue shimmery shade. "That one."

"Good choice." Sunshine nodded, dipping a brush into the shadow. "Close your eyes."

As she applied the color, the room fell into a comfortable silence, but it didn't last long. "Is Tate your boyfriend?" Addy asked suddenly.

Sunshine froze, the brush hovering mid-air. She hadn't expected that question. "I didn't know you knew Tate."

"I talk to him when he comes here for his head shrinking,"

She nodded slowly as she dipped the brush into the powder and tapped it lightly against the side to release the excess. "To answer your question... no," she began, trying to keep her tone casual, though her heart raced a little faster at the mere mention of him. "I wouldn't even really consider us friends."

"He likes you. I can tell," Addy stated with certainty.

Sunshine's hand faltered again, the brush hovering inches above Addy's face as her cheeks flushed pink. The warmth spread across her skin, and she felt the heat creeping up to the tips of her ears. She tried to play it off, keeping her expression neutral, but the corners of her lips betrayed her, twitching upward.

"You think so?" she asked, trying to sound nonchalant, though her voice came out softer than intended.

Addy nodded eagerly, as if she held some undeniable truth. "He thinks you're a pretty girl,"

The blush deepened on Sunshine's cheeks, her heart doing little somersaults in her chest. She lowered the powder brush, her gaze falling away from Addy's inquisitive eyes as she tried to collect herself.

But just as the warm feeling settled in, Addy cut through the moment. "Are you a virgin?"

By now, Sunshine was used to Addy's random, unfiltered questions, so she didn't react much. "Never really had the time for it, so yeah. What about you?"

"Hell no,"

Sunshine shook her head with a grin as she found the perfect lipstick shade, applying it to Addy's lips with a careful hand. Once finished, she leaned back and admired her work. "Alright, take a look in the mirror."

Addy jumped off the bed and hurried to the mirror on the wall, her face lighting up with pure joy as she gazed at her reflection. "Sunshine, I'm beautiful!"

"You've always been beautiful," Sunshine said softly, standing up to join her. "Now the rest of the world can see it too."

CHAPTER 12

Sunshine stood by the kitchen counter as she sipped on a glass of water. Violet appeared suddenly in the doorway, dressed like she was ready to go out, her arms crossed with a sheepish smile on her face.

"Hey, so I just realized," Violet began, her voice carrying an almost-too-casual tone that Sunshine immediately clocked. "I totally forgot I promised Tate we'd hang out in the basement today."

Sunshine raised an eyebrow, already sensing that something was off. "And you're telling me this because...?"

"Because," Violet shrugged. "I also promised Leah I'd meet her like... right now. We have plans, and I kinda double-booked myself."

Sunshine set her glass down, her suspicion growing. "So, you're ditching Tate?"

"I wouldn't say ditching," Violet said, waving it off like it wasn't a big deal. "I just... won't be here. And you know, since you're around, you could just... hang with him for a bit. Make sure he's not down there alone."

Sunshine blinked, her voice faltering slightly. "Hang out with him? In the basement? Alone?"

Violet, as always, brushed off Sunshine's apprehension with a casual wave. "I'll be back after Halloween."

Sunshine's brows furrowed, suspicion growing. "Wait, you're spending the night there?" Her lips curved into a knowing chuckle as she leaned back against the counter, crossing her arms. There was no hiding the teasing glint in her eyes.

"I don't know what you're insinuating," Violet said, attempting to sound nonchalant, but Sunshine could see though it.

"Mhmm," Sunshine hummed.

Before Violet could respond, a car honked loudly from the driveway, cutting through the moment. Sunshine watched her sister spin toward the back door, grabbing her bag.

"Right, well," Violet muttered, her pace quickening as she opened the door. "That's my ride."

But before disappearing outside, Violet paused, turning back. "Oh, and by the way—midnight. Tate."

Sunshine's chuckled, her posture straightening. "Wait, what? Midnight? What do you—"

"Midnight!" Violet called back, her voice echoing through the kitchen as she slipped out, the door clicking shut behind her.

Sunshine stood there, mouth open, caught somewhere between confusion and exasperation. She hadn't even agreed to anything, and yet, here she was. Midnight. Tate. Alone. In the basement.

Sunshine stood in front of the mirror, her eyes scanning over her reflection as she smoothed down her hair for what felt like the hundredth time. Her dirty blonde waves, usually tied up, now cascaded down her back, reaching just past her shoulders.

The faint glow of her phone caught her attention, and she picked it up, checking the time. Midnight was approaching, and with it, the thought of Tate waiting for her in the basement. Her heart gave a quick, nervous flutter.

A sigh escaped her lips as she tossed her phone onto the bed, trying to steady the jittery feeling in her stomach. The thought of being alone with Tate tonight sent her nerves into overdrive. There was a chance—an undeniable chance—that her little crush could be reciprocated, and that terrified her more than anything.

What if he felt the same? What if something shifted between them? She wasn't sure possibility if she was ready for that. The idea of ▨▨▨▨it thrilled her, but it also made her afraid of what she might do—or allow—if she let her guard down.

With one final glance in the mirror, Sunshine took a deep breath and left her room. Her heart raced with anticipation as she padded quietly down the stairs, each step bringing her closer to the basement. She hesitated when she reached the door. The memories of that night—of the thing she and Violet had convinced themselves was just a mask—lingered in her mind.

The stairwell yawned into darkness below, the air cold and stale. Sunshine's hand hovered on the light switch, flicking it on as her eyes darted down the steps, half expecting to see Tate waiting at the bottom. But the stairs were empty, the basement quiet.

She swallowed the lump forming in her throat. It's fine. It's just Tate, she reassured herself. Her voice was soft as she called out, "Um... Tate?" Her words echoed down the staircase, bouncing off the concrete walls. Silence greeted her in return.

Sunshine took another deep breath, stepping carefully down the stairs, the wooden steps groaning beneath her weight. Flicking on the basement light, she scanned the room.

"Tate?" she called again as she cautiously turned a corner, peering into one of the subsections of the basement.

Suddenly, before she could fully register what was happening, a hand clamped over her mouth, another arm wrapping tightly around her waist. Sunshine's scream was muffled, her eyes wide with panic as she thrashed against the grip. Her heart pounded in her chest, adrenaline spiking as she struggled. But just as quickly, her terror shifted into seeing things anger as her eyes caught sight of his face—Tate's face.

He pressed her against the stairs as he stifled his laughter.

"That's so not fucking funny," Sunshine grumbled, pushing him back slightly, her chest still rising and falling as she tried to catch her breath and calm her racing heartbeat.

"I scared you," Tate teased, his voice low and amused as he towered over her.

Sunshine glared up at him through narrowed lashes, her pulse still hammering in her ears. She bit the inside of her cheek to keep from smiling, refusing to give him the satisfaction. "Seeing as I'm home alone and standing in the world's most scariest basement, I'd say it's perfectly reasonable for me to be scared," she retorted, sarcasm dripping from her voice.

Tate's eyes lingered on her face for a moment before drifting down her form, taking her in with a quiet intensity. His gaze, dark and piercing, returned to meet hers, and a small, appreciative smile curled his lips. "You look pretty," he said softly, his voice taking on a different, more genuine tone.

Sunshine felt a sudden warmth bloom in her cheeks, the flush creeping up her neck as her irritation quickly dissolved under the intensity of Tate's gaze. His eyes seemed to linger on her a second too long.

Oh God, stay calm, she thought, her heart now racing for an entirely different reason. Trying to break the thick tension swirling between them, she blurted out, "Oh! I forgot to mention. Violet's at Leah's."

Tate nodded, his expression unchanging as he casually shoved his hands into his jean pockets. "I know,"

Sunshine's brows furrowed in confusion, her lips parting. "You know?"

A small, knowing smile tugged at the corner of Tate's lips as he took a step closer, his presence suddenly overwhelming. "I asked her to get you to come down here," he admitted, his eyes never leaving hers.

She let out a nervous laugh, her heart pounding in her ears. "Why would you do that?" she asked, her voice waving, unsure of where this was going.

He lowered his voice, his eyes dark and locked on hers. "Don't ask questions you already know the answer to... you're smarter than that."

Sweet fuck, she thought, her mind reeling as she tried to process what was happening. The way he was staring down at her, the low rasp of his voice—it was making her feel like she was about to explode. Sunshine swallowed hard, her mouth suddenly dry as she tried to steady her breathing.

"Well," she began, her voice wavering slightly, "since you went out of your way to get me down here..." Her eyes flickered over the basement. She clasped her hands tightly behind her back, her fingers twitching nervously. "What did you have planned?"

Tate shifted his weight awkwardly, his gaze darting from the shadowed corners of the room to Sunshine's face. His lips twisted into a faint, unsure smile. "I hadn't really gotten that far," he admitted. "Honestly... I wasn't sure you'd even show up."

A small smile flickered across Sunshine's lips, her expression softening as she reached out to place a gentle, reassuring hand on Tate's arm. The warmth of her touch lingered for a brief moment, her fingers squeezing lightly as if to say I'm here. Then, without another word, she stepped past him.

As she walked further into the basement, her eyes scanned the shadowy corners and dusty shelves. The low, oppressive ceiling made the space feel smaller, as though the walls were closing in, but Sunshine was undeterred. Her fingers trailed across a nearby shelf, leaving small streaks in the dust, as she searched for something that could break the tension between them.

Suddenly, her gaze fell on a weathered wooden box, half-buried beneath a pile of old books. She carefully pulled it free, blowing away the thick layer of dust that coated the surface. As the dust settled, the faded lettering became visible: Ouija.

In the spirit of Halloween, Sunshine decided this was perfect. She turned, holding the box up.

"How about this?" she asked, her voice playful but laced with the thrill of the unknown.

"You sure?" Tate asked as he stepped closer. "Wouldn't want you to be scared."

Sunshine scoffed, rolling her eyes with playful defiance. "I can handle it," she replied, nudging him lightly in the ribs as she brushed past. Her touch was brief but enough to make him glance back at her, curious. She made her way toward an old table she had spotted tucked in the far corner of the basement. It was worn, the wood splintered and dulled with age, but on top of it rested three red candles, their wax frozen in mid-drip from who knows how long ago.

Sunshine set the Ouija board down gently, the wood making a soft thud against the table. She moved around the table and sat cross-legged on the floor.

Tate lingered for a moment, watching her settle in. Without a word, he shrugged off his flannel shirt, revealing the snug black t-shirt underneath that clung to his lean frame as he lowered himself across from her.

From the pocket of his jeans, Tate pulled out a matchbox. The sound of the match striking against the rough strip was sharp, and in the darkness of the basement, the sudden flicker of the flame cast light across the walls. One by one he lit the old red candles.

Sunshine watched the flames for a moment, then reached for the board. She lifted the planchette carefully, feeling its smooth, cool surface beneath her fingers as she placed it gently in the center of the board. She glanced up at Tate.

"So, how does this work?" she asked, her voice quieter now.

"You have to put your fingers on the other side," Tate instructed, his voice soft yet commanding as he absentmindedly brushed a lock of hair away from his face. Sunshine hesitated for a second, then followed his instructions, placing her fingers lightly on the opposite side of the planchette.

"Charles is going to answer all your questions," Tate continued, his tone dropping to something more ominous. "He used to live here."

Sunshine's lips twisted into a smirk, but the bitterness was unmistakable. "Maybe Charles can tell me what happened to the people that tried to kill us." Her voice was laced with thinly veiled hostility. She hadn't forgotten Tate's role in that night, nor the part he played in the chaos. It gnawed at the back of her mind, especially since one of the women that had come after her was found mutilated a couple of blocks away—nearly sliced in half. It makes a girl wonder, she thought.

The detectives had chalked it up to infighting, theorizing that the accomplices turned on each other, but that explanation never quite made sense to her. There were too many unanswered questions. Her eyes flicked back to Tate, narrowing slightly. "Or maybe you can tell me," she added, her voice low and challenging. "Since you said you had it all handled that night."

Tate's expression didn't shift, but there was something unsettling about the way his dark eyes bore into hers, as if he could see straight into her soul. "I'll tell you what I told Violet," he replied evenly, his voice calm but carrying an edge. "I didn't do anything."

Sunshine's eyes narrowed, shooting him a look that clearly said she wasn't buying it.

He paused, letting the words sink in before adding, "I had some help."

Sunshine leaned forward slightly, her eyes narrowing further. "Help from who?" she asked, her posture shifting into something more confrontational—like she was interrogating him.

"The ghosts that live here," Tate said flatly, his voice devoid of emotion, as if daring her to take him seriously.

"Haha. Very funny," she replied, rolling her eyes as if brushing off his attempt to scare her.

A slow, knowing smile spread across his face.

"And what about the thing in here?" Sunshine asked, her tone half-joking, but there was a subtle shift in her voice that hinted at a sliver of doubt. "Is that a ghost too?"

Tate's smile faded, his eyes growing serious once more. "What I'm about to tell you," he said, his voice dropping to a near whisper, "might scare you... to death."

Sunshine arched an eyebrow, her smirk returning but with a flicker of unease in her gaze. "I sure hope so,"

"Dr. Charles Montgomery built this house," Tate began, his voice dropping to a low, chilling tone. "And here in this basement is where he worked."

He paused drawing Sunshine further into the story. "Charles was a doctor to the stars, known for his brilliance, but he was also a drug addict. His wife, Nora, wasn't going to let that get in the way of her lifestyle."

Tate leaned in slightly, his expression serious. "So she set up a little secret side business. Charles would take care of girls who didn't want to be in trouble anymore."

"This went on for some time until one day, one girl couldn't keep the secret to herself. She told her boyfriend what happened, and he wanted revenge. So he kidnapped Charles and Nora's baby."

Sunshine gasped. "Terrified, the doctor and his wife waited for ransom demands. Driven insane by grief, the doctor used all his experience and surgical skills to try and cheat death."

"But what he created was ungodly, monstrous. And even after their tragic end, that 'thing' remains down here, to this day."

"That's... really sad," Sunshine finally said, her voice barely above a whisper. She frowned as the story lingered in her mind, leaving her more depressed than scared.

"You're not scared?" Tate asked, a hint of disbelief in his tone.

"I mean, sure, it's a creepy story, but it just makes me feel bad for Nora... the baby... even Charles," Sunshine replied, her voice thoughtful and steady.

Tate's expression shifted slightly, surprise flickering across his face before a smile appeared. "You really feel for the monsters, don't you?"

"I guess so," she said, a small smile playing at the corners of her lips. "Monsters are just people. It's kind of tragic, really."

Tate nodded, his expression softening as he watched her. "You've got a big heart, Sunshine."

Footsteps echoing from upstairs suddenly interrupted their intimate exchange, drawing both of their gazes upward. The muffled sound of voices and the creak of the floorboards broke the spell that had enveloped them, a gentle reminder of the world outside the basement.

"My parents are back," Sunshine said, her tone disappointed as she stood. Tate followed suit, rising to his feet, but something in his expression made her pause.

As Sunshine turned toward the stairs, Tate gently grasped her hand, a quiet urgency in his touch that stopped her in her tracks. "Your father agreed to see me again, but I'm not supposed to be here," he explained.

Sunshine glanced down at their entwined fingers, a small smile curling on her lips at the warmth radiating from him. "I won't let them see you," she assured him, her tone confident as she motioned toward the door.

But just as she tried to pull away, Tate tightened his grip, drawing her back to face him. The intensity in his gaze made her heart flutter as he searched her eyes. "What are you doing tomorrow night?" he asked, his thumb gently tracing the softness of her skin, sending electric sparks through her.

"Giving out candy with my parents," she replied, trying to keep her voice steady despite the warmth blooming in her cheeks.

"Let's go out after," he suggested, a playful glint in his eye. "You and me."

Sunshine's heart raced at his words, her smile widening. "Like a date?"

"Yeah. Like a date."

Chapter 13

As Sunshine put the finishing touches on her Halloween look, she took a deep breath, her nerves buzzing with anticipation. She stared at her reflection in the mirror, trying to calm herself. Tonight was her date, and the excitement was colliding with anxiety, sending her spiraling.

The sudden sound of a Halloween decoration going off downstairs startled her, snapping her out of her thoughts. With a casual hop, she made her way down the stairs, the faint rustling of her outfit accompanying her movements.

Coming up behind her parents, she immediately noticed one of the fluffers, Chad, eyeing her outfit with undisguised disdain, his gaze crawling up and down her figure with judgment.

"What?" Sunshine asked, raising an eyebrow, glancing between her parents, who both looked like they had just been criticized for a crime.

"He doesn't like our costumes," Vivien explained her voice tinged with frustration as she turned and headed toward the kitchen.

Sunshine exchanged a knowing look with her father, both of them stifling their amusement as Chad dramatically followed Vivien.

"Well, there's nothing to be done about it now." Chad continued, his voice rising in exasperation. "The doorbell's going to start ringing soon, and we still haven't finished setting up the bobbing station." He gestured dramatically toward the spread of a half-decorated Halloween game, clearly unimpressed. His eyes landed on the apples, and his face twisted in disgust. "What the hell is this?"

"What?" Vivien asked, her tone weary, as if she were already exhausted by the conversation.

Sunshine shook her head, deciding she didn't want to be caught up in whatever drama was brewing. She nonchalantly grabbed a lollipop from the candy bowl, unwrapping it before popping it into her mouth.

Patrick, Chad's husband, cautiously entered the kitchen, his voice soft but apprehensive. "Chad?"

"Gala apples," Chad finally spat out, looking at the fruit like it personally offended him. "We specifically talked about Granny Smiths."

"They didn't have any at Gelson's," Ben replied with a shrug, pulling one of the offending apples from the bobbing bucket.

Chad's eyes widened in outrage, his temper flaring. "Then you go to the farmer's market or drive out to an off-ramp in Valencia and buy a bag from Pedro! Where's the effort?" His voice grew more agitated, his arms flailing as he stared down both Ben and Vivien as if they had ruined Halloween itself.

"I think you're overreacting," Vivien sighed, stepping up next to Ben, her patience clearly fraying.

"I second that," Sunshine chimed in, pointing her lollipop lazily in Chad's direction before tucking it back between her lips.

Chad's face twisted in fury as he stepped closer to Vivien. "Because I'm the only one who actually gives a shit?" He spat, the space between them shrinking. "I think you should just leave."

Vivien blinked, genuinely taken aback. "You think we should just leave our house?" she asked, her voice shaky but firm.

"It's not your house," Chad snapped back, his eyes flashing with a manic certainty. "We know it, you know it, and the house knows it. Frankly, you don't deserve it."

Sunshine stood frozen for a moment, her eyes wide with disbelief. "Wow," she finally muttered, gaping at the escalating tension. "You guys are fucking nuts."

Vivien's emotions, once restrained, started to boil over. "Get out!" she shouted.

"Yeah, leave," Ben added, his tone low but insistent, stepping closer to his wife.

"We are not leaving this house." His words were almost a growl, his stance rigid, his refusal absolute.

Vivien, now beyond reason, began to pull things off the shelves in the kitchen, her frustration manifesting in a wild flurry of motion. Plates and decorations crashed to the floor, shattering into jagged pieces. "Get out! Get out! Get out! I don't care about any of this. Just go!" Her voice cracked as she screamed, and tears started to well up in her eyes.

Patrick, standing by the doorway, glanced nervously between his husband and Vivien. He stepped forward, gently placing a hand on Chad's arm. "You shouldn't have to watch this," he whispered to Chad, urging him to leave before things got worse.

"Get out of here!"

Patrick tugged on Chad's arm, finally pulling him toward the door. After a moment of resistance, Chad allowed himself to be led out, his furious mutterings trailing behind him as they left the house.

As the door slammed shut, the silence that followed was almost unbearable. Sunshine stood there, her heart racing, wide-eyed and stunned by what had just unfolded.

"Are you okay?" Ben's voice was quiet, tentative, as he approached Vivien, concern lining his features.

Vivien turned, her face flushed, her breath heavy. Her eyes locked on Ben's. "I don't believe you, Ben," she said, her voice quivering with restrained emotion.

Ben glanced at Sunshine, a silent plea in his eyes. "Honey," he said gently, "you should go upstairs."

"No," Vivien shook her head, her words cutting through the tension. "She can stay."

Sunshine shifted uncomfortably, glancing between her parents. Her mom's word was final, and despite the awkwardness, she stayed rooted in place, watching them both cautiously.

Vivien's face contorted with sorrow, her voice softening, but still edged with bitterness. "You tell me your story, but there's a little glimmer in your eye, a little... lie, a little darkness." Tears welled up in her eyes, and she fought to keep her composure. "I don't want to live with suspicion anymore, so I want you to go. I want you to go." Her voice broke, and the fight in her seemed to collapse into raw grief.

Suddenly, Vivien's expression changed. Her face twisted in pain as she clutched her stomach, her breaths coming in short gasps.

"Oh, God. Aah!" Her knees buckled slightly, and Sunshine rushed forward, panic flashing in her eyes.

"Mom!" Sunshine's voice trembled as she reached out, supporting her mother as best she could.

"What's wrong?" Ben asked, his worry mounting as he stepped closer.

Vivien grabbed onto Sunshine's arm, her grip tight and desperate. "Something's not right," she gasped, shaking her head. "Okay, I need to go to the hospital."

Without hesitation, Ben took hold of Vivien. He glanced at Sunshine, his tone commanding. "Stay here," he instructed, his eyes serious. "And don't answer the door."

"O-okay," Sunshine nodded as she watched her father help Vivien out the door.

Sunshine stood in her room, her fingers trembling slightly as she fumbled through her school bag, searching for the small pill bottle. The moment she found it, her heart slowed just a fraction. She popped one pill into her mouth, swallowing dry. Closing her eyes, she let out a shaky breath, yearning for something to dull the sharpness of reality. Just a little relief. Just for a moment.

The doorbells sharp chime pierced the quiet, jolting her out of her thoughts. Sunshine jumped as if she'd just been caught doing something forbidden. She grumbled, deciding to ignore it at first, hoping whoever it was would just go away.

But then it rang again. And again.

"Fuck," she muttered under her breath, tossing her bag onto the bed with an irritated flick of her wrist. Reluctantly, she made her way down the stairs.

As she neared the door, a man's voice cut through the stillness, loud and demanding. "Goddamn it, Ben, I want my money! I'm not leaving here till I have my thousand dollars! Hello! Ben Harmon!"

The voice was followed by a sharp pounding on the door that made Sunshine freeze in place. She hesitated, then moved closer to peer through the peephole. There was a man wearing a fedora, his face twisted and half-burnt. At first, she thought it was some Halloween prank, but something about the way it looked—too real—made her skin crawl.

"Ben Harmon! I am not leaving here till I have my thousand dollars!" the man continued, voice growing more impatient by the second. "Screw you! You owe me! Oh, here, take one and go! Come on, come on!"

His fist pounded against the door, and the doorbell rang again and again, filling the house with its shrill, maddening sound.

Her hands shaking, Sunshine fumbled for her phone, yanking it out of her leather jacket. Her fingers slid over the buttons as she quickly dialed her dad's number, her heart hammering in her chest. She pressed the phone to her ear, each ring feeling like an eternity.

"Hey, honey," her father's voice finally came through, calm but laced with concern.

"Dad," Sunshine's voice was barely above a whisper, her gaze darting toward the door where the pounding continued. "There's a man at the door... he says you owe him money. Should I call the cops?"

There was a pause on the other end, long enough for her to feel a rising sense of dread. "No!" Ben's voice was suddenly sharp, urgent. "No. Just... just keep the door closed. Is it locked?"

Sunshine glanced toward the lock, quickly checking. "Yeah, it's locked."

"We're on our way home right now," Ben reassured her, his tone still tense. "Just... keep the door locked. Sunshine, do not open that door."

"Okay, Dad." She swallowed hard, ending the call with a shaky thumb. Her hand clenched around the phone, her eyes never leaving the door. The pounding had stopped, but the man's voice didn't.

"I know you're in there," he called out, his voice almost sing-song, sending a chill crawling up her spine. "Is that your daughter? Hmm?"

Her eyes scanned the room, her mind racing, and that's when she saw it. Something in her peripheral vision—black, slick, a nightmare come to life.

The Rubber Man.

Her breath caught, her body frozen with fear. She turned her head sharply to look, but the space where he'd stood was now empty, as if he'd never been there at all. Her mind reeled. Was she losing it?

The pounding resumed with a sudden violence, the doorbell ringing incessantly now, and Sunshine felt like the walls were closing in.

Fear began to seep into her every muscle, her legs feeling weak as she backed away from the door.

Deciding it was safer upstairs, Sunshine made her way back to her room, her steps quick and quiet. Once inside, she shut the door with a soft click and turned the lock, sealing herself in. Leaning her back against the door, she exhaled shakily, eyes closed as if that might somehow block out the chaos of the world outside.

Her palms rubbed over her face, the coolness of her fingers grounding her just slightly. It felt like she was losing it—like she was on the verge of unraveling. Her mind played tricks on her, convincing her that the Rubber Man was real, lurking somewhere in the shadows of the house.

But he couldn't be real. He wasn't real.

She tried to reason with herself, clinging to logic even as her pulse raced and her body betrayed her with trembling hands. Maybe it was just a side effect of sleep paralysis, a hallucination bleeding into her waking hours. She'd heard of that happening before—her mind struggling to separate dreams from reality. But even that thought didn't offer much comfort. She felt the burn of tears pricking her eyes and let out a defeated sigh, her body slumping slightly against the door.

Just as she was sinking deeper into her thoughts, a soft sound broke through—the faint tap of something hitting her window. She tensed.

Slowly, cautiously, she moved toward the window and peered out.

There, standing in her backyard, was Tate. He was tossing pebbles up at her window, his expression as calm as ever. When he caught sight of her, a crooked smile spread across his face, and he motioned downward.

"Basement," he mouthed, his voice quiet but carrying enough for her to hear.

A small smile tugged at her lips despite everything. She gave him a quick nod before closing the window again.

Chapter 14

Sunshine flew down the basement steps, her feet barely touching the ground as excitement coursed through her. She tried to keep her expression composed, but the smile tugging at her lips was impossible to suppress. Reaching the bottom, she called out into the basement, her voice playful, "Don't even think about scaring me."

From the shadows of a small, dark subsection, Tate emerged with a grin on his face. He held one hand behind his back. "Who would do such a thing?" he teased as he sauntered toward her. He stopped just before her, close enough that she could feel the warmth radiating off him.

Without thinking, Sunshine stepped forward, wrapping her arms around him and burying her face in his chest. It felt natural, like it was exactly what she needed at that moment. His scent, the soft fabric of his sweater against her cheek—it was grounding. Tate immediately returned the hug, one arm wrapping around her, holding her close as his hand rubbed her back in soothing circles.

"Is everything okay?" he asked quietly, his voice filled with genuine concern.

Sunshine let out a deep sigh, her cheek pressing further into his chest. "Today's just been all over the place," she admitted. "There was this guy with a burnt face, banging on the door, yelling about money..."

Tate pulled back just enough to meet her eyes as he brushed a strand of hair behind her ear. "Hey," he said gently, his voice steady and reassuring. "Shit like that tends to go down on Halloween. Probably just some asshole trying to scare people. It's fine now. I'm here."

And it was. With him standing there, holding her like that, Sunshine felt the anxiety she'd been carrying all day evaporate. Everything in her body relaxed, the tension melting away as his presence filled the space around her. The way he looked at her made her heart flutter. She couldn't help but smile, unable to hide how happy and safe she felt in that moment.

Then, as if remembering something important, Tate took a small step back. His hand, which had been hidden behind his back, came forward, and in it was a single white rose. He held it out to her.

Sunshine blinked, surprised. She stared at the delicate bloom in his hand, its pale petals soft and perfect. "White roses represent purity... innocence," Tate explained, his voice softer now. "They remind me of you."

Her chest swelled at the gesture, warmth spreading through her like sunlight. Slowly, she reached up and took the rose from his hand, twirling it between her fingers before bringing it to her nose to inhale its gentle fragrance. "Thank you, Tate," she murmured, her voice barely above a whisper. "This is the sweetest thing anyone has ever done for me."

Tate chuckled softly, clearly flustered but trying to play it cool. His cheeks tinged with the faintest blush, dimples appearing as he smiled. His gaze dropped to his feet for a moment before flicking back up to meet hers. "You ready to go on our date?"

Sunshine licked her bottom lip as she nodded eagerly, her smile widening.

As the cool breeze rolled in from the ocean, Tate and Sunshine walked side by side and Sunshine hugged her jacket a little tighter around her body, the chill of the evening brushing against her skin.

Tate walked a step ahead before slowing his pace to fall in line with her. He kicked a small seashell out of his path, sending it skittering across the sand. "I've always liked the beach at night," he said, his voice low and contemplative, almost swallowed by the sound of the ocean. "It's like the world goes quiet, and you can actually hear yourself think."

Sunshine glanced at him, her lips curving into a small smile. "It's peaceful... kind of lonely, too."

Tate tilted his head, his eyes flicking over to her. "You think so? I kind of like the loneliness of it. It's like the world disappears, and it's just... you."

Sunshine nodded thoughtfully, tucking a loose strand of hair behind her ear as the wind played with it. "I get that. I guess I just don't like being alone." She paused, her gaze falling to her feet as they walked, toes sinking into the cool sand. "Sometimes I feel like... when everything gets too quiet, it's when my thoughts get the loudest."

Tate stopped walking for a moment, turning to face her. "I feel that way too," he admitted, his voice soft. "Like when it's quiet, everything you're trying to avoid just... catches up with you." He paused, his dark eyes searching hers. "But it doesn't feel that way when I'm with you."

Her breath hitched slightly at his words, matching his gaze. "It doesn't feel that way when I'm with you either," she admitted, her heart fluttering as she spoke. The beach felt endless, the stretch of sand and water creating a world just for them, separated from reality, from everything else.

As they walked, Tate occasionally drifted away, bending down to pick up small, weathered sticks from the ground. He added each one to a growing collection cradled in his arms, examining each piece before tucking it under his elbow.

Sunshine watched him with curiosity, her eyes flicking to him every few steps as he wordlessly hunted for the perfect fragments of driftwood. She couldn't help but smile, her earlier nerves easing into a gentle calm.

Tate nodded toward a nearby lifeguard post and Sunshine followed without question, their steps quiet in the sand as the waves whispered in the distance. When they reached what seemed like the perfect spot, just far enough from the water's edge but close enough to feel the cool mist, Tate crouched down and began arranging the sticks he'd collected earlier.

Sunshine lowered herself into the soft sand, not caring that her white costume would inevitably get dirty. She let out a breath, the coolness of the beach air clinging to her skin.

Tate finished setting up the fire pit, glancing up at her for a moment with a half-smile before pulling out a matchbox from his jacket pocket.

He struck the match, the flame flaring to life with a sharp hiss before he tossed it onto the pile of sticks. The dry wood caught almost immediately, crackling as the fire sparked to life. A soft orange glow began to spread across their small corner of the beach, flickering and dancing.

The warmth of the fire radiated toward her, chasing away the evening chill. The smell of burning wood mixed with the saltiness of the ocean air as Sunshine pulled her knees to her chest, resting her chin on them as she watched the flames grow.

Tate bounded over to the lifeguard post with a burst of childlike energy, his converse kicking up sand as he moved. It was as if the simple act of being outside had breathed new life into him.

Sunshine's eyes followed his every move with a soft, contented smile. She had never seen him like this—so carefree, so happy. The way his smile widened with each step, his arms swinging loosely at his sides, made her heart swell.

Sunshine dug into her pocket, her fingers brushing against the cool surface of her phone. Pulling it out, she saw the screen light up with missed calls from her mother. She bit her lip, hesitating for a moment before pressing the call button, lifting the phone to her ear as she glanced over at Tate, who was still lost in his own world on the lifeguard post.

"Sunshine, where are you?" Her mother's voice came through the line, tight and concerned.

"Uh," Sunshine hesitated, deciding it was probably best not to mention who she was with. "With a friend."

"We told you not to leave," her mother's tone grew sharper.

"I know, I'm sorry," Sunshine sighed, her free hand absentmindedly playing with the sand beneath her. "Do you want me to come home?"

"Are you safe?" Her mother's voice softened slightly, but there was still an edge to it.

"Yeah, Mom, of course," Sunshine assured her.

"Are you having fun?"

Sunshine's fingers stilled, and a small, genuine smile tugged at the corners of her lips. "Yeah," she said softly, her voice lighter.

Sunshine's smile faltered slightly, her thoughts drifting back to earlier in the evening when her mother had been in so much pain. "Is the baby okay?"

There was a pause on the other end, then,

"Yeah, everything's fine," her mother replied, though the exhaustion was clear in her tone. "I'm just stressed."

"That's good, Mom," Sunshine said, relieved, her shoulders relaxing as she sunk her fingers deeper into the cool sand.

"I want you home in an hour,"

"Okay. I'll see you later," Sunshine nodded, even though her mother couldn't see. She ended the call, flipping the phone shut and sliding it back into her jacket pocket.

Tate appeared at her side, his energy drawing her out of her thoughts. "Who was that?"

"Just my mom," Sunshine replied, but she grew more aware of how close he was. His face was just inches from hers, and her heartbeat quickened, her nerves suddenly on edge.

Tate's gaze flickered down to her lips, the tension between them growing thick. "Aww," he whispered softly.

Before she could process what was happening, he leaned in, his lips brushing against hers with a tenderness that caught her completely off guard. For a split second, she froze, her mind racing, but then something inside her melted, and she found herself leaning into him, her lips softening as they met his in a kiss.

The world around them faded into the background, the ocean waves and the cool breeze barely registering as her senses focused entirely on him. The warmth of his breath, the feel of his hand gently brushing against her cheek—it all felt like a dream she didn't want to wake from.

Tate pulled away slowly, his gaze locking onto hers. He searched her eyes, looking for any hint of what she was feeling. Sunshine felt a pang of disappointment wash over her as the warmth of his lips left hers.

Unable to hold back any longer, she leaned in again, her heart pounding as she pressed her lips against his with a newfound urgency.

Tate gently guided her onto her back, the coolness of the sand contrasting against the warmth radiating from their bodies. As they kissed, the urgency of their connection intensified, each moment feeling more electric than the last.

Her legs instinctively opened to accommodate him, allowing him to settle comfortably against her. Sunshine's hand found its way to his jawline, her fingers tracing the sharp contours of his face with a delicate touch. She felt the subtle pulse beneath his skin, each heartbeat echoing her own rising excitement. As her fingers brushed against the soft skin behind his earlobe, the kiss deepened.

Sunshine bucked her hips against him, a desperate plea for more, an instinctual reaction that sent ripples of exhilaration coursing through her. This feeling was entirely new, a whirlwind of emotions and sensations that scared her. Yet, amid the intensity, there was an undeniable comfort in his presence—something familiar that made her feel anchored and safe.

As she pulled her heated kisses from his lips, a trail of soft, lingering touches adorned his jawline, gradually making their way to the tender curve of his neck. Each kiss was a gentle exploration, her heart racing as she felt him melt against her.

But then he spoke, his voice thick with breathlessness. "We should... we should slow down."

Sunshine's heart sank. Did he not want her as much as she craved him? Was she not enough? "Oh," she whispered, insecurity creeping in.

"I just—" Tate started, hovering above her, his dark eyes searching her face for understanding. "Sunshine, I swear. I want to be with you so badly. And that's never happened with me, with a girl."

Sunshine blinked, looking away from him, unsure of what to believe.

Tate climbed off of her, turning toward the ocean before talking over his shoulder. "Sunshine, I really like you," he continued, his voice steady yet soft. "I just... I want you to know that you mean more to me than just this moment,"

Sunshine felt a wave of warmth wash over her as she realized that he was just as vulnerable as she was. It wasn't about lack of desire but a yearning for something deeper, something more meaningful.

"It's okay," Sunshine breathed out, feeling the weight of their conversation lift slightly as she sat up and scooted closer to him. She nestled her head against his shoulder. Tate instinctively wrapped his arm around her, drawing her in.

The two sat in a comfortable silence. The moon hung low in the sky, casting a glow over the ocean, illuminating the soft ripples as they danced under the night.

"I used to come here…when the world closed in and got so small I couldn't breathe," Tate began, his voice a low murmur.

"I'd look out at the ocean and I'd think… 'Yo, douche bag. High school counts for jack shit.'" His expression was earnest, his confidence shining through as he named the figures that had inspired him. "Kurt Cobain… Quentin Tarantino… Brando, De Niro, Pacino—" He turned to look directly into her eyes. "All high school dropouts."

A small smile crept onto her lips as their gaze drifted back to the vast ocean before them.

"I… hated high school. So I'd come here… and I'd look out at this endless, limitless expanse. And it's like, that's your life, man. You can do anything. You can be anything. Screw high school. That's just a blip in your timeline. Don't get stuck there."

Sunshine felt her heart resonate with his words. She hated high school, too. The oppressive hallways, the judgmental stares, and the relentless pressure to conform. It was suffocating, and it only fueled her desperation to escape back to the East Coast, to attend Juilliard, to immerse herself in a world where her dreams could flourish, far away from the harsh realities of her life.

Sunshine closed her eyes, relishing the warmth of the moment, when a sudden snap shattered the tranquility. Instinctively, she turned her head, her eyes narrowing as she spotted a group of teens approaching them.

"Uh, Tate..." she murmured, a knot of apprehension forming in her stomach.

Tate turned to look where she was looking, his expression shifting from calm to alert as the group finally closed the distance. The moonlight glinted off their garish Halloween makeup, transforming their faces into grotesque caricatures.

"You know, there's a whole lot of beach, guys," Tate stated coolly, his gaze sweeping around the group.

"Good job, Tate. You finally came out of hiding." The guy in the letterman jacket stepped forward, a smug grin plastered across his face. "We've been waiting for years for you to show your face. But you like Mommy's little safe house, don't you?"

Sunshine turned her gaze onto Tate, confusion knitting her brows together. He seemed just as lost, his eyes darkening with unspoken thoughts as he replied, "I don't know you."

The cheerleader leaned in, her voice dripping with mockery. "I'm actually surprised you have the balls to show your face around here." She squatted down to meet his gaze.

"Yeah. Maybe you should have worn a mask," a blonde goth girl added, invading Tate's personal space, her eyes glinting with a twisted kind of amusement.

"I'm not really into Halloween," Tate replied, attempting to remain unfazed.

"But this year's different, right?" The goth girl shifted her focus to Sunshine, who watched cautiously, irritation brewing beneath her skin. "You have a date. How cute is that?"

"Leave her alone," Tate warned, rising from the sand.

"We don't want her. We want you," the jock interjected, his voice dripping with disdain.

"How about we drown him?" the goth girl suggested.

"No, we should shoot him right between the eyes," the jock countered, pointing to his fake makeup depicting a bullet wound in his forehead, laughter bubbling up from the group.

"Okay." Sunshine stood tall, closing the distance to the jock, her eyes ablaze with defiance. "It's time to cut the bullshit. I'm getting bored."

"Will somebody please waste this bitch?" the goth spat, venom lacing her words, but Sunshine met her with a saccharine smile, defiantly flipping her off.

"Yeah. Why does he get a girlfriend?" a guy in a leather jacket chimed in, his tone mocking. "I don't have a girlfriend. Do you, Kyle?"

"Nope. I haven't had sex in a long time," Kyle stated, his gaze shifting menacingly toward Tate, as if daring him to respond.

"Shocker," Sunshine retorted, her words sharp enough to cut.

"Come on. Let's go." Tate placed a firm hand on Sunshine's shoulder, urging her to move forward. "This beach sucks. Someone should pick up the trash."

Chapter 15

The door shut softly behind Sunshine, pausing for a moment as she processed everything that had happened. Turning to Tate, she searched his face for answers, her mind spiraling with questions as the silence stretched between them.

After a long moment, she broke the stillness. "They knew you, Tate."

"But I don't know them."

"How can they hate you, then?"

"Th-They're just high school assholes," he finally managed, his voice strained. "I mean, the world's full of 'em. It's popular kids who get off on being mean and cruel. I thought you understood that."

He cast his eyes down, focusing on his hands as he nervously picked at his nails, his weight shifting as he leaned against her dresser. When he finally met her gaze again, his eyes were filled with a sadness that pierced her heart.

Sunshine sighed, taking a tentative step toward him. "I do understand, I ju—"

The sound of laughter and shouts from outside her window sliced through the moment, freezing her mid-sentence. Sunshine turned her head sharply, dread pooling in her stomach as she walked toward the window. She peered outside, her heart sinking when she saw the group of teens from earlier had found her home. Tate moved closer, peering over her shoulder, his body tense and rigid.

Sunshine looked up at Tate for a brief moment, her anger radiating from her features. Without another word, she stormed past him, her footsteps thumping angrily down the stairs, echoing in the otherwise quiet house. She pushed through the kitchen side door, stepping out into where the group stood.

"Oh, great. He sends his little girlfriend out," Kyle mocked, a smirk playing on his lips as he leaned casually.

Sunshine squared her shoulders. "You all have about five seconds to leave, or I'm calling the cops,"

"Go ahead. Call them. You'll probably need them," the cheerleader taunted as she perched on the brick wall.

"Screw that. She deserves whatever happens to her," Kyle spat.

"Yeah. She's like those lonely, fat chicks who marry guys on death row," the goth girl chimed in, her voice dripping with disdain. "You're deeply, deeply disturbed."

"Just go home," Sunshine pleaded, her voice wavering slightly but still firm.

The cheerleader skipped over to her. "Home? Where is that?" she asked, her voice rising sharply. "I'm an only child. After what happened, my parents split up, sold the house, moved away. No forwarding address. So I don't have a home." Without waiting for a reply, the cheerleader flounced over to the steps and plopped down.

"I'm sorry... but I can't help you," Sunshine replied, her voice softer now, almost pleading.

"Can you help this?" Kyle interjected, pointing to the fake blood smeared across his forehead. "Can you give me back my scholarship to Georgia Tech? I'm supposed to be starting quarterback freshman year."

"She doesn't care. She's in love, and she'll do anything for him, including giving him her virginity," the cheerleader scoffed, crossing her arms and regarding her with condescension. "Tonight was the night, wasn't it?"

Sunshine clenched her jaw, her frustration boiling over. "Shut up," she spat back.

"You stupid slut. She's worse than he is. She thinks it's okay what he did to us," Kyle berated as he prowled around her.

Sunshine rolled her eyes, trying to project confidence despite the pit of anxiety in her stomach. "What could he have possibly done to you?"

The cheerleader stepped forward, a flicker of realization crossing her face as she stood up to join the others, closing in around Sunshine. "She doesn't know,"

"Know about what?" Sunshine asked.

Before anyone could answer, a member of the group who had been silent until now stood up, attempting to speak. But as he opened his mouth, fake blood pooled and dripped from the corners, causing him to instinctively clutch his grotesque mouth.

"It's okay," the cheerleader said, her voice adopting a soothing tone.

"Have you seriously not heard about Westfield High?" Kyle continued, his gaze piercing through her as if searching for an answer within her eyes.

Sunshine took a step back. "We just moved here,"

"Pick up a yearbook, bitch,"

"Or read a newspaper,"

"We're kind of famous,"

Sunshine narrowed her eyes, struggling to hold back a laugh at the absurdity of it all. "Are you seriously mad that I don't know who you are?"

"Let's put her down, get her out of her misery," the goth girl threatened, stepping forward and invading Sunshine's personal space.

"Leave her alone!" Tate's voice cut through the tension as he emerged, positioning himself protectively in front of Sunshine.

"Finally. The prodigal son returns," Kyle sneered. "We've got some questions."

"Go inside." Tate shot a glance over his shoulder at Sunshine, his voice firm "I can handle this."

"What? No." Sunshine shook her head vehemently.

"Go inside!" Tate's sudden burst of authority made her flinch.

"I'm not leaving you," she insisted.

"Karma's a bitch, Tate," the goth girl hissed, her eyes narrowing as she took a step closer.

"You want to talk to me? Let's see how fast you can run," Tate challenged, adrenaline coursing through him as he turned on his heel and sprinted away. The teens erupted into a frenzy, trailing after him as they surged forward like a pack of wolves on a hunt.

Sunshine stood frozen, unsure of what to do next. Panic clawed at her as she pulled out her phone, fingers shaking as she dialed for help. "Hello? There's a bunch of kids chasing after my friend," she explained as she ran a hand through her hair. "I think they want to kill him."

Unexpectedly, she felt a grip on her arm, spinning her around to face Constance, who loomed over her like a storm cloud.

"Come with me to my house now," Constance demanded, her grip painfully tight as she tugged at Sunshine.

"What? Are you crazy?" Sunshine protested, discomfort surging through her as she struggled against Constance's iron grasp.

"Addy is dead because of you,"

"She wanted to be a pretty girl." Constance began, her voice tremulous yet steady as she sat across from a visibly shaken Sunshine in her kitchen.

"Of course, she didn't look so pretty lying on that table, under those harsh, energy-efficient lights," Constance said, her voice thick with grief. She paused before continuing, "One of the few comforts of having children is knowing your youth hasn't disappeared... it's simply been passed on to the next generation. Something you'll understand for yourself soon enough."

Sunshine felt a wave of confusion wash over her, but she chose not to react to the strange comment, remaining silent instead.

"They say when a parent dies... a child feels his own mortality. But when a child dies... it's immortality that a parent loses."

Sunshine sniffled, a shuddered breath escaping her as she quickly wiped away her tears. "I'm so sorry, Constance. I didn't think this would happen," she murmured, her voice laced with guilt.

"Well, you did encourage her," Constance replied, her voice quavering as she poured steaming tea into a cup. "That's true. But you were just trying to be kind, weren't you? I was the one who sent her out into the world tonight. And it did what it will do."

Sunshine frowned, a pang of empathy piercing her heart as she absorbed Constance's pain. "It's not your fault."

"Go ahead, drink your—drink your tea, honey." Constance commanded softly, pushing the steaming cup closer to Sunshine. Nodding, Sunshine lifted it to her lips, the heat enveloping her face as she blew gently at the steam before taking a sip.

"You know, Adelaide was a willful child. I suppose if she... inherited anything from me, it was that," Constance mused, her gaze drifting into the distance as she took a spoonful of sugar, the grains dissolving in the liquid when she stirred. "In truth, I think my little monster was more like me than any of my other children."

"You have other children?" Sunshine asked, surprise threading through her voice.

Constance brushed a stray hair from her face, her expression solemn. "Tate is my son."

Sunshine nearly dropped her cup, her eyes wide with disbelief. "What?"

"He cannot know about this, Sunshine." Constance's urgency heightened, her eyes glistening with unshed tears. "He cannot know... that his sister has passed. Not now. He doesn't... react well to certain things. So you— you have to promise me." Desperation tinged her tone as she grasped Sunshine's hand, her grip firm yet pleading.

"I—" Sunshine shook her head, confusion washing over her. "I don't—"

"He's a sensitive boy. You've seen that. He—he's a young man with... too deep feelings... the soul of a poet... but none of the grit or steel that acts as a bulwark against these horrors of this world. The steel that has protected me... that Adelaide possessed. And that— that you have too."

"I, uh... I think— that's why he's taken so with you. He craves your strength. Look, maybe he misses his sister. But we must protect him, Sunshine." Constance's eyes locked onto hers, conveying a depth of vulnerability that made Sunshine's heart ache.

Chapter 16

"Sunshine Harmon."

Her name sliced ▨▨through the murmurs of the crowded hall and Sunshine's head jerked upward. From her place among the sea of ▨▨faces, she felt dozens of eyes shift toward her. They were indistinct, blurring together like smudges of paint on a canvas. She couldn't make out a single expression—just the weight of their collective gaze.

Her limbs felt heavy as she rose from her seat, the auditorium's oppressive silence closing in around her. Each step down the aisle seemed endless, her senses heightened. She could feel the scrutiny of watchful, faceless figures as she passed.

When she reached the stage, Sunshine ascended the steps with trembling legs, the distance between her and the grand piano shrinking yet somehow feeling insurmountable. She reached the piano, the smooth surface cool beneath her fingertips as she lifted the fallboard.

"Whenever you're ready," a voice called from the admissions panel, cutting through the suffocating quiet.

Taking a slow breath, she stretched out her fingers, letting them hover just above the keys. As her fingers descended, the first delicate notes of Tchaikovsky's Swan Lake poured from the piano.

With each note, the world around her began to dissolve. The music wrapped around her, pulling her deeper into the melody. Her fingers danced effortlessly across the keys, as if she were no longer in control but simply a vessel for the music. A strange sense of euphoria washed over her, leaving her weightless.

But then, without warning, something felt wrong. A strange pressure bloomed in her abdomen. It started as a subtle sensation, almost like an itch, but quickly grew into something more alarming. Her fingers hesitated, faltering over the keys, yet the music continued, as if the piano were playing itself.

The pain intensified, sharp and undeniable now. Instinctively, Sunshine glanced down at her stomach, eyes widening in horror. Her abdomen had swelled grotesquely, the fabric of her shirt stretched tight across what now resembled the bulging belly of a woman eight months pregnant.

Frantically, she lifted her shirt, revealing her bloated stomach. It wasn't just the size—beneath her skin, something moved. The unmistakable outline of hooves pressed against the inside of her belly, pushing, clawing as though whatever was inside her was trying to escape.

The music grew louder, deafening, drowning out her cries. The audience remained still, their blank faces frozen in sickening smiles. And then, they began to laugh. A hollow, mocking chorus that echoed in her ears. She screamed, her voice cracking with terror.

Her eyes shot open, breathless. Her bedroom surrounded her, bathed in the sunlight filtering through the window. It had been a dream—a twisted, surreal nightmare.

Sunshine let out a shuddered breath, frantically tossing her sheets aside. Her hand instinctively flew to her stomach, half-expecting to feel a kick, but there was nothing. Just the familiar softness of her skin. A wave of relief washed over her, and she exhaled deeply, her head dropping forward as she dangled her feet off the edge of the bed, grounding herself back into reality.

But the calm couldn't hold back the flood of memories from last night. The revelation about Tate—it rattled her. Tate... Constance's son? It spun through her mind like a broken record, questions mounting. Why had Tate never mentioned it? Why had none of them said anything?

Sunshine's bottom lip quivered, her chest tightening as the image of Addy resurfaced.

Addy was dead.

Her throat tightened as guilt twisted inside her. Rationally, she knew it wasn't her fault, but the memory of Addy dressed up, yearning to be a "pretty girl" before meeting her end—it gnawed at her. Sunshine couldn't help but dwell on the role she played, no matter how small.

Then her mind snapped to another dark corner—the teens from the beach. Her body stiffened, and her gaze drifted toward her laptop sitting innocently on the desk.

Their words. Their anger. It had seemed so much more than teenage cruelty. Their fury had felt visceral, raw. She wanted to trust Tate, wanted to believe his version of things, but... those kids weren't just acting out. They were... grieving.

Her fingers twitched, uncertain. She couldn't ignore it anymore. Sunshine hesitated, then, almost involuntarily, grabbed her laptop and fell back onto the bed. Her fingers hovered over the keys, debating whether she really wanted to know the truth.

She began to type and a click brought her to the school's website. A memorial page loaded slowly. And then—faces. Rows of young faces stared back at her, their smiles frozen in time. She swallowed hard, recognizing a handful of them. Her heart hammered in her chest, and she quickly clicked out of the page, trying to push the rising nausea back down.

She clicked on an article and there, staring back at her, was a school photo of Tate. She scrolled down with shaking hands, her breath hitting in her throat as she read:

'In a tragic and shocking incident, Tate Langdon, a 17-year-old student at Westfield High School, opened fire inside the school on the morning of October 10, 1994, killing 15 students and injuring several others before being shot and killed by law enforcement at his home residence.'

Her eyes stung with unshed tears as her vision blurred. She could barely process it, her body trembling with disbelief. Panic surged through her, and she bolted up from the bed, her movements frantic.

She couldn't just sit here and read about it. She needed to know for sure, to see it with her own eyes. Her hands fumbled as she pulled on her clothes.

Sunshine quickly slipped on her shoes, grabbing her bag as she swiped at the tears that kept falling. She rushed down the stairs, her mind in a fog, barely noticing anything around her. All she could think of was getting out of the house. To school, she needed to get to school.

She rounded the corner into the kitchen, ready to tell her mom she was leaving when she froze.

"She's not here." Constance's voice broke the silence as she took a slow drag from her cigarette, her back facing Sunshine.

Sunshine blinked, the words sinking in slowly. "Where is she?" she asked, glancing around the kitchen like her mother might suddenly appear from behind a corner.

Constance exhaled smoke, the curl of it rising lazily toward the ceiling. "She's probably at the grocery store," she said coolly, her voice devoid of any real concern. "Buying some frozen fare to reheat for your supper tonight." She flicked the ash from her cigarette. She didn't need to turn around to see the turmoil etched across Sunshine's face. "You found out about Tate, didn't you?"

Sunshine's lips parted—another confirmation of the truth she desperately wanted to deny. Her head spun, and she fought back the bile building in her throat.

"I knew you would," Constance continued, her tone flat.

Sunshine shook her head violently, stepping up beside the older woman. "I don't know what kind of sick joke this is, but I'm fucking tired of it,"

Constance finally turned her gaze toward her, her icy eyes meeting Sunshine's with a hint of pity. "I questioned my sanity when I first found out. But this house..." Her eyes flickered, an unsettling calm in them. "This house will make you a believer."

Sunshine stood frozen, her mind screaming at the absurdity of it all. How could this possibly make sense? But deep down, through all the chaos and confusion, Constance's words began to gnaw at the edges of her reality.

Ever since she and her family had moved into this house, everything had been wrong—twisted in ways that logic couldn't explain.

"You see, Sunshine," Constance continued. "we were living here when Tate lost his way." She gestured around her with a delicate hand, the cigarette still smoldering between her fingers. "And I believe that the house drove him to it ."

Sunshine's legs threatened to buckle beneath her. Her mind was at war with itself—desperate for this to be some cruel joke, but unable to fully shake the doubt that crept in. Had Tate really killed all those people? Her heart screamed no, but the evidence... the faces of the kids... Tate's name in the articles... it was all too real.

"I don't believe this." Sunshine breathed.

Constance's gaze sharpened. "You're a smart girl. How can you be so arrogant to think there's only one reality you're able to see?" She flicked the cigarette into the ashtray.

Constance stood, smoothing her skirt before meeting Sunshine's gaze once again. "I want you to meet someone,"

"Sunshine Harmon, meet Billie Dean Howard," Constance announced as she guided Sunshine into her kitchen.

Billie, seated calmly at the table, flashed a warm, reassuring smile as Sunshine waved awkwardly in return.

"Billie is a gifted medium," Constance continued, setting the kettle on the stove. "She can help."

"You're confused. Overwhelmed. Why wouldn't you be?" Billie observed with a gentle nod, her eyes studying Sunshine.

Sunshine shifted uncomfortably, her bag still slung over her shoulder as she glanced down at her wrinkled sweatpants. "That obvious, huh?"

Sunshine hesitated before accepting the seat Billie offered, slumping down beside her and dropping her bag on the floor.

Billie's gaze lingered, almost like she could see through Sunshine, picking up on something that unsettled her.

Constance busied herself, placing teacups in front of her guests. "Billie has been helping me for years. I first found her on Craigslist, believe it or not. I've been through all the phonies, but she is 100% authentic."

"I've just come from a meeting at Lifetime; they're interested in making a pilot with me." Billie glanced back at Constance, a proud glint in her eye.

Constance poured tea in Sunshine's cup, then pushed it toward her. "Have some chamomile. It'll calm the nerves."

"I feel like I'm in a never-ending nightmare," Sunshine admitted.

"I used to be like you. Confused. Lost. Until I was 25. Then, out of the blue, my cleaning lady shows up while I'm brushing my teeth." Billie leaned forward slightly, her eyes taking on a faraway look as she recalled a memory. "Except she's not holding a toilet brush or wearing rubber gloves—she's naked and bloody. Her husband murdered her with an ice pick."

"It's hard to keep good help." Constance, unfazed, added.

Billie's hand went to her pearls, clutching them. "Do you think I wanted a bloody Mexican ghost in my bathroom?"

Sunshine shook her head before Billie continued. "All I wanted was to improve my tennis game and unseat Charlotte Whitney as president of my book club. But I was chosen. And when you're chosen, you either get with the program or you go crazy. Understanding the truth is your only choice."

"What even is the truth?" Sunshine whispered.

Billie's gaze turned serious as she grabbed a cigarette, leaning toward Constance for a light. After a slow, deliberate drag, she exhaled a plume of smoke and leaned back in her chair.

"There are some spirits—those who were murdered in violent, tragic ways—who cannot move on. They refuse to leave until they've exacted their pound of flesh." Her voice was calm as she explained. "Then there are a few, like Tate, who don't even realize they're dead. They wander in a childlike confusion, stuck between worlds."

Constance stirred her tea slowly. "That's why I wanted your father to see him. I hoped he might help Tate achieve some clarity about himself... so that maybe, just maybe, Tate could see the truth on his own."

Billie leaned forward, her tone soft but urgent. "We must help him cross over, Sunshine."

Sunshine shot up from her seat before Billie could touch her, her chest tightening as a tear slipped down her cheek. "I can't do this." Her voice broke, and the room seemed to close in around her, the pressure unbearable.

Constance and Billie exchanged a knowing look before Billie spoke up again, her voice calm and steady. "Who is Mary?"

Sunshine's heart sank. Mary. Memories of her late grandmother flooding back— You'll never be good enough. The words echoed in her mind, the painful sting of an unresolved wound.

Billie's voice was gentle, but her question cut deep. "Does that mean anything to you? You'll never be good enough?"

Sunshine backed away, her breath quickening as she fought to hold back the flood of emotions threatening to overtake her. It was too much.

Without another word, Sunshine spun on her heel, her feet carrying her out of the kitchen. The door slammed shut behind her.

Chapter 17

Sunshine stood motionless before the memorial plaque, her eyes tracing the engraved names of the students who had been killed. A total of fifteen were written, but all she could focus on were the names attached to the faces that haunted her from last night.

Kyle Greenwell. Chloe Stapleton. Stephanie Boggs. Amir Stanley. Kevin Gedman.

Her stomach churned violently, and she swallowed hard, trying to push back the overwhelming nausea that crept up her throat.

"You're not the first one to come here."

Sunshine spun around at the sound of the voice, startled out of her thoughts. Behind her sat Mr. Carmichael, her calculus teacher, his wheelchair creaking as he rolled closer.

"What?" Sunshine blinked, trying to make sense of his words.

"Your sister," he clarified, nodding toward the plaque. "Violet. She was already here. Came in a an hour ago asking questions about the shooter."

Sunshine's heart skipped a beat, confusion sweeping over her. Violet? Why would Violet have come here? Why would she ask about this?

"Tate Langdon?" she asked, though the answer was already burning in the pit of her stomach.

Mr. Carmichael nodded, his face slightly annoyed. "She seemed pretty upset."

Sunshine's vision blurred, the nausea that had been bubbling up finally taking hold. Her body betrayed her, and before she could stop it, she bolted for the nearest trash can. The retching sounds filled the library as she doubled over, her body convulsing as she emptied the contents of her stomach.

She wiped her mouth shakily with the back of her hand, leaning over the trash can, gasping for air. Tears welled up in her eyes as the weight of everything came crashing down on her. The truth was too heavy to bear.

She squeezed her eyes shut, willing herself to breathe, but the image of those faces—their names etched into the plaque—was seared into her mind. She couldn't escape it. She couldn't run from the truth.

Ms. Peggy, with her warm Southern drawl and sharp eyes, glanced at the thermometer. "Well, you don't have a fever," she glanced at her with a raised brow, the question coming out casually but pointedly. "Any tenderness in your breasts?"

Sunshine blinked, shrugging her shoulders. Maybe? It was hard to tell. Tenderness came and went with her period, so she never really thought much of it. "I guess," she muttered, not really seeing the relevance.

Ms. Peggy continued, undeterred. "Frequent urination? Weight gain?"

Sunshine's brow furrowed. Weight gain? She hesitated, her mind running back over the past few weeks. She had been running to the bathroom more often and, come to think of it, her clothes had felt a bit snug lately. But she chalked that up to stress-eating or just not paying attention.

Sunshine nodded slowly.

Ms. Peggy studied her, eyes narrowing in suspicion. "When was the last time you had your period?"

Sunshine blinked, caught off guard by the question. The words almost made her laugh. Did she really think she was pregnant?

"I don't know. Life's been pretty stressful," she muttered, brushing the question aside.

Ms. Peggy, however, was unfazed by Sunshine's attempt to downplay the situation. After a beat, she walked over to one of the counters. Sunshine's eyes followed her as she bent down and rummaged through the lower cabinets. When she stood up, Ms. Peggy held a small box—a pregnancy test.

Sunshine's stomach twisted, confusion flickering in her eyes. She stared at the box, then up at the nurse. "I don't need that,"

"You're not leaving this office until you do," Ms. Peggy said, pushing the box into Sunshine's hands.

With a dramatic roll of her eyes, Sunshine sighed, clearly not in the mood for this argument. She snatched the test from the nurse, muttering under her breath, "This is stupid."

She trudged into the small bathroom connected to the office, slamming the door behind her with more force than she meant to.

Sunshine ripped open the box, scoffing at the absurdity of the situation. Pregnant? Really? The idea felt ridiculous. The only reason she was going through with this was to prove Ms. Peggy wrong and finally get out of here. She skimmed the instructions, though they weren't exactly rocket science.

Sighing, she sat down on the cold toilet seat, lowering her sweatpants to her knees. She relieved herself onto the stick and then placed it on the counter, her movements robotic and detached.

She washed her hands and splashed cold water onto her face, trying to shake off the lingering queasiness that had been gnawing at her since this morning. Her reflection stared back at her, pale and tired.

Without even glancing at the test, Sunshine grabbed it from the counter, fully expecting to hand over a negative result. She pushed open the bathroom door and placed the test in front of Ms. Peggy with a casual shrug. "See? I'm fine,"

Ms. Peggy leaned forward, peering at the test, she pointed at the plastic stick. "Those two pink lines tell me otherwise."

The room seemed to tilt around Sunshine. Her stomach dropped, a hollow pit forming in her gut. She whipped her head around, staring down at the test.

Two lines.

"That's impossible," Sunshine blinked, her pulse thundering in her ears. "I've never had sex."

Ms. Peggy arched an eyebrow, her skepticism cutting through Sunshine's rising panic. "You really expect me to believe you're pregnant with the second coming of Christ?" she asked, her tone half-amused, half-disbelieving. "Nice try."

But Sunshine wasn't lying. This can't be real.

She opened her mouth to speak, but nothing came out at first. Her throat felt dry, her stomach twisted in knots.

Ms. Peggy leaned back in her chair, crossing her arms with an exasperated sigh. "Honey, I've heard it all before. If I had a nickel for every girl who said she didn't know how it happened..." She trailed off, rolling her eyes as if the entire situation was mundane. "Let's be real here. Did something happen and you just don't want to admit it?"

Sunshine shook her head violently. "No. I'm telling you, nothing happened." Her voice cracked with desperation. "I've never... I've never even..."

Suddenly, the air felt too thick, the room too small. Sunshine stumbled backward, hitting a chair. "I need to go," she blurted out. She grabbed her bag, fumbling with the strap, her hands shaking uncontrollably.

"Wait, hold on—" Ms. Peggy stood up, alarm flashing in her eyes. "You can't just leave. We need to—"

But Sunshine was already heading for the door, her breath shallow, her heart racing as panic swallowed her whole. She pushed through the door, entering the hallway. She couldn't stay. She couldn't face this. Whatever this was, it wasn't normal, and she had to get away from it.

But deep down, Sunshine knew there was no escaping the truth. There never had been.

Chapter 18

Sunshine stepped into her home, the familiar creak of the door echoing in the quietness as she shut it firmly behind her. Leaning against the door, tears stung her eyes, but she was tired of crying; the release felt pointless now, an exhausting cycle she couldn't afford to indulge. She didn't want to come home, but there was nowhere else to go.

With a soft thud, she leaned her head against the door, wishing desperately that this nightmare would end. She dropped her bag to the floor with a dull thump.

A flicker of movement caught her eye—a shadow darting across the hallway. She took a deep breath, forcing herself to muster the courage to investigate. "Tate?" she called out, a part of her hoping he wouldn't answer.

The hallway stretched before her guiding her toward the dining room where she spotted Tate again, just out of reach. Without thinking, she followed him as he slipped down into the basement. She hurried after him, skipping down the steps two at a time, only to find the basement empty and silent.

"Tate?" she called again, her voice echoing against the cold, concrete walls.

No response.

Panic began to set in, and Sunshine shook her head, feeling the warm tears finally spill over as her fingers tangled in her hair, frustration and despair swirling within her.

The sound of children laughing broke through the heaviness, punctuated by the sharp pop of party snaps. Sunshine turned instinctively toward the noise, her eyes widening in shock as she saw twin boys dashing past her, their laughter echoing. Compelled to follow them, she rushed forward, but stopped short as a woman in a nurse's uniform stepped into her path, her expression a mask of anguish.

"Look at what he did to me," the woman cried, her voice filled with pain.

Sunshine gasped in horror, instinctively turning to flee, but she was confronted by the ringleader of the invasion, her neck slashed and bloodied, standing beside the man who had also terrorized her that night.

"Excuse me, ma'am, I don't want to bother you, but I'm hurt and needing some help,"

Sunshine screamed, terror igniting her senses as she dashed around the corner, her heart pounding in her chest. She stumbled into another figure—a doctor.

"Has my wife medicated you? Are you here for the procedure?"

Fear thumped through her veins, propelling her to sprint past him and up the basement stairs. As she reached the top, she could hear the haunting notes of Beethoven's Moonlight Sonata resonating from her room.

Sunshine ran up the steps to her room before she opened her door slowly, relief flooding her as she found the room empty. She stepped inside and shut the door behind her, feeling a momentary sense of safety. Moving toward her radio, she turned it off, silencing the music that seemed to taunt her.

Collapsing onto her bed, Sunshine's entire body trembled with the force of her sobs. Each cry seemed to intensify her distress. She gasped, her hand flying to her chest in a desperate attempt to steady herself. But it wasn't working. Her breathing came in shallow, jagged bursts, her throat constricting painfully as if it were closing in on itself.

Her heart raced, pounding violently against her ribcage, each thud echoing in her ears. The sensation was overwhelming, as if her chest might explode at any second. She choked on her breath, her vision blurring with the intensity of her tears, her body giving in to the sensation of being utterly consumed. The room around her spun, her dizziness making everything feel far away, as though the world was slowly slipping from her grasp.

I'm dying, she thought in her panic, her mind spiraling as she struggled to control the storm raging inside her. It felt like everything was being stripped away, piece by piece, until all that remained was her fear, raw and suffocating.

She squeezed her eyes shut, curling into herself as if she could hide from the relentless onslaught of emotions. Today was not a good day.

As she sat there, something in her peripheral vision caught her attention. Slowly, she turned her head, her breath still coming in ragged gasps.

On the bed beside her, partially tucked beneath her pillow, was a small piece of paper.

Her tear-filled eyes narrowed as she stared at it, the edges crumpled as if someone had hastily left it for her to find.

With shaking hands, she reached for it, heart pounding as she unfolded the note. The words "I love you," written in Tate's handwriting, blurred before her eyes as fresh tears spilled down her cheeks. A teardrop fell onto the paper, smudging the ink and blurring Tate's confession.

Sunshine felt a rising desperation; she needed relief, something—anything—to dull the ache that throbbed in her chest. The painkillers her dealer had given her weeks ago came to mind. Just one pill, she thought. It would help her sleep, help her escape this never ending nightmare, even if only for a few hours.

With renewed urgency, she rushed to her bag, rifling through its contents. Her heart sank as she came up empty-handed. No pills. In a panic, she dumped the entire bag onto her bed, the contents spilling out in a chaotic mess, but still, there was no sign of the precious little capsules.

Frustration clawed at her insides, and a wave of anger surged through her as she tore apart her room, searching desperately for any trace of the pills, including her Adderall.

"Violet!" Sunshine yelled, her voice echoing through the house as anger boiled over. Her sister had to have taken them.

Without a moment's hesitation, she swung open her door and stormed into Violet's room. "Violet." she repeated, but her sister remained curled up in bed, the shadows of sleep enveloping her.

"Vi?" Sunshine's voice dropped, a tremor creeping in as she stepped further inside. The sight of two empty pill bottles scattered on Violet's bed caused her heart to plummet.

She rushed to Violet, shaking her frantically. "Violet!"

But there was no response; her sister lay still, too still.

Sunshine pressed two fingers against Violet's neck, desperately searching for a pulse, but her heart sank further when she felt nothing.

Panic surged through her as tears streamed down her cheeks. Sunshine bolted out of Violet's room, her mind racing.

"Somebody help!" she screamed, racing to her parents' room, but it was empty, amplifying the dread curling in her stomach. She ran through the hallways, calling out for anyone, her heart hammering in her chest. If Tate really was dead... He would be here... wouldn't he?

"Tate!" she cried out, desperation lacing her voice as salty tears dripped into her mouth. "Help me! Tate!"

"Sunshine?" His voice cut through the chaos behind her and she snapped around to face him.

"It's Violet," Sunshine sobbed, panic clawing at her throat. "She took a bunch of pills."

Worry flashed across Tate's face, and without a second thought, they rushed to Violet's room together. Sunshine's cries filled the air as Tate shook Violet gently, urging her to respond, but her sister remained unresponsive.

In a flurry of movement, Tate grabbed Violet, pulling her down to the floor. Sunshine's heart shattered at the sight of Tate's tears beginning to flow as he struggled to pull Violet into the bathroom. "Don't you die on me, Violet!" he sobbed.

"No! Don't you die!" Tate pulled them both into the tub and turned on the water. "Don't you die on me," he repeated as he shoved his fingers down Violet's throat, and Sunshine watched as her sister began to throw up a small amount of the pills.

Sunshine knelt beside the tub, relief flooding through her as Violet regained consciousness, her eyes blinking open in confusion and fear.

"Violet!" Sunshine gasped, taking her sister's face in her trembling hands, brushing away the water and tears mingling on her skin.

Violet's gaze locked onto hers, and she began to sob, relief and horror filling her eyes. Sunshine rested her forehead against her sister's wet skin, tears cascading down her cheeks as she whispered, "I love you. I love you."

Violet glanced back at Tate, her eyes wide.

"It's okay," Tate reassured, his voice steady despite the tears streaming down his cheeks.

Sunshine tapped lightly on Violet's bedroom door, hesitating for a moment before poking her head inside.

Violet glanced up from where she lay curled on her bed, engrossed in a book about birds.

Sunshine stepped into the room. "How are you feeling?" she asked, her voice a soft murmur as she moved to sit on the edge of the bed, feeling the mattress shift slightly under her weight.

"Sad," Violet replied as she traced her fingers over the illustrations of the birds.

"Me too," Sunshine confessed.

Violet forced a smile, but it didn't reach her eyes as she returned her gaze to the book.

"You found out about Tate?" Sunshine ventured, breaking the silence that felt too thick to slice through.

Violet's head shot up as if she couldn't fathom how her sister could possibly know. "Mr. Carmichael said you came by this morning... looking for the same thing I was,"

"Leah mentioned what happened at the school," she said, her voice quaking as she recalled the moment. "I was curious, so she showed me this article." A shuddering breath escaped her as she pushed the book aside, burying her head in her hands. "And then I saw a picture of Tate. I feel like I'm going crazy."

"You're not going crazy," Sunshine reassured her. "Constance confirmed it."

Violet looked up, confusion etched across her features. "What?"

Sunshine's heart sank as she realized her sister hadn't known about that connection. "Tate's her son," she explained gently.

"What the fuck?" Violet's voice was barely a whisper, disbelief and shock washing over her.

Sunshine nodded, glancing down at her hands as she contemplated the weight of what to say next. "Are you gonna tell Mom and Dad... about the pills?" she asked hesitantly, bracing for Violet's response.

"No," Violet replied firmly, shaking her head. "I won't tell them where I got them from either."

Sunshine's pulse picked up as realization struck her; Violet had to know that she was still using if she went into her room to look for her pills. "I'm sorry," Sunshine whispered, the guilt tightening around her throat.

"Don't be." Violet sighed, the heaviness of her words settling between them.

A beat of silence passed.

"I'm tired," Violet said finally, lying down on her side. "Will you lay with me?"

Sunshine didn't respond verbally; she simply moved behind her sister, wrapping her arms around Violet's slender frame, seeking comfort in the closeness. As she held her, her eyes caught sight of Violet's long sleeve riding up slightly, exposing angry scars that marred her skin. A wave of sorrow washed over Sunshine as the realization hit her: her baby sister had been in so much pain.

Gently, she reached over and traced the scars with her fingertips, her heart aching for the struggles Violet had endured. Violet didn't move or react, but the soft sniffle that escaped her indicated that she too had been crying.

"I love you, Sunshine," Violet murmured.

"I love you too, Violet," Sunshine replied, her own tears spilling over as she tightened her grip around her sister, wishing she could shield her from all the pain in the world.

Chapter 19

Sunshine sat cross-legged on her bed, her fingers danced across the keyboard as she scrolled through pages of medical forums and articles. The words "false positives" flashed on the screen, and with each click, relief washed through her. She clung to the notion that the test could be wrong, that this was all a mistake. Yet, in the back of her mind, the nagging truth lingered: she had experienced almost all the symptoms.

Unless she was the next Virgin Mary, something else had to be happening with her body. The absurd thought made her snort quietly, shaking her head in disbelief. Religion had never been a guiding force in her life; it always felt too distant, too abstract. But now, with the knowledge that ghosts were real, her mind spiraled with unanswerable questions. If spirits existed, what else was possible? Was there a God watching over all this chaos? And, of all people, would that God seriously pick her to carry out some divine miracle?

The thought felt ludicrous, and yet, the uncertainty gnawed at her. She shook her head again, trying to shove the idea out of her brain. The rational part of her screamed that there had to be a logical, medical explanation.

A sudden knock at her door shattered the silence, jolting her out of her spiraling thoughts. Her heart leapt in her chest as her body flinched, startled. She hastily slammed her laptop shut, its screen fading to black just as Tate's head appeared in the doorway.

"Hey,"

Sunshine forced a smile. "Hey," she replied, hoping her voice sounded steadier than she felt.

"Can we talk?" Tate asked as he hesitated in the doorway.

Sunshine straightened her posture, trying to shake off the heaviness in her chest. She nodded, her throat suddenly dry.

Tate stepped inside, the door shutting behind him. He settled onto the edge of her bed, a few inches away, and for a moment, they both seemed lost in their thoughts.

"I wanted to check on you," Tate finally said, his voice soft. "After everything… you know, with Violet."

She gave a small nod, forcing herself to stay composed despite the rising lump in her throat. Her fingers fidgeted in her lap as she tried to keep her emotions at bay. "I'm okay," she managed but the lie tasted bitter on her tongue.

"Did I do something wrong?" Tate asked gently.

Sunshine couldn't bring herself to meet his gaze, her eyes shifting away.

"No…" Sunshine whispered, shaking her head as if the simple action could erase the turmoil churning inside her. Despite her words, she was burdened by emotions she couldn't fully comprehend.

Every time she looked at Tate, it was like looking at two different people—two distinct realities. One was the boy she was falling for, the one who made her heart race, who made her want to giggle and kick her feet like a school girl. The other was the boy who had taken fifteen lives in cold blood, something she couldn't ignore now matter how hard she tried.

She recalled Billie's words. Tate didn't remember how he died, or even that he was dead. That knowledge was something she clung to, a small sliver of understanding she couldn't let go of.

Maybe it wasn't entirely his fault. Maybe there was more to it than she knew. For a brief moment, the tension in her shoulders eased, as if the weight of what he'd done could be softened by his ignorance. But that relief never lasted long.

And then there was the secret she carried—a truth that knotted her stomach and twisted her insides with guilt. His sister was dead. Constance had told her not to reveal the truth. How could she keep something like that from him? If it were her own sister, she would want to know. She would need to know.

How could she reconcile these things? How could she look him in the eyes, knowing what he had done and knowing what she was hiding from him?

Tate swallowed hard. "Sunshine... something's changed in you... toward me," he murmured, his eyes searching her face for a hint of what she was feeling. "You're distant, cold."

He looked down at his hands, as if trying to gather the right words. "I don't know what I've done but... I'll leave you alone from now on, if that's what you want." His voice faltered, and when he glanced up, his eyes glistened with unshed tears. "Is that what you want?"

Her heart clenched painfully at his words, her bottom lip trembling. She shook her head, fighting to keep her emotions in check, but the lump in her throat only grew.

"You know why I'd leave you alone? Because I care about your feelings more than mine." He paused, taking a shaky breath. "I love you."

The tears Sunshine had been holding back broke free, spilling down her cheeks. His confession pierced through her defenses, crumbling the walls she had so carefully constructed around her heart.

"There, I said it—not just on some piece of paper," Tate continued, his voice thick with emotion. He reached for her hand, holding it between his. "I would never let anyone or anything hurt you. I've never felt that way about anyone."

Something shifted inside her, a surge of raw emotion that she couldn't quite explain. Maybe it was because she was a sad, broken girl, desperate to feel loved. Or maybe, in some inexplicable way, she wanted to be the one who loved him—through all the dark, twisted parts of his soul.

Without thinking, she reached out, cradling his face in her hands. Her fingertips grazed his damp cheeks, brushing away the tears that had fallen. A deep longing tugged at her chest, pulling her toward him, as if this moment was the only thing that made sense in the chaos of everything else.

"I love you," she whispered, her voice barely audible as she searched his eyes. Leaning in, she pressed her lips softly to him, and in that instant, the world seemed to stop. Tate's arms wrapped around her, pulling her closer, and Sunshine melted into his touch.

Sunshine pulled away slightly, locking eyes with Tate. This was the moment she had been waiting for—a point of no return where everything else faded into insignificance. With a steadying breath, she stood up, pulling Tate's gaze along with her as he turned his head.

Standing in front of him, she gazed down into his deep, almost black eyes. Sunshine brushed her fingers gently through the mess of his hair, tucking it away from his forehead.

She grabbed the hem of her dress and with a swift pull, she removed it from her body, letting the fabric fall to the floor. Sunshine felt a rush of vulnerability. She was laying herself bare, not just physically but emotionally.

Tate's eyes roamed her figure, but there was no sense of judgment in his gaze. Instead, it was filled with reverence, awe even, as if he were seeing her for the first time. His Adam's apple bobbed as he swallowed

"Are you sure?" he asked, searching for any trace of doubt or hesitation in her eyes.

With a gentle nod, she leaned closer, the distance between them shrinking further. "I'm sure," she whispered as her lips brushed against his.

Their lips met, and Sunshine moved between his parted legs and Tate's hands found the back of her thighs. She placed her hands on the back of his neck, fingers tangling in his hair as they explored one another's lips, their kisses softening and swelling with every breath.

She had imagined this moment a million times before, but each fantasy had always centered around Tate—his dimmed smile, his touch, the way he made her feel. In her mind, it had been a dream, an unreachable desire that felt so far away.

But now, it was real.

And nothing could compare to the sweet yet salty taste of his lips, still tinged with the remnants of the tears they had shared together. Every kiss carried that lingering trace of their shared pain, binding them in a way words never could.

Sunshine's fingers traced the collar of Tate's green flannel before she pushed it down his shoulders, exposing the soft fabric beneath. He surrendered to her touch, letting the flannel slip to the bed.

Tate pulled away from their kiss, rising to his full height. Their eyes locked as he slowly removed his gray shirt, revealing his chest and the subtle definition of his muscles.

Every inch of his skin seemed to glow in the soft light of her room, and Sunshine's fingers found their way to his bare skin, tracing the lines of his shoulders and down his arms.

Sunshine looked up at Tate through her lashes, moving her hands away from his body. Her fingers fumbled behind her back, deftly undoing the clasps of her bra and letting the fabric slip away.

Tate's eyes lingered on her figure, tucking her long hair behind her shoulder. He lowered his head to her neck, and Sunshine felt the warmth of his breath against her as he kissed the spot right behind her earlobe.

Sunshine licked her lips as Tate's hand rested possessively on her jaw, his fingers gently tilting her head to the side, granting him better access.

He trailed hot, lingering kisses along her neck, each one deeper than the last. Her pulse quickened beneath his mouth as his lips danced their way up her jawline, teasingly halting just inches from her waiting lips.

"Get on the bed,"

Sunshine nodded, unable to find her voice as nervousness overtook her. She did as he instructed, settling herself onto her bed, her head sinking into the pillows and her knees bent in an inviting position.

Tate kicked off his converse before he climbed onto the bed, positioning his hands on either side of Sunshine's head. He looked down at her and she couldn't help but smile up at him.

Sunshine reached up, placing a hand on his cheek, the warmth of his skin beneath her fingertips grounding her in the moment. Her thumb brushed against his bottom lip, savoring the softness as she took in the way his eyes devoured her.

He really was here, wasn't he? The thought echoed in her mind. Everything she knew about ghosts made her half-expect her hand to pass right through him, as if he was just an illusion. But he wasn't. He was solid, real. His presence was undeniable, as tangible as the way her heart raced when their skin touched.

Tate placed a light, feather-soft kiss on her lips before he trailed kisses down to her neck, continuing his descent down between her breasts. His lips found her belly button, planting a tender kiss that made Sunshine suddenly acutely aware of her body. She felt a wave of self-consciousness wash over her as she became aware of how much her body had changed.

He looked up at her, his expression earnest and full of adoration, as if he could sense her hesitation. Tate lifted himself onto his knees, his hands sliding to the sides of Sunshine's underwear.

Slowly, he began to drag the fabric down her thighs, the tension in the air thickening. A rush of heat overtook her but alongside that warmth, an unwelcome sensation crept in—a familiar feeling that made her blood run cold.

Images of the Rubber Man invaded her thoughts, threatening to tarnish the purity of the moment they were sharing. Sunshine felt a knot of anxiety tighten in her stomach, but she quickly pushed those thoughts aside. Taking a deep breath, Sunshine focused on Tate's gentle touch as he lowered himself to place a heated kiss on her inner thigh.

Sunshine's head fell back against the pillows when his tongue made contact with her clit. Her breath hitched at the sensation and her fingers instinctively intertwined with his blonde hair, feeling the softness of the strands against her skin.

As Tate's tongue moved in slow, deliberate strokes, a soft moan escaped Sunshine's lips, her body trembling beneath his touch. His free hand began to glide upward, the roughness of his fingertips contrasting with the smoothness of her skin as they trailed along the curve of her hip.

With every flick of his tongue, her body reacted, and as his hand caressed higher, reaching her stomach, she felt the tension build. His hand made contact the soft skin of her breast, his thumb grazing her hardened nipple as he massaged the supple flesh.

Pleasure overwhelmed her, a wave of sensations crashing over her as he inserted a finger in her wet heat. The room spun around her, and all she could focus on was him slowly pumping in and out of her. A string of pleasurable cries escaped her lips, bucking her hips slightly as she felt the pressure in her abdomen build.

But just as Sunshine teetered on the edge of release, Tate suddenly pulled away. A playful smirk curled at his lips as he looked up at her.

"Not yet," he whispered, his voice low and teasing.

Sunshine whined, her body trembling with frustration, her breath coming in shallow, rapid bursts. She locked eyes with Tate, silently pleading for more, her body aching from the sudden denial of her orgasm.

Tate's smile widened as he drank in the sight of her, vulnerable and desperate beneath him. His eyes darkened with something deeper, more primal, as his fingers traced a slow, teasing line along the soft skin of her inner thigh.

Her body responded instinctively, a soft whimper escaping her lips as she arched into him, craving more of his touch.

Tate lifted himself up, his eyes never leaving Sunshine's. With a swift tug, he undid his belt and tossed it aside, the sound of the leather hitting the floor barely registering as Sunshine was flush with need. In one fluid motion, he shed the last pieces of clothing, his body now fully exposed to her.

Sunshine's eyes widened as she took in the sight of him. She wondered how it could even fit but before she could say anything he lowered himself on top of her, wedging himself between her spread legs. Tate moved slowly, inserting himself into her, but still giving her a moment to adjust.

Sunshine winced at the sharp sting of pain as Tate stretched her, opening up her walls to accommodate for his size. His lips moved tenderly against her collarbone, trailing soft, reassuring kisses along her flushed skin.

Tate paused, sensing her tension. His lips lingered against her neck, his breath warm. "You okay?" he whispered softly, his voice filled with concern.

"Mhm," Sunshine gave a small nod, biting her lower lip as she willed herself to relax.

Tate nodded as he slowly built up his rhythm, his touch firmer yet still tender. The pain began to ease, replaced by a slow, building pleasure. Sunshine let out a shaky breath, her fingers gripping tighter as her pleasure began to crest again.

His lips brushed against her neck, leaving a trail of heated kisses that made her arch beneath him. The pressure inside her built with every passing second, her moans growing louder, more urgent.

He kissed her deeply, their lips meeting in a passionate, breathless exchange. Sunshine moaned into his mouth, her voice muffled by the kiss but filled with pure pleasure.

Sunshine's body tensed as she felt the familiar heat coiling low in her abdomen, spiraling upward in waves that made her toes curl and her head fall back into the pillows. The sensation was all-consuming, her body trembling as she clung to him, lost in the moment.

Tate's grip on her outer thigh tightened, his fingernails digging into her skin. Sunshine gasped, her hands clutching at his back, feeling the muscles tense beneath her fingers.

The mounting pleasure was overwhelming, her senses blurring as the pressure became too much to bear. She let out a soft, breathless moan, knowing she was on the verge of release. "Tate,"

"I know," Tate whispered against her lips, pushing her even closer to the edge.

In that moment, everything around her disappeared—her thoughts, her worries, the pain she'd been carrying. All she could feel was him, and the white-hot pleasure flooding her entire body.

Her vision blurred, stars dancing at the edges of her sight as she finally reached her peak. A soft cry escaped her lips as her body trembled beneath him, consumed by a rush of pure, dizzying nirvana.

Chapter 20

Sunshine lounged comfortably on her side atop Violet's bed, her head propped up by her hand, elbow sinking softly into the mattress as she listened to her sister complain.

"They planned some brutal family dinner for tonight," Violet vented, her tone a mixture of frustration and resignation. "Like that's going to make me feel better."

"Ugh. That's tonight?" Sunshine grumbled, extending her arm flat against the bed before allowing her head to rest on it.

Tate perched at the edge of the bed, his feet dangling just above the floor, flipping absently through one of Violet's books.

"Do you believe in ghosts?" Tate asked suddenly, turning his gaze toward Violet.

Sunshine and Violet exchanged a puzzled glance.

Violet raised an eyebrow and turned her attention back to Tate. "Why are you asking me?"

Tate turned away for a moment, lost in thought, before glancing back at Violet. "I don't know," he admitted. "It can't all be shit, right?"

Violet shrugged.

"There's got to be someplace better, somewhere. For people like you guys, at least," Tate continued, glancing back and forth between the sisters, his gaze lingering on Sunshine for a fraction longer.

"Not you?" Sunshine asked, her voice tinged with sadness as she sensed a deeper truth behind his words. Tate's stare softened momentarily before he turned back to the book in his lap, a faint frown creasing his brow.

"Ever since you guys got here, this is the better place,"

Sunshine sat directly across from her sister at the dinner table, their parents on either side, the tension thick enough to choke on. She forced herself to take another bite of her food, each chew feeling more mechanical as the silence stretched on, becoming heavier with each passing second.

Violet, on the other hand, didn't even pretend to engage. She leaned her head on her hand, her gaze distant, the untouched plate in front of her a silent protest.

"You're not eating anything," Vivien said, breaking the silence, her eyes flicking over to Violet with concern.

"I'm not hungry," Violet mumbled, barely glancing at their mother. "Pretty stuffed on bullshit."

"Your mother and I know that you're upset. Maybe there's some things you want to talk about?" he suggested, his voice calm but loaded with professional undertones.

Oh God, not the shrink talk. Sunshine rolled her eyes, trying to disappear into her water glass as she took a sip.

Violet's eyes darkened as she turned her gaze to Ben, then Vivien. "Like who I'm going to live with after you get divorced?" she shot back. "Is there a third option? 'Cause both of you kind of make me want to kill myself."

Sunshine nearly choked on her water.

Violet's tone was flat, almost disturbingly nonchalant as she continued. "Is that what you guys are afraid of? Why else would you want to actually deal with the problem?"

Ben's voice softened even more, leaning into his professional training. "You never leave your room. You barely eat. These are textbook signs of depression. We're very concerned, Vi."

Sunshine's heart clenched. She understood where her parents were coming from. They had every reason to be worried. They didn't know about Violet's previous attempt, but Sunshine did.

She felt for them—how scared they must be. But at the same time, she knew how Violet felt too. Their parents weren't happy together, and pretending otherwise only made things worse.

Violet's frustration boiled over as she stood abruptly from the table, her chair scraping loudly against the floor. She made it halfway to the door before turning on her heel, crossing her arms defiantly.

"Look, you guys drag me all the way out here to save our family, then you decide to break up. You buy a house that I actually like, then you're telling me you're selling it without even asking what we want. So, fine, I'm depressed. But I'm not going to off myself. So, you can go back to your policy of benign neglect."

Her words struck like a dagger, leaving Vivien and Ben momentarily speechless As Violet stormed out of the dining room. Both parents exchanged a helpless look before glancing toward Sunshine.

Sunshine felt the eyes on her, and she cleared her throat awkwardly, pushing her plate aside. "May I be excused?"

Vivien gave a small nod, not arguing, clearly needing the space to talk privately with Ben.

Sunshine sat at her desk, one earbud in, the other dangling as soft music played in her ear. She tapped her pencil against the edge of her notebook, trying to focus on her homework. For the first time in what felt like ages, she was doing something that felt... normal.

"Sunshine."

Her mother's voice pulled her out of her thoughts. Sunshine glanced up as she turned to see Vivien standing in the doorway.

"Yeah, Mom?" she replied, dropping her pencil onto the paper and swiveling her position to face her.

Vivien glanced over her shoulder, as if checking to ensure no one was eavesdropping, before stepping further into the room.

"I got a call from the school nurse today," Vivien said, her tone calm but weighted.

Sunshine's stomach dropped. Fuck. She tried to keep her face neutral, though panic started to simmer beneath the surface. "It's nothing, Mom, seriously," she said quickly, hoping to brush it off.

Vivien's eyes narrowed, rubbing her temples as if the conversation itself was giving her a headache. "A positive pregnancy test isn't nothing, Sunshine."

The room felt like it was closing in on her. Sunshine's mind raced, searching for the right words, the right explanation. Could she even explain this? She had only recently lost her virginity, and even then, she didn't believe she could be pregnant. Not with the timing... not with everything that had happened.

"When were you going to tell me?" Vivien asked, her voice laced with disappointment, her hand resting on her hip as she sighed heavily. She looked hurt, as if their bond had fractured in ways Sunshine hadn't realized.

"Mom, it was defective or something," Sunshine said, shaking her head in frustration, her voice rising defensively. "There's no way."

Vivien studied her for a moment, her expression softening. She let out a deep breath, nodding slowly. "Okay," she said, her tone more gentle now. "Well, let's just get you to a doctor, just in case."

Sunshine hesitated, but then again, she needed to know too. She couldn't let this consume her thoughts any longer—it was driving her mad. With a reluctant nod, she agreed.

Chapter 21

The sterile smell of antiseptic filled the waiting room at Planned Parenthood as Sunshine sat next to her mother, her leg bouncing with nervous energy.

Sunshine glanced at the laminated pamphlets scattered across the small table in front of her, all filled with information she didn't want to read. Even though she knew, deep down, that she wasn't pregnant, the anxiety gnawed at her anyway.

Vivien sat silently beside her, flipping through an outdated magazine, but Sunshine could feel the tension radiating off her mother. She kept shifting in her seat, eyes flicking occasionally to her daughter, as if ready to ask another question but holding back. She stared down at her hands, which had grown clammy.

A nurse behind the front desk called someone else's name, and Sunshine watched as another girl—a little younger than her—stood up, looking just as anxious.

Why am I nervous? She asked herself, though the answer was obvious. The symptoms, the fear, the pressure of what it would mean if she was—it all weighed on her, even though she'd told herself a hundred times it wasn't possible. She hadn't even had sex until recently, and there was no way the timeline matched up. It had to be a false positive, she kept reassuring herself, over and over.

The door to the back opened, and another nurse stepped out. "Sunshine Harmon?"

Sunshine's feet dangled off the edge of the exam table, her sneakers grazing the sterile paper. The fluorescent lights buzzed overhead, casting a clinical glow over everything.

The nurse stood by the counter, flipping through her folder with a practiced detachment that made Sunshine feel more like a file than a person.

"I'm just going to ask you a couple of questions," the nurse said, barely looking up.

Sunshine nodded, swallowing the lump in her throat. Her hands fidgeted in her lap, fingers twisting together. She wasn't sure if the tightness in her chest was from nerves or the unbearable tension of waiting. Every minute stretched into what felt like hours.

"Last period?" the nurse asked, finally glancing up as she scribbled in the folder.

Sunshine's mind scrambled, trying to remember. The days had blurred together so much lately. "Uh... late August, I think."

"Any drugs or alcohol?" The nurse's voice was monotone, professional, but Sunshine felt a sudden surge of defensiveness rise in her chest. She hesitated for a second too long, her mind flicking to the little pills hidden in her room. She kept her expression neutral.

"No," she lied, her voice firmer than she expected.

The nurse didn't seem to notice the slight tension in her tone. She continued. "Are you currently on any medications?"

"No," Sunshine repeated, this time more certain.

The nurse made a final note in her folder before setting it aside, her expression unreadable. "Okay, temperature and blood pressure look good," she said, slipping the cuff from Sunshine's arm and reaching for the door. "The doctor will be in shortly. Go ahead and change into the gown and cover your legs with the cloth."

Sunshine nodded again, but the moment the door clicked shut behind the nurse, a wave of unease rolled over her. She stood up slowly, her limbs feeling too heavy for her body, and walked to the counter.

Once the gown was on, she sat back down, the crinkling paper beneath her loud in the deafening silence of the room. Her legs, now covered by the thin paper cloth, felt cold, exposed. She stared at the closed door, every second stretching longer than the last.

Sunshine's heart picked up as the door creaked open, revealing the doctor, clipboard in hand. The doctor didn't look up immediately, eyes scanning the paperwork before she glanced over at Sunshine.

"Ms. Harmon?" the doctor asked, her tone polite but professional.

Sunshine managed a smile, though it felt forced and hollow. "That's me," she replied, trying to steady her breathing.

"How are you doing today?" Dr. Martinez asked, stepping fully into the room and closing the door behind her.

Sunshine shrugged, feeling the coolness of the paper gown against her skin. "Fine," she said, though her voice betrayed her. She was anything but fine.

The doctor, still smiling kindly, nodded. "I'm Dr. Martinez. I'll be doing your ultrasound today."

Sunshine gave a stiff nod, feeling exposed in more ways than one.

Dr. Martinez began prepping the equipment, her movements fluid and practiced as she pulled out the leg holders from the exam table. "Lay back for me," she instructed, motioning toward the table.

Sunshine did as she was told, lowering herself onto the exam table. She placed her feet in the rests, the cool air brushing against her as her heart pounded in her chest.

The doctor moved to sit in her rolling chair, now at eye level with the ultrasound machine. She snapped on a pair of gloves before grabbing the ultrasound probe, the squelch of the gel filling the silence as she applied it to the tip of the instrument.

"This'll be a little cold, and you'll feel some pressure," Dr. Martinez said softly, glancing up at Sunshine to gauge her readiness.

"Okay," Sunshine barely managed to say, her voice tight. She braced herself, and within moments, the cool probe was inserted. Sunshine winced, her fingers dug into the edges of the exam table as she stared up at the dark ceiling, trying to ground herself in anything other than the discomfort she was feeling.

A loud thumping sound echoed in the room, steady and rhythmic. Sunshine's head snapped toward the doctor, panic flooding her veins. "What's that?"

Dr. Martinez glanced at her with a calm expression. "That would be the heartbeat," she said, her tone gentle but matter-of-fact. She adjusted the screen so Sunshine could see it better. "This is the amniotic sac," " and this..." Dr. Martinez's finger hovered over the screen, pointing at a small, barely formed shape. "This is the fetus."

Her gaze locked onto herself the tiny, indistinct figure on the screen—fragile and real. "What?" she whispered as she lifted up slightly on her elbows, trying to get a better look at the image in front of her.

"You look to be about nine weeks," Dr. Martinez added, her eyes focused on the screen.

Nine weeks. Pregnant. The words echoed in Sunshine's head, bouncing around like some surreal nightmare she couldn't wake up from. The room spun around her, a dizzying tilt that made her stomach churn. This couldn't be real. It couldn't be happening. She hadn't even fully processed Tate being dead, let alone this.

A wave of nausea overtook her, her face draining of color as she struggled to catch her breath. She felt faint, her body growing weaker by the second. Dr. Martinez must have noticed because, without missing a beat, she slid over and handed Sunshine a trash can.

Sunshine barely had time to grip it before she doubled over, vomiting into the can as her mind raced a mile a minute. Her whole world was spiraling, collapsing in on itself with every retch, with every harsh, unrelenting thought. Pregnant. It was impossible.

She pulled the trash can closer, gripping it tightly as her thoughts twisted in every direction.

Maybe God was real after all.

Sunshine sat in the waiting room, nervously picking at her nails, her mind still reeling. Her mother had just been given the news, and now the weight of it all pressed down on her. Sunshine felt numb, the tears that had earlier streamed down her cheeks now replaced by a hollow emptiness.

Vivien, sitting beside her, looked at her daughter with a mixture of concern and heartbreak. Gently, she placed a hand on Sunshine's back, her voice soft as she asked, "Are you sure you want to go through with this, right now? You don't want to think about it a little longer?"

Sunshine blinked, her puffy eyes glazed over from crying. "I can't bring a baby to Juilliard, Mom." Her voice was steady, but the exhaustion and sorrow in her words were undeniable.

Vivien's expression softened, her heart breaking for her daughter. "I'm sorry, sweetie," she murmured, tucking a loose strand of hair behind Sunshine's ear, trying to offer comfort in whatever way she could.

Sunshine swallowed hard, her throat tight. "Mom?" Her voice was small, hesitant. "Can you... can you not mention any of this to Dad?"

Vivien paused, studying her daughter's face for a long moment before nodding. "Of course," she said softly, understanding the depth of Sunshine's plea.

"Thank you," Sunshine whispered, her voice barely audible.

Vivien stood, clutching her purse. "I'll get this paid for," she said, heading toward the front desk.

Sunshine watched her mother walk away, feeling an ache settle in her chest. The thought flickered through her mind—was she defying God? Was it wrong to take control of her own future like this? Maybe, but if God was real, wouldn't He know that there was no room for a baby in her life right now? She had dreams—dreams that had no space for a child.

When Vivien returned, a nurse appeared, calling Sunshine back into a quieter room with a small desk and a single chair. The room felt even more isolated than before. Sunshine sat down, her fingers twisting together in her lap as she tried to steady her breathing.

The nurse settled across from her, flipping through paperwork, her pen clicking as she prepared to ask the next round of questions. "Any history of depression?" the nurse asked, glancing up from the form.

"Um, no," Sunshine replied, her voice flat.

"Family history of depression?"

"My sister," Sunshine said quietly, her thoughts briefly drifting to Violet.

"Any history with drugs or alcohol?" the nurse asked, eyes still on the paper.

"No."

"Any family history with addiction? Alcohol? Other substances?"

Sunshine shook her head, feeling her heart pick up speed. The room felt colder with every question, every pause between her responses.

"Okay." The nurse scribbled down her answers before looking up. "How do you feel about being here today?"

Sunshine shifted in her seat, swallowing hard. "Nervous, I guess."

"Any reservations about the procedure? Any second thoughts?"

Sunshine bit her lip, then shook her head. "No."

The nurse gave her a small, understanding nod, finishing up the last of her notes before pushing her chair back slightly. She reached for a small, square box as she explained, "I'll be administering the mifepristone now, and then when you get home—or within 48 hours—you'll need to insert the four misoprostol pills vaginally."

Sunshine nodded, her hands fidgeting nervously in her lap. "Okay."

The nurse stood up, filling a small plastic cup with water before placing it on the table in front of Sunshine. "You've been prescribed hydrocodone for the pain. You'll want to take that about 30 minutes before you insert the pills."

The nurse opened the box and handed Sunshine a single pill.

Sunshine stared at it, the small pill feeling like the heaviest thing in the world as it sat in her palm. Without giving herself more time to think, she popped the pill into her mouth and chased it down with a quick gulp of water.

Night had fallen and the usual quiet felt thicker as everyone but Sunshine slept. She moved slowly, her limbs heavy and dulled from the painkiller. The misoprostol had done its job, and though the pain had been unbearable at first, now it was numbed, distant, like something that had happened to someone else.

She could breathe now. No more wracking sobs, no more agony coiling through her body. Just... relief. And maybe, she thought with a hazy smile, a little happiness, though she knew it was most likely the pills.

Her mind felt lighter too, disconnected from the chaos of the past few days. She hadn't even thought about her so-called immaculate conception since the medication took effect.

Her bare feet padded down the steps, the wooden floor creaking beneath her toes as she wandered into the kitchen. She moved almost on autopilot, her thoughts a swirl of floating fragments, as she poured herself a glass of water. Her vision blurred slightly, and she blinked, trying to clear her head.

"Where's my baby?"

Sunshine froze, staring at the water spilling across the floor as the glass slipped from her hand.

The voice was soft, broken by grief. Sunshine's breath hitched, and she spun around, her eyes wide. A woman stood behind her—blonde, with tears streaking down her pale cheeks, her dress something from another era.

Sunshine's pulse thundered in her ears, her feet throbbed where the glass had bit into them, but the pain barely registered against the terror crawling under her skin.

The woman's tear-filled eyes locked onto hers, her voice trembling. "Where's my baby?" she asked again as if Sunshine held the answer to a loss so deep.

"I...I don't know," Sunshine stammered, shaking her head but the woman's desperation only grew more frantic, more aggressive. Her eyes wild with grief, the blonde woman lunged forward, grabbing Sunshine by the shoulders and shaking her violently.

"Give me my baby!" the woman demanded, her voice breaking, every word sharper than the next.

Sunshine whimpered, her body trembling as she tried to pull free. "Let go of me," she pleaded, panic rising as the woman's grip tightened, her nails biting into her skin. Tears welled up in Sunshine's eyes as she struggled against the woman's relentless hold.

A voice cut through the chaos. "Go away! You're scaring her!"

Tate appeared behind her, his voice firm, and the moment Sunshine heard it, she turned and clung to him, her body shaking as she buried her face into his chest. Tate's arms wrapped protectively around her, anchoring her in the storm of emotions swirling inside.

He placed a gentle hand on her cheek, cradling her head as she cried into him.

Sunshine turned her head slightly, her breath still ragged, and saw that the woman had vanished. She hadn't even realized she was crying until her breath shuddered painfully.

"Sunshine, it's okay," Tate soothed, his voice soft as he pulled back just enough to look into her tear-streaked face. His thumb brushed away her tears with gentle strokes. "Calm down, okay?"

"I'm going crazy," Sunshine whispered. The remnants of the painkillers still dulled her senses, mixing with the emotional exhaustion of the day, making everything feel unreal, as if she were drowning in her own mind.

Tate shook his head softly, his eyes full of understanding. "You're not crazy. They're from the past. The ghosts of people who've died here. They're appearing to you now because you're... evolved," he explained, his voice steady. "Don't be scared. All you have to do is tell them to go away. And they will."

Sunshine swallowed hard, her chest rising and falling as she fought to regain control. She nodded slowly, stepping back slightly from Tate's embrace. But a sharp pain shot through her, and she winced, looking down at her feet. Blood dripped from the small cuts where she had stepped on the shattered glass, painting the floor red.

"Let's get you cleaned up, okay?"

Sunshine lay on her back, her body heavy and sore, watching through a sleepy haze as Tate gently cleaned the wounds on her feet. The sight of blood had long lost its shock, but exhaustion from the day made her grateful for his help.

He worked in silence as he wiped away the blood and wrapped her cuts with care. It was strange—comforting, yet surreal—to see him, someone who wasn't supposed to be here, tending to her as if it were the most natural thing in the world.

Tate finished, getting up to pull open her sock drawer as if he'd always known where it was. He found a pair before walking back to the bed. Without a word, Sunshine lifted her foot slightly, and Tate slid the sock on, repeating the process with her other foot.

When he finished, Tate moved closer to her and placed his hand on her cheek. His thumb stroked her skin gently. "You doing okay?" he asked, his voice quiet.

Sunshine blinked up at him, the words forming in her mind but too tangled to speak. She shook her head, the smallest motion, but it said everything.

Tate's expression softened, his hand slipping away as a small frown pulled at his lips. He didn't push, didn't ask any more questions. Just waited.

"Will you lay with me?" Sunshine's voice cracked.

Tate watched her for a moment, as if weighing her request, before he nodded. "Yeah."

He climbed onto the bed beside her, and Sunshine rolled onto her side, facing the wall. His arm draped over her waist, pulling her close, his warmth settling against her back. The tension in her body began to melt away, her breathing evening out as his presence washed over her. It felt safe, here with him. For the first time that day, she felt okay.

Sunshine's fingers found his, interlocking with them. She could feel the exhaustion tugging at her, but her mind briefly flashed to the basement, to Tate's words about the house's history.

The thought lingered, twisting in her drowsy brain. "Was that Nora?" she asked softly, her voice thick with sleep.

There was a beat of silence before Tate responded. "Yeah, it was."

"Hmm," was all Sunshine could manage, her eyes growing heavier, her body surrendering to the warmth and comfort. Her thoughts began to blur, floating on the edge of sleep.

"Where were you today?" Tate asked quietly, his breath warm against her neck.

"Doctors," she mumbled, her words barely making it out as sleep tugged harder at her. She felt his hand gently brushed her hair back, his lips pressing a soft kiss to the side of her head.

Chapter 22

"Vi! It's time for school, let's go!" Sunshine called up the staircase, her voice echoing through the hallway from her spot by the front door.

After a moment, Violet appeared, hesitating midway down the steps, her expression stubborn. "I'm gonna hang with Tate today. Go without me."

Sunshine's gaze flickered over to Tate, who was just descending the stairs behind Violet. Her irritation flared up as she turned back to her sister.

"You've skipped all week. I can't keep covering for you and I'm fucking tired of picking up your shit so you don't fall behind." The words spilled out with a sharpness that surprised even her. Lately, she'd been on edge, and this small situation was just the latest to trigger her.

Violet let out a heavy sigh, her frustration palpable. "Fine. Whatever." She turned on her heel, storming back up the steps, leaving Tate standing midway.

"You're a bad influence," Sunshine pointed at Tate, the accusation half-hearted but laced with playful irritation.

"I really don't think it's a good idea for her to go to school today," he replied, hopping down the last few steps to approach her.

Sunshine frowned, crossing her arms defiantly. "Why?"

"School sucks. Kids suck. She's better here," he replied, his voice steady as he looked down at her, as if trying to assert his opinion with some kind of authority.

Sunshine's eyes widened, anger bubbling up inside her. "Who gives a shit? Kids have been assholes since the beginning of time. That's not gonna change. But what will change is a truancy officer showing up here, and me getting blamed for it because I'm the one supposed to make sure she's there every day."

"What's up with you?" Tate asked, confusion knitting his brows together. "Why are you being mean?"

Sunshine closed her eyes, taking a deep breath to steady herself. "She needs to go to school, Tate." When she opened her eyes, they were steely, filled with determination. "What were you two even planning, anyway?"

Ah, there it was—the jealousy creeping in, unsettling and unwelcome. She knew logically that they were strictly friends, but the chaotic whirlwind of her emotions clouded her judgment.

"Oh, I see," Tate said slowly, a knowing smile creeping onto his face, as if a light bulb had just flickered on in his head. "You're jealous."

"No, the fuck I'm not." Sunshine spat, but his smile only widened, and he stepped forward, pulling her into an embrace that caught her off guard. She struggled for a moment, but the warmth of his body seeped into her, and she melted against him, the tension in her shoulders easing slightly.

"I love you, remember?" Tate murmured, lifting his head to look at her, sincerity in his eyes.

"I'm not jealous," Sunshine grumbled against the soft fabric of his sweater, though her heart fluttered in her chest, both comforted and conflicted.

"Am I interrupting something?" Violet interjected, a teasing smirk spreading across her face as Sunshine pulled away from Tate to see her sister standing there, ready for school with her bag slung over one shoulder and a stylish hat perched on her head.

Sunshine exhaled sharply, caught between embarrassment and amusement as she made awkward eye contact with Tate.

"So, what, are you guys dating now?" Violet asked, strolling down the remaining steps with her arms crossed.

Tate hadn't officially asked her to be his girlfriend, but she didn't want to be the one to bring it up. She turned to look at him, Violet's expectant gaze shifted to him as well.

Tate glanced between the two sisters before settling on Sunshine. "I mean… yeah? Aren't we?"

Sunshine blinked. "You never asked."

"Am I supposed to ask? I thought it was obvious." His genuine confusion made her chuckle softly, and she shook her head, a smile breaking through her earlier frustration.

"Boys are so dumb," Violet observed, shaking her head as if she were a wise sage. "This is why I like girls."

"Lucky you," Sunshine teased, stepping back and opening the front door, her mood feeling lighter. "See you later, Tate."

She waved at him as Violet stepped through the threshold, Sunshine following closely behind before shutting the door with a soft click.

"I'm surprised," Violet remarked, glancing sideways at her sister as they walked across the front yard, the grass still damp from the morning sprinklers.

"What?" Sunshine asked, curiosity piqued.

"Well, I knew about Tate. He wouldn't shut up about you," Violet explained, her tone teasing but sincere. "But I thought you hated him."

Sunshine shrugged, pulling open the creaky gate that led to the sidewalk. "Things change."

As she motioned for Violet to walk through so she could shut the gate behind her. But the moment Violet stepped off the property, she vanished into thin air.

Sunshine's eyes widened, her mouth parting in shock as her mind struggled to comprehend what she had just witnessed. One second her sister was there, and the next—nothing.

Sunshine dropped her backpack to the floor as she dashed for the front door. "Violet!" she shouted, her voice ringing with urgency.

She burst through the threshold, scanning the area of any sign of her sister. "Violet!" she called again, panic clawing at her chest. She rushed through the house, glancing into the kitchen, but the space was empty.

As she moved into the hallway, a sobbing Violet rushed past her, barreling out the front door, her face streaked with tears and confusion. Sunshine's heart plummeted.

"Violet, what the fuck?" Sunshine called out, her voice laced with concern, but her sister didn't respond, just continued to run.

Violet reappeared, sprinting from the kitchen with wild eyes, her hair a disheveled halo around her face. Sunshine blinked in disbelief, struggling to process how she had crossed the house so quickly.

Violet rushed into Sunshine's arms, burying her face in her sister's shoulder, her sobs desperate and frantic. "I don't know what's happening."

Sunshine wrapped her arms around her sister, holding her tight as confusion swirled in her mind. "It's okay, Vi. Just breathe," she murmured, her heart aching at the sight of her sister so distraught, feeling utterly helpless.

Tate appeared in the hallway, his face drawn tight with worry. He looked between the two sisters, concern evident in his eyes.

Violet pulled away from Sunshine, her gaze turning sharp and accusatory at Tate. "Why am I running around like a crazy person? Did you drug me?"

"What? No!" Tate exclaimed, shaking his head vehemently, his voice rising slightly. "Violet, listen to me. I was hoping you wouldn't have to find out this way, but... I have to show you something. You have to trust me."

"It's so disgusting down here," Violet complained, her voice laced with revulsion. The darkness of the cramped space seemed to amplify her discomfort, the air heavy with dampness and an unsettling mustiness.

"Okay, come on," Tate urged gently, his tone calm yet insistent.

Sunshine watched as Tate extended a hand, carefully assisting Violet down from a brick platform. Tate then turned to Sunshine, raising his arms up to help her down.

When Sunshine hopped down, Tate's hands slipped away from her waist. Dust particles danced in the faint beam of light from Tate's flashlight, and Sunshine felt as if she were inhaling death.

Tate looked between the sisters. "Close your eyes. And remember... everything's going to be okay."

Sunshine nodded, locking eyes with Violet, whose fear was palpable. Tate took Violet's hand firmly while Sunshine grasped her other hand. With Tate leading the way, the light from the flashlight flickered and bounced off the damp, wooden beams. Sunshine squeezed her eyes shut tightly, the oppressive darkness intensifying her anxiety.

After a while, Tate halted, and the atmosphere shifted. The air thickened with the buzzing of flies, a chorus of disquiet that made Sunshine's skin crawl. The foul stench invaded her nostrils, sharp and acrid, twisting her stomach in knots.

"Open your eyes," Tate instructed, his voice steady yet strained.

Sunshine reluctantly peeled her eyes open alongside Violet, and what met her gaze sent a wave of horror crashing over her. The sight of her sister's lifeless body sprawled on the ground, partially decayed and covered in a swarm of flies and writhing maggots, struck her like a physical blow.

"Oh my god." A hand shot to Sunshine's mouth, the shock rendering her momentarily breathless as she instinctively dropped Violet's hand, turning away in sheer disbelief.

Her baby sister was dead.

Violet's anguished wails echoed painfully in the confined space, her hands desperately clutching at her hair. "I died when I took all those pills..." she gasped, the realization hitting her.

Sunshine stood frozen, her back to the horror, her hand pressed tightly against the wall for support. Tears streamed down her face as her chest heaved, her throat constricting as nausea churned violently in her stomach.

The stench of decay filled the air making her swallow hard to keep her bile from rising. The suffocating weight of grief wrapped around her, and for a moment, she couldn't breathe.

"I tried to save you. I did. I tried to make you throw them up. You threw up some. Not enough," Tate explained, his voice thick with remorse as tears rolled down his cheeks. "You took so many, Violet."

"I hardly feel anything," Violet shuddered, her voice thick with mucus, retreating further into her own despair.

Violet stumbled toward Sunshine, collapsing into her sister's arms as they both fell into a pit of sorrow. They sobbed together, Sunshine's fingers weaving through Violet's hair in a feeble attempt to calm her sister.

"It's gonna be okay," Sunshine whispered, her face splotchy from crying.

Tate approached them, rubbing Violet's back through his own tears. "I didn't want you to find out this way, Violet. You or your family. I never wanted you to see this. I'm so sorry, Violet..."

Sunshine opened her free arm, inviting Tate into their embrace. The three of them held each other, their cries echoing in the stillness of the dark space beneath the house.

Chapter 23

Sunshine lay sprawled across her bed, her head gently rising and falling with the rhythm of Tate's breathing as it rested on his chest. His fingers moved slowly through her hair, each stroke calming but also sending a ripple of questions through her mind.

She stared absently at the wall, now burdened with the knowledge that Tate had been aware of his death all along. A creeping confusion tugged at her, pulling her deeper into thought.

"Why didn't you tell me?" she asked softly.

Tate's fingers briefly paused, as if her question had jolted him from his own thoughts. "Hmm?" he murmured, his hand shifting from her hair to her shoulder, pulling her slightly closer.

"That you knew... that you were dead," Sunshine clarified.

Tate took a long, deep breath, his chest expanding beneath her cheek. "Hey, I'm Tate. I'm dead... wanna hookup?" he quipped, his lips twitching into a half-smile. He shook his head softly. "I don't think so."

A small, involuntary smile tugged at Sunshine's lips at the absurdity of his joke, though it quickly faded as darker thoughts crept in. Her mind flashed back to the article she had found—the one about him, about the tragic way he had died... and why.

She hesitated before asking the question that had been gnawing at the edges of her consciousness. "Do you remember how you died?" Her voice was quieter now, fearing the answer but needing to know all the same.

There was a long stretch of silence.

"Nope," he finally answered, his voice flat and emotionless.

As the year drew to a close, Sunshine sat at her desk, diligently filling out her Juilliard application. Her pen glided across the form, carefully filling in each section, working to ensure no detail was overlooked. She still had a couple of months before the deadline, but the weight of her dreams pushed her to stay ahead.

A faint knock at the door pulled her from her focused haze. She glanced up to see Violet standing in the doorway, her familiar face tinged with the same melancholy that always lingered since the truth of her death had surfaced. Every time Sunshine looked at her sister, a pang of grief shot through her chest.

Violet was forever trapped in this house, while Sunshine still had the chance to move forward—to leave. The guilt gnawed at her heart whenever she even thought about the future, let alone spoke about it.

"What are you doing?" Violet asked as she stepped into the room, her eyes flickering to the papers on Sunshine's desk.

Sunshine glanced awkwardly down at her application, feeling a sudden wave of discomfort. "Oh, um," she hesitated, her fingers tightening around the pen, "it's my application for Juilliard."

Violet's gaze stayed on the papers before she frowned slightly. "I thought those weren't due till January?"

"Yeah," Sunshine shrugged, trying to sound nonchalant, "just wanna make sure everything's perfect."

Violet's eyes softened as she looked at the form, the sadness in her expression deepening. "Being dead kind of makes me miss school," she muttered, her lips pressing into a thin line.

Sunshine's heart clenched, a flood of guilt rising in her throat. "I'm sorry, Vi," she whispered loud enough to carry across the room.

Violet leaned against the doorframe, resting her head against the wood, her face unreadable. "Don't be," she said with a sad smile, shrugging it off. "I did it to myself."

Sunshine tried to return the smile, but it felt forced, hollow. She didn't know what to say—how to comfort her sister when the truth hung between them.

Violet sighed, the mood shifting. "Mom wanted me to tell you... the cunt is here." Her voice dripped with disdain as she crossed her arms.

Sunshine's brow furrowed in confusion. "Aunt Jo?"

"Yup," Violet replied, her eyes rolling dramatically.

Sunshine let out a deep sigh, setting her pen down with a soft clatter before standing. The two sisters headed down the stairs, their footsteps in sync as they approached the living room. Vivien sat on the couch, mid-conversation with Aunt Jo, whose overly familiar voice filled the air like nails on a chalkboard.

"There they are!" Aunt Jo's voice chimed as she spotted them, immediately making a beeline for Sunshine. The woman's presence was overwhelming, her perfume thick and her demeanor scrutinizing.

"Hey, Aunt Jo," Sunshine forced out, her voice stiff but polite, masking the irritation bubbling beneath the surface.

Aunt Jo grasped Sunshine by the elbows, her sharp eyes scanning her as if assessing her from head to toe. Her gaze lingered a little too long on Sunshine's body, her lips pursed in an expression of disapproval.

"Oh my," Aunt Jo finally said, her tone heavy with judgment. "You've definitely gained a few."

Sunshine felt the heat rise to her face. Her smile faltered as she instinctively glanced down at herself, feeling self-conscious. She'd struggled with her body ever since everything had happened, and despite no longer being pregnant, the weight hadn't disappeared as she'd hoped.

"Joanna!" Vivien snapped, her voice sharp with disapproval, glaring at her sister.

Aunt Jo turned slightly, feigning innocence as she glanced over her shoulder at Vivien. "What?" she said, as if she had done nothing wrong.

She turned her attention back to Sunshine, who stood there trying not to let the comment fester, but the insecurity clawed at her chest. Aunt Jo had always been dramatic, but that didn't stop her words from stinging.

"Well, sweetie, I suppose it happens to the best of us, doesn't it? Life just catches up, especially when you're not... you know, keeping an eye on things," she said with a tight-lipped smile, her eyes flicking down to Sunshine's midsection. "But no need to worry, dear. There are always solutions for these things."

Sunshine bit the inside of her cheek as she fought to maintain her composure. She knew what Aunt Jo was doing—this wasn't new. Every visit was laced with these backhanded comments, always finding some way to make Sunshine feel like she wasn't enough.

"I'm fine, really," Sunshine said, her voice strained but polite. "Just focusing on my music and school."

Aunt Jo's lips curled into a thin smile. "Good to hear. We were all a little... concerned for a while, you know? With everything that happened last year."

Sunshine's heart dropped into her stomach.

Aunt Jo glanced back at her sister. "You know, Viv, it must've been so hard for you to handle everything back then—what with Sunshine going off the rails like that. Pills are no joke, after all."

Sunshine stiffened as a wave of shame washed over her. She could still remember those days—when everything felt like it was crumbling around her. Her baby brother was born dead, her family barely holding it together, and the pressure from every angle had pushed her to the brink. Pills became her escape. She was desperate for a way to silence the noise in her head, to numb the constant ache.

She still struggled with it sometimes, the urge lurking in the corners of her mind, even now. But having Aunt Jo bring it up like this, in front of everyone, made her feel exposed and raw, like the room had tilted, leaving her off-balance.

Vivien's voice cut through, cold and controlled. "Joanna, that's enough."

But Aunt Jo was already in full swing, ignoring the warning. "I just think it's important to keep an eye on these things. After all, stealing your own father's prescription pad to get pills... that's a serious cry for help."

Violet scoffed at Aunt Jo's words. "Seriously? leave her alone,"

Aunt Jo turned her sharp gaze toward Violet. "Oh, Violet, sweetheart, I'm not trying to upset anyone. I'm just trying to be helpful."

"Sure you are," Violet deadpanned, crossing her arms tightly over her chest. "Because that's what you're known for, being helpful."

The dining table was laden with the comforts of a Thanksgiving meal—turkey golden and crisp, mashed potatoes whipped smooth, stuffing fragrant with herbs, and a boat of thick gravy.

Sunshine sat stiffly, her hands folded in her lap as she stared at the plates of food that had long since lost their appeal. Her mind drifted as Vivien and Aunt Jo's conversation floated across the table. They were deep in talk, reminiscing about their childhood, though it seemed less about fond memories and more about the ghosts that lingered in them.

Sunshine's grandmother had always been a source of pain—a woman musically gifted but ruthless in her expectations. She'd once told Sunshine that she would never be good enough, never live up to the talent the family supposedly carried.

Those words had carved a scar deep in Sunshine's heart, one that still bled, even as she worked relentlessly to prove her wrong. Her mother had eventually bowed out of the pressure, only playing music now and then for fun. But Sunshine couldn't let go. She couldn't let her grandmother win. Not in memory, not in spirit. She had to keep fighting to prove herself, no matter how hard it was.

She glanced at Vivien who seemed at ease in the conversation, though a faint edge of bitterness lingered in her voice when their mother was mentioned.

Beside Vivien, Aunt Jo laughed, her cackle grating against Sunshine's nerves. She turned toward her father who sat awkwardly at the far end of the table, nursing his glass of wine. He kept taking sips, his eyes darting nervously between his wife and her sister, as if unsure how to insert himself into the conversation without causing a scene.

On the other side of the table, Violet was hunched over her plate, fork in hand but doing little more than pushing the food around in slow, disinterested circles. Her mashed potatoes had become a swirling mess of gravy, but she didn't seem to notice.

Violet was still adjusting to her death. Yet here they all were, pretending things were normal, pretending life hadn't been turned upside down in the walls of this house.

Aunt Jo's laughter suddenly rose, pulling Sunshine back to the present. "I still can't believe you stayed with him... and moved into this house. You're stronger than me," Aunt Jo said, her tone full of passive-aggressive mirth as she gestured loosely toward Ben.

Ben, sitting with a forced smile, waved a hand weakly, trying to maintain some semblance of grace. "Hey, Jo," he said, his voice strained as he leaned forward slightly. "I'm right here."

"Oh, I know, Ben." Aunt Jo didn't even bother to look at him, her eyes instead flicking back to Vivien, who offered a strained chuckle of her own, as if used to her sister's digs. "I'm just saying, Viv deserves a medal for putting up with... well, everything."

The subtext wasn't lost on Sunshine. Aunt Jo had always held a quiet disdain for her father, the psychiatrist husband who, in her eyes, never quite measured up. And moving into the infamous Murder House only seemed to cement her low opinion of him.

The snide remarks about his profession, his choices—none of it was new, but tonight they seemed sharper, crueler. Maybe it was the wine.

Sunshine looked back down at her plate, her appetite long gone. It was supposed to be a family dinner, but the air felt oppressive. She could feel Violet's silent frustration simmering beside her. Sunshine knew they'd both rather be anywhere else, doing anything else than sitting through this disaster.

She finally let out a quiet breath, forcing herself to say something, anything, to diffuse the growing tension. "So, Aunt Jo," she began, her voice calm but brittle, "how's work been?" It was a flimsy attempt, but anything to steer the conversation away from her father.

Aunt Jo turned her sharp gaze toward Sunshine, raising an eyebrow. "Work's fine, dear. Busy, as always. But thank you for asking." There was a pause, and her eyes flicked down to Sunshine's plate before she added with a smile, "Though I do hope you're finding time for more... active pursuits. Sitting at a desk all day isn't great for the waistline, you know."

Sunshine's jaw clenched as the familiar sting of her aunt's words settled in. Before she could respond, Violet let out a loud, exaggerated sigh and set her fork down with a clatter. "For the love of god, can we not talk about waistlines for five minutes?" she snapped, her voice dripping with irritation.

Aunt Jo blinked in surprise, but before she could retort, Vivien intervened, her voice tight and controlled. "Alright, let's all just calm down. It's supposed to be a nice dinner."

"Is it?" Violet muttered under her breath, stabbing her fork into her mashed potatoes with a little more force than necessary.

Sunshine stood abruptly from the table, the tension in the room too suffocating to endure any longer. "I'll be right back," she mumbled, not bothering to wait for anyone's response. Her chair scraped loudly against the hardwood floor as she stepped away from the table.

She moved quickly into the kitchen, the low hum of her mother's voice carrying faintly from the dining room as she skillfully redirected the conversation back to safer topics. Sunshine barely registered it, her focus solely on escaping the negative energy behind her.

Without thinking, she slipped into the pantry, the small space offering a moment of solitude. She shut the door behind her, cutting off the outside world.

Sunshine pressed her back against the cool wall, closing her eyes and taking a deep breath, letting the stillness wrap around her. But before she could fully calm down, the door creaked open, and Tate slipped inside, shutting it quietly behind him.

Sunshine's eyes snapped open, wide and surprised. "What are you doing?" she whispered.

"Don't worry," Tate reassured in a low voice, "they can't see me unless I want them to."

Before she could respond, he was already advancing on her, his presence filling the small space as he closed the distance between them. Her back pressed further against the pantry wall as he leaned in, towering over her.

Sunshine tilted her head up to meet his gaze. His eyes were dark, hungry, staring at her as if he wanted to devour her whole.

Realization hit her all at once, her cheeks flushing with heat. "My family is in the next room, Tate,"

"So," Tate murmured in reply, his voice dropping to a husky whisper. He lowered his head, his lips brushing against the soft skin behind her earlobe. His hands slid to her waist, gently pulling her closer as he whispered against her ear, "You're upset... let me make you feel better."

Sunshine's mind raced, torn between the urge to pull away and the intoxicating pull of his presence. His lips lingered just behind her ear, and she could feel her defenses crumbling with every second he stood so close.

Tate's hand slipped down her side, his fingers brushing over the soft fabric of her dress before inching lower, teasing the edge of her hem. His fingers traced a slow, deliberate path up her inner thigh, lifting the fabric of her dress.

She bit her lip, trying to stifle the soft gasp that escaped her as his hand ventured higher. Her heart pounded in her chest, her body responding despite the voice in her head reminding her of the dining room just a few feet away.

"Tate..." she whispered but the words barely left her lips before his hand delved into her underwear, his fingers pressing gently into her clit.

Sunshine's lips parted, a heated breath escaping as he maintained eye contact with her. Her hips instinctively pressed into his hand when he moved his fingers in a circular motion.

A soft moan escaped Sunshine's lips before she could stop it, the sound quickly stifled by Tate's hand as it pressed gently over her mouth. "Shh," he whispered as his other hand continued its slow, tantalizing movements. "You don't want them to hear, do you?"

Tate's gaze remained locked on hers he watched every subtle shift of emotion flicker across Sunshine's face. His smirk grew wider, as her cheeks flushed deeper beneath his hand. He relished in the control, in the way her body responded to his touch, helplessly surrendering to the sensations he was creating.

His fingers moved with more urgency now, picking up speed as he rubbed her with deliberate precision. He could feel her hips instinctively roll into his hand, her body betraying her need despite the tense atmosphere.

The sensation was overwhelming, her breath coming out in ragged gasps through her nose, muffled by the hand that silenced her. She could taste his skin, warm and rough against her lips, adding to the dizzying haze that clouded her mind.

Sunshine's hands pressed against the pantry wall, searching for something to steady herself as she felt her control slipping away. Her body responded on its own, caught in the rhythm he set, and she found herself lost in the intensity of it all—his hand, the darkness of his eyes watching her every reaction.

The world outside the pantry seemed to fade away—the faint murmur of voices from the dining room, the clatter of dishes—it all blurred into the background, drowned out by the deafening rush of her own pulse and the intoxicating feeling of Tate's hands on her.

Tate's hand slipped away from her mouth just as she reached the brink, replacing it with his lips in a fierce, silencing kiss. The moment his mouth met hers, Sunshine's legs began to tremble, the tension inside her unraveling all at once.

A soft, muffled moan escaped her, melting into Tate's lips as her body surged with the overwhelming sensation.

She clung to him as the wave of release crashed over her, her chest heaved against his as she desperately tried to catch her breath. Tate didn't pull away, instead keeping his lips locked with hers, deepening the kiss as if feeding off her pleasure.

As the last tremors faded, she pulled back from the kiss, her lips parted and swollen, her breathing still ragged. Tate stared down at her, the corners of his mouth quirking up in a satisfied grin. He wiped a stray lock of hair from her flushed face.

"Feel better now?"

Sunshine awkwardly re-entered the dining room, trying to shake off the lingering tension from the pantry. Violet glanced up from her seat, her brow furrowing with impatience.

"What took you so long? You left me here to suffer through this alone," Violet whispered.

Sunshine forced a smile and mouthed, "Sorry," as she moved to sit back down.

Just as she reached for her chair, a sharp, searing pain shot through her abdomen, making her freeze mid-step. Her hand instinctively flew to her stomach, her expression contorting into confusion and alarm. It felt like something kicked—no, someone kicked her from the inside.

"Sunny, are you okay?" Ben's voice cut through the conversation, noticing the sudden change in her posture and the way she clutched her stomach.

"I—I'm fine," she started to reply, but her words were cut short as a white-hot pain erupted once more, this time more intense, forcing her to double over. Sunshine's body folded in on itself, her arms wrapping tightly around her middle as if trying to shield herself from whatever was happening. A gasp of pain escaped her, her face paling as the room spun.

"Sunshine?" Vivien's voice trembled with concern, her fork clattering onto her plate as she stood up quickly.

Violet shot up from her seat, her eyes wide with panic. "What's happening?" she demanded, looking around the table as if someone had the answers.

Sunshine whimpered as tears welled in her eyes. The pain was unbearable, like something was tearing her apart from the inside. Her knees buckled beneath her, and she gripped the edge of the table, trying to steady herself, but her body was no longer responding the way it should.

"Ah!" Another cry slipped from her lips, more desperate this time, as the agony tore through her again. Her vision blurred with tears. Something was horribly, horribly wrong.

Chapter 24

Sunshine sat on the hospital bed, her legs dangling off the edge of the exam table as she stared at the stark white curtain that separated her from the other patients. The sharp, relentless pain had subsided since they'd given her pain medication, but the nausea still lingered.

Her mother and father sat nearby in stiff chairs, their faces drawn with concern. The silence in the small, curtained-off space felt suffocating, broken only by the faint beeps of machines and the distant murmurs of hospital staff.

They waited in uneasy quiet until a doctor finally pushed through the curtain holding a clipboard, a hurried look on her face. "Sorry to keep you waiting," she said, her tone brisk but not unkind as she walked over to Sunshine, immediately directing her attention to her stomach. "Are you currently experiencing any abdominal pain?"

Sunshine shook her head. "No, not anymore. I just…feel sick." Her voice was quiet, almost apologetic, as if the nausea were a burden she shouldn't be admitting to.

The doctor nodded, setting down the clipboard and prepping the sonogram machine. "Have you had any procedures recently?" she asked casually, turning on the device.

A sudden panic fluttered in Sunshine's chest. She glanced at her father, knowing full well he had no idea what she was about to reveal. Her eyes then darted to her mother, seeking some sort of permission or reassurance. Vivien gave a subtle nod, urging her daughter to speak.

"I, uh..." Sunshine stammered, her hands nervously gripping the thin hospital blanket draped over her. "I took the abortion pill two weeks ago."

Ben's face contorted in confusion, his eyes darting to Vivien. "What?" he asked, his voice rising in both disbelief and hurt.

"Ben," Vivien warned softly, her tone pleading for patience.

The doctor, unfazed by the family tension, continued with a professional nod as she prepared the ultrasound. "Okay. And how far along were you when you took the pills?"

Sunshine swallowed hard, her mouth suddenly dry. "The doctor said nine weeks."

"Well, the pills aren't always 100% effective," the doctor explained matter-of-factly. "There's a chance you could still be pregnant, though it could just be gas. Let's take a look to be sure."

Sunshine laid back on the bed, her dress already hiked up to reveal her stomach, the blanket modestly covering her lower half. She watched in dread as the doctor squirted the cold ultrasound gel onto her abdomen and pressed the probe against her skin.

The room felt like it had shrunk as the doctor scanned her belly. The rhythmic hum of the machine filled the silence, but Sunshine's mind was racing, her breath shallow. She stared at the ceiling, trying to hold onto some thread of calm, but everything felt surreal.

The doctor's face scrunched in concentration, her eyes fixed on the screen. "And you're certain about the timeline?" she asked, glancing at Sunshine.

"I... I think so. Nine weeks." Sunshine's voice cracked slightly. She had no idea how any of this was happening, but the doctor at Planned Parenthood had been clear. She should be eleven weeks by now if the pregnancy had persisted.

But the doctor's expression was growing more concerned as she moved the probe across Sunshine's stomach. "I see the fetus, but... the baby looks much bigger than it should at this stage," she murmured, her voice tinged with confusion.

Sunshine's heart sank. Still pregnant? How could this be? Her mind spiraled. The abortion had failed. This wasn't normal. None of this was normal. The immaculate conception, the strange occurrences... something beyond her control was taking over.

The doctor's eyes suddenly widened, her face draining of color as she stared at the ultrasound screen, transfixed by something on the monitor. A flash of fear rippled across her features.

A cold dread washed over Sunshine. "Is... is everything okay?"

Before the doctor could respond, her body went rigid, and then, without warning, she collapsed, hitting the floor with a sickening thud.

"Oh my god!" Vivien gasped, her hand flying to her mouth as she stared at the unconscious doctor in horror.

Ben jumped up from his chair, rushing to the doctor's side before standing up and moving toward the curtain. "I'm going to get help,"

Sunshine remained frozen, her wide eyes darting between the doctor sprawled on the floor and the sonogram machine.

What did she see?

Sunshine lay curled on her side in her room, her fingers gently cradling her cheek as she gazed blankly at the wall. It felt like an eternity since she'd come home. She replayed the events of the past few weeks over and over, each thought dragging her deeper into a pit of despair.

Planned Parenthood had offered to perform another procedure for free, a second chance at escaping this unexpected reality, but part of her felt it was pointless. It was as if fate had already laid its claim on her.

God, it seemed, intended for her to carry this child. Sunshine felt her grip on reality slipping, spiraling into what she could only describe as a spiritual psychosis. Nothing made sense anymore.

Was there truly a hell? Would she be condemned for her attempt to end what had now become a divine burden? And what about Tate and Violet—did they dwell in some limbo, caught between heaven and hell, forever lingering in a world that felt just out of reach?

She had never been opposed to having children; in fact, she had always envisioned a future where motherhood would be a joy rather than a shackle. But now, at seventeen, with dreams shimmering like distant stars, those aspirations felt like dust scattering in the wind.

Sunshine's hand slipped down to cradle her stomach, the slight bump she had tried to ignore now undeniable. This was real. There was a baby growing inside of her—a magic baby, as absurd as that sounded.

"Who's the dad?"

The voice pierced through her thoughts, drawing her attention to the doorway.

"Not now, Violet," Sunshine sighed, closing her eyes in a futile attempt to block out the reality of the situation.

How could she even begin to answer that question? The thought of telling Tate—her now boyfriend—that she was pregnant, and not by him, felt like a confession that could shatter everything. Oh, by the way, I'm having a baby that isn't yours, but it isn't anyone else's either. She imagined the look on his face, the confusion and disbelief.

"Is it Tate's?" Violet pressed, inching further into the room.

"God, Violet, no!" Sunshine snapped, a wave of frustration washing over her as she sat up.

"Are you keeping it?"

Without thinking, Sunshine sprang to her feet, grasping her sister's shoulders gently yet firmly, and guided her back toward the door before shutting it, locking her sister out.

Chapter 25

Sunshine stood before her mirror clad only in underwear. Today was her doctor's appointment since her mother had insisted it was crucial to ensure the baby's well-being, regardless of the choice Sunshine would ultimately make.

Her gaze fell to her stomach, the subtle curve taking her main focus. She reached out, hesitantly placing her palm against the skin. As she rubbed her belly gently, she swore she could feel a flutter—like a butterfly's wings beating softly against the walls of her womb. A small smile curled on her lips at the sensation.

Sunshine's eyes widened as she caught a glimpse of Tate's reflection in the mirror, standing just behind her.

She spun around to face him and Tate's gaze drifted downward to her stomach, and she felt a rush of shame wash over her. There was no hiding it now.

"Tate," she breathed before hastily moving to her closet. She rifled through the hangers, tugging a loose-fitting dress over her head, desperately trying to cover the evidence.

Tate remained silent, an unreadable expression etched across his features as she caught his eye.

Sunshine moved to sit on the edge of her bed, her hands fidgeting in her lap as she stared at the floor, trying to find the right words. She had rehearsed this conversation in her head countless times, but now that Tate was here—standing just a few feet away, looking at her with such tenderness—she felt her throat tighten. This wasn't going to be easy.

Tate's gaze softened as he noticed her unease. "Is that why you've been avoiding me?" His voice was gentle, patient, but there was a flicker of concern in his eyes as he moved to sit beside her on the bed.

Sunshine's fingers twisted together nervously, and she took a deep breath, steadying herself. She turned to face him, her eyes meeting his. "Tate, I was going to tell you," she started, her voice wavering. She could see the worry deepen in his expression as he waited.

"I'm pregnant." The words hung in the air between them, heavy and thick with meaning.

She felt her breath catch, her throat tightening as she pushed forward. "But it's... it's not yours. I—I know it's not." Her voice trembled slightly as she explained. "The timeline doesn't add up, and... I don't know." Sunshine's eyes dropped to the floor again, her heart aching with the guilt she felt. "I just didn't want to keep it from you."

For a moment, there was silence. Sunshine braced herself for the anger she thought might come—the frustration or sadness.

Tate shifted uncomfortably, his jaw tightening for just a split second before his calm, comforting demeanor returned. "It's okay,

Sunshine," he said, his voice soft and reassuring. "I'm not mad." He reached out, taking her hand in his, his thumb gently brushing over her knuckles.

Sunshine shifted uneasily, her gaze flickering over Tate's face as she tried to process his reaction. He hadn't questioned her virtue—not once—and for that, she was deeply grateful. The relief of not having to explain the unexplainable was a relief. How could she tell him the truth, even if she wanted to? If she even attempted to explain what she thought had happened—she'd sound like a madwoman.

And yet, here he was, calm and composed, offering her nothing but love and reassurance.

"You're really not upset?" she asked cautiously, still wary of how easy it all seemed.

Tate shook his head, a small smile tugging at the corner of his lips. "No, Sunny. I'm not upset. This... this baby, it doesn't change anything between us. I'll still be here, with you."

Sunshine exhaled, relieved by his response, though a small part of her still wondered why he wasn't more affected by the news. Maybe it was because she had imagined the worst—rejection, anger—but instead, he was calm, even supportive.

"I want to help you, with all of this," Tate continued, his hand still warm in hers. "You're not alone in this, okay?"

Sunshine felt her chest tighten, emotions all over the place. She nodded, leaning into him, resting her head on his shoulder. "Thank you, Tate. I was so scared to tell you."

He wrapped his arm around her, pulling her closer. "You don't ever have to be scared with me," he murmured into her hair.

A knock sounded at the door, pulling them out of their conversation.

"Sunshine? Are you ready?" Vivien's voice echoed from the hallway.

Sunshine looked toward the door. "Yeah, Mom. I'm coming."

Sunshine sat in the sterile, cold exam room, her hands nervously gripping the edges of the paper-lined table beneath her. The walls were an uninviting pale blue, a color meant to soothe, but only serving to make the room feel more clinical.

Sunshine glanced down at her stomach, where her baby was growing—an impossible, inexplicable baby. She had tried to make sense of it all, but nothing in her life had been "normal" since she moved into that house. She'd convinced herself that whatever was happening, it was beyond her control.

The doctor entered the room, a kind smile on her face as she wheeled the ultrasound machine closer to the bed. "Good morning, Sunshine. How are you feeling today?"

"Nervous," Sunshine admitted, biting her lip.

"That's completely understandable. We're just going to have a look and see how things are progressing, alright? You can relax, this won't take long."

Dr. Novak squeezed a cool blob of gel onto Sunshine's belly, and the sudden chill made her shiver. As the probe touched her skin, her eyes glued to the screen, waiting, terrified, and strangely excited to see the baby she still wasn't sure she wanted.

The black-and-white image flickered to life, fuzzy at first, but then slowly coming into focus. A shape emerged—small, but unmistakable. Her baby. Sunshine's heart skipped a beat as she stared at the image on the monitor, a lump forming in her throat.

She hadn't expected to feel this... connected, this suddenly overwhelmed by the reality of it all.

"There's your baby," Dr. Novak said softly, her voice filled with quiet awe. "Let's get a closer look."

Sunshine blinked away tears, her chest tightening as the tiny form on the screen moved.

"Is... everything okay?" she asked.

Dr. Novak smiled, her eyes studying the screen. "Everything looks perfect. Strong heartbeat, good movement."

Vivien leaned in closer, her own eyes misting over. "Sunshine... look at him," she whispered, pointing at the monitor. "He's beautiful."

"Him?" Sunshine asked.

Dr. Novak nodded. "Yes, it looks like you're having a boy."

A boy. Sunshine's mind reeled. She hadn't let herself imagine this—what the baby would be like, who they would become. But now, seeing him, seeing the shape of him, the way he moved so effortlessly inside her... everything shifted.

Dr. Novak's brow furrowed slightly as she moved the probe around Sunshine's belly, focusing on measurements. "According to the size of the fetus, you're measuring around 24 weeks. That's... a bit farther along than you originally thought, isn't it?"

"Twenty-four weeks?" Sunshine echoed. That was impossible—she had been nine weeks when she took the pills, and she'd taken them three weeks ago. "But... that can't be right, I mean..."

This pregnancy wasn't normal. It never had been. Whatever this was, it wasn't going to follow any rules. She definitely didn't feel five months pregnant.

Vivien glanced at her daughter, concern etched into her features. "What does that mean?"

Dr. Novak paused, her expression carefully neutral. "Well, every pregnancy is different. Sometimes women don't find out they're pregnant until they're farther along, and measurements can vary. But based on what I'm seeing, everything looks healthy."

Sunshine stared at the screen. Twenty-four weeks. That meant she was past the point of no return. This baby was real, and growing fast, and soon, he would be here.

She gazed at the image of her son, tears welling up in her eyes again. This was her baby. All hers. He had a heartbeat. He had little arms and legs. And he was growing—against all odds, despite everything. Maybe this was God's plan. Maybe this baby was meant to be.

"I think I'm keeping him," Sunshine whispered, her voice trembling. She looked up at her mother, tears finally spilling over as she spoke the words aloud, making it real. "I'm going to keep him."

Ben's concerned expression tightened as he leaned against Sunshine's desk, staring at her with a mixture of frustration and worry. "Sunshine, have you even really thought about this?"

Sitting on the edge of her bed, Sunshine exhaled, her fingers idly picking at the fabric of her comforter. "All I've done is think about it, Dad," she replied, her tone thick with exhaustion. She glanced at her mother, who sat beside her, offering quiet support with a comforting hand on her knee.

Vivien turned toward Ben, her voice firm yet understanding. "It's her decision, Ben."

He let out a long breath, rubbing his temples as though trying to alleviate the tension building behind his eyes. "I understand that, Viv, but she's seventeen," he pressed, pushing off the desk and pacing slightly. "What about Juilliard?"

Juilliard. The word felt like a distant echo of a dream she'd been holding onto for so long. Sunshine's chest tightened at the mention of it, but she quickly suppressed the growing doubt. "I'll take a gap year," she responded, trying to sound confident, though the weight of the decision gnawed at her.

Ben folded his arms across his chest, glancing between Sunshine and Vivien. "And what about the cost?" His voice softened again, a fatherly concern leaking through his frustration. "We're already struggling as it is, kiddo. Between trying to sell this house and the fact that your mother is pregnant..."

Sunshine knew Ben wasn't wrong. Their finances had been tight for months, and the house—well, that was another matter altogether. The idea of bringing another baby into their current situation made her stomach knot, but it didn't shake her decision.

"I'll get a job," Sunshine said, her voice quiet but resolute. "Whatever I need to do."

Ben's brow furrowed deeper, his frustration inching toward desperation. "And school? Are you going to drop out?"

"Ben," Vivien cut in again, her tone sharper this time, as if scolding him for pushing too hard.

Sunshine shook her head, meeting her father's eyes with all the certainty she could muster. "No. I'm not dropping out. Daddy, I've taken everything into consideration. I tried to do what I was supposed to, but it didn't work. And maybe... I don't know, maybe it's a sign from God or something."

Ben let out a low, exasperated groan, rubbing his face with his hands as though he couldn't quite believe what he was hearing.

"Oh my god," he muttered under his breath before looking back at her, his eyes searching for something—anything—that made sense. "Where's the father? Have you told him?"

Sunshine averted her gaze, her silence betraying more than she could find the strength to say. Her mother's eyes darted toward her, that same question written across her face.

"He's...not in the picture," Sunshine managed as she stared down at her hands, hoping that would be enough to end the discussion.

Ben's shoulders slumped slightly. He sighed, rubbing the back of his neck, trying to soothe the tension that wouldn't leave.

"Being a single mom is tough work, Sunshine. It's going to be a challenge—one of the hardest things you'll ever do. But if this is what you want," she paused, locking eyes with her daughter, "then we will be here for you."

Chapter 26

Sunshine sat at the kitchen island as Moira quietly cleaned around her, and her mother prepared tea. Her phone was pressed to her ear as she spoke with the hospital, her mind still fixated on the strange turn of events during her visit to the emergency room.

Something had happened—something that wasn't normal. Sunshine felt it deep in her bones, and now she needed answers.

"Yeah, I think her name was Angie? I'm not sure, but she fainted during my ultrasound." Sunshine's voice wavered as she recounted the incident, her eyes darting toward her mother, who was stirring sugar into her tea with an air of quiet concern. The voice on the other end of the line seemed to pause, and then Sunshine's brows furrowed. "She quit?"

Vivien looked up, her eyes sharp with interest. "Tell them to ask her to call you," she instructed gently.

Sunshine nodded, following her mother's lead. "Could you ask her to call me? Sunshine Harmon. Okay, yeah, thank you," she replied before flipping her phone shut with a sigh. Turning to

Vivien, she exhaled again, running her fingers through her hair. "They said they'd give her my number."

"That's good," Vivien replied, offering a reassuring nod as she took a measured sip of her tea.

Before they could say more, the kitchen door swung open, and in strode Constance, holding a covered plate as if she owned the place. Her presence was commanding as always, the scent of something metallic and raw filling the air.

"Hi, Constance," Vivien greeted, her tone resigned. Sunshine could tell her mother was slowly getting used to Constance's sudden, unannounced visits.

Ignoring Vivien's pleasantries, Constance zeroed in on Sunshine, her sharp gaze softening slightly. She set the plate down near the island with a flourish. "Your mother tells me you've been suffering terribly. That every time you step outside, you're racked with violent morning sickness?"

Sunshine hesitated, glancing over at Vivien for confirmation, mildly annoyed that everyone seemed to know about her pregnancy now. She sighed, brushing it off. "Um, yeah, something like that."

"Well, you know, my mother always recommended a big platter of offal during the second trimester of pregnancy. She preferred pork," she declared, her fingers moving quickly as she began unwrapping the plate. As the parchment came undone, it revealed a pile of bloodied meat—so red and raw that Sunshine's stomach turned.

Sunshine's mouth fell open, her expression torn between horror and disbelief.

"Sweetbreads," Constance explained, pointing to different sections of the meat with delicate precision. "Now, these two are thymus glands, one from the heart, one from the throat. And this," she gestured to the thickest piece of tissue, "is the pancreas. So good for mother and child. Full of protein, vitamin C, all the B vitamins, and iron. I gifted some to your mother not too long ago."

Vivien gave her daughter an encouraging look. "It's really not that bad,"

Sunshine wasn't convinced, her gaze fixed on the plate of organs that now sat ominously before her.

"You were such a dear, sweet child," Constance continued, her voice softening in an almost maternal way. "Such a comfort to me when Addie passed." Her eyes lingered on Sunshine, brimming with a strange mixture of fondness and intensity. "I wanted to do something nice for you—and for your baby. Though I knew long before you did."

Sunshine's brow furrowed, suspicion creeping into her voice. "What do you mean?"

Constance touched the end of her nose, as if revealing a secret. "I've got the nose of a truffle pig... all those pheromones," she said with a knowing smirk.

Sunshine swallowed hard, her skin crawling at the thought. Oh.

Without skipping a beat, Constance turned to Moira, who had just closed the dishwasher. "Moira, why don't you sauté these for Sunshine's lunch? Do 'em the way you used to for me, remember? With sweet butter."

Moira looked over at Sunshine with a resigned nod. "I'd be happy to do that for Ms. Harmon."

"Thanks, Constance..." Sunshine said through gritted teeth, forcing politeness through the discomfort as she watched Constance walk toward the door.

"It's no trouble at all," Constance replied dismissively, leaving as suddenly as she had arrived.

As soon as the door clicked shut, Sunshine's stomach dropped. She turned to her mother with wide eyes, silently pleading for an escape from the absurdity. But Moira had already moved to the stove, pulling out a pan and placing the raw meat into it. The sizzling sound filled the air as Moira glanced back over her shoulder at Vivien.

"May I say something that could be considered out of turn, but that is sincerely heartfelt?" Moira asked.

Vivien set her teacup down carefully, watching Moira with a raised brow. "I guess so."

Moira's tone dropped, taking on an edge that was sharper than the knife she used to stir the offal. "Cheating on one's pregnant wife qualifies as an unspeakable criminal act. It's on a par with murder. And I'll tell you one thing I know—if I know anything at all—Dr. Harmon will cheat again, if given half the chance."

Sunshine shifted uncomfortably in her seat as she exchanged a quick glance with her mother, whose face had hardened into a mask of forced composure. The wound was still fresh—Sunshine knew that. She had never forgiven her father for what he'd done, and now, with everything spiraling out of control, her parents separating had slipped her mind.

When Moira finished her task, walking over to the island and placing a plate of the sautéed meat in front of Sunshine. "Just a pinch of sea salt, a tiny squeeze of lemon, if you like. Though I prefer it without," Moira said, her voice light. "And ma'am, I've left the pancreas uncooked. They say it's the tenderest organ of them all, especially when eaten raw."

Sunshine stared at the plate, then let out a nervous laugh. "Are you serious?"

Moira nodded. "Think of the baby."

The crisp December air bit at Sunshine's skin as she stepped out of her mother's car, her breath visible in the cold. She shoved the keys deep into her pocket, wrapping her jacket tighter around her body as she walked across the pavement, her boots echoing faintly against the concrete.

She stopped for a moment, her gaze lifting to the imposing structure of the Catholic church where the doctor had agreed to meet her. The towering stone walls and stained glass windows loomed overhead.

She hadn't expected to be brought here. A church. The irony of it twisted in her mind. Did the doctor think she was carrying a divine miracle, too? The very thought made her stomach churn, her hand instinctively resting over her growing belly as she took a deep breath and pushed forward.

The heavy wooden doors groaned as she opened them, stepping into the interior. The faint scent of incense filled the air, mingling with the cold draft that swept in behind her. The church was vast, the rows of wooden pews stretching out on either side of the aisle that led down to the altar.

Votive candles flickered and above, a massive cross hung from the ceiling. Sunshine's eyes lingered on it for a moment before she spotted the doctor standing near the candles, clutching something to her chest.

"Angela?" Sunshine called out softly, her voice echoing slightly in the quiet expanse of the church as she walked down the isle.

Angie flinched at the sound of her name, her body stiffening as she turned to face Sunshine. "Sunshine,"

Sunshine shoved her hands into her pockets as she finally reached the woman. "Um, thanks for agreeing to meet with me."

Angie took a step back, her knuckles white around the edges of the Bible as she held it close to her chest. "That's, uh, probably close enough,"

Sunshine blinked as she tried to process the doctor's unease. "Okay..." She swallowed hard, her eyes drifting around the church. "Why... why the church?"

"It's where I feel safe," Angie replied quickly, her voice brittle, as though it might crack at any moment. Her eyes darted nervously around, never lingering on Sunshine for long.

"The hospital said you quit your job... and that the machine malfunctioned, but I've been worried about it." Her voice wavered. "I don't know, you just seemed... scared?"

"Yes," Angie whispered. "And I've been praying about it ever since. I saw the unclean thing... what you carry in your womb. The plague of nations. The Beast."

Sunshine felt her blood run cold, her limbs stiffening as her mind tried to grasp what Angie was saying. The Beast? Plague of nations? This was insane. This whole pregnancy was already a whirlwind of confusion and fear but now Angie was spewing religious prophecy? All this time, Sunshine had tried to convince herself that maybe, just maybe, it was God's baby. But what if she had been wrong?

"What?" Sunshine's voice came out in a breathless whisper, her lips parted in shock as she stared at the woman before her.

"I saw the little hooves,"

Sunshine's world tilted. Her stomach dropped as the words hit her. A nightmare she had had not long ago resurfaced in vivid clarity—the memory of her swollen belly, the feeling of something clawing from within, hooves scraping against her insides. She hadn't told anyone about it. It was too disturbing, too real, but now...

Her chest tightened, her breath quickening as panic overtook her. "I... I have to go," she stammered as she backed away from Angie, her legs shaky beneath her. She turned, bolting down the aisle, her footsteps echoing like thunder in the empty church.

As she neared the doors, Angie's voice rang out behind her. "And the woman was full of the filthiness of her fornication!" she cried, her words steeped in Biblical fervor. "The mother of harlots and abominations of the Earth!"

Sunshine's hands fumbled with the doors, her breath coming in short, panicked gasps. She stumbled outside into the cold air. The wind stung her cheeks as she hurried back to the car, her mind reeling, the words echoing in her skull.

The Beast. Hooves. The mother of abominations.

Her hand instinctively moved to her stomach, the life growing inside her now feeling more alien than ever.

Chapter 27

Dr. Novak entered the exam room with a warm smile. She wore her usual calm demeanor, clipboard in hand as she glanced over Sunshine's chart. "Sunshine, how are we doing today?"

Sunshine sat on the edge of the examination table, her hands resting awkwardly in her lap. She had come to this appointment alone, feeling more isolated than she cared to admit. "Um... I've been taking the B6 like you said ," she began, her voice carrying a hint of weariness. "But honestly, it's not really helping. I'm fine when I'm at home, but every time I step outside, I feel like I'm going to be sick ."

Dr. Novak nodded sympathetically, setting her clipboard down and crossing her arms as she leaned against the counter. "It could just be your body's way of telling you to slow down," she suggested, a hint of concern in her tone. "Or it's a sign to stay home and take it easy."

Sunshine let out a soft, humorless laugh, shaking her head slightly. "Well, I can't exactly drop everything. I still have school, and... well, there's a lot going on." Her eyes flicked toward the ceiling as she tried to push back the real reason for her anxiety, the gnawing fear she couldn't bring herself to say out loud.

Because what if it wasn't just normal pregnancy symptoms? What if there was something wrong ? The strange dreams, the fainting doctor, the hooves. A part of her wanted to confide in Dr. Novak, to tell her everything—but how could she explain something so terrifying, so impossible? How could she admit that she feared there might literally be a little demon growing inside her?

Dr. Novak studied her carefully, sensing the underlying tension. "You know, if you're feeling particularly worried, we can always run some tests," she offered, her voice softening. "It might help ease some of that anxiety, though I can't guarantee it'll make you feel any better."

Sunshine chewed on her bottom lip, weighing the offer. She was already swimming in uncertainty, desperate for any reassurance, even if it was fleeting. "Yeah, I think it will," she murmured, her voice steadying as she met the doctor's gaze . "I think I need to know."

Dr. Novak nodded, her expression understanding. "Alright, we'll get everything scheduled this week. I'll make sure we cover all the bases." She scribbled something quickly on her chart before looking back at Sunshine with a reassuring smile.

"Thank you." Sunshine offered a small smile in return, but her heart still weighed heavy. Even with tests, even with answers, nothing could quell the storm inside her mind.

Sunshine sat cross-legged on the floor, surrounded a scattering of sheet music. Lost in thought, she was startled by a soft knock on her door.

Looking up, she was greeted by Tate, his silhouette framed by the doorway. He wore a shy smile, his eyes sparkling with warmth. "Hey,"

"Hey," she replied, a smile spreading across her face. Slowly, she moved onto her knees, struggling a bit as her pregnancy made even the simplest tasks feel more challenging. Tate stepped closer, offering his hand to help her up. "Thank you. What's up?"

"I actually wanted to give you something," he said, dicking in one of his pockets. He revealed a small velvet pouch.

Sunshine gasped. "For me?"

"Yeah," Tate nodded, a dimmed smile blooming on his face at her reaction. "I found it in the attic. I thought you might like it." With a gentle tug, he opened the pouch, revealing a delicate silver necklace.

Her eyes widened in delight as she looked at it. It was simple yet beautiful, featuring a charm shaped like a sun. "Tate..." Her voice trailed off as she looked back up at him, her heart swelling with affection. " It's beautiful."

"I thought it suited you," he said. "You know, you're like this... light in the darkness."

A warmth spread through her, filling her with joy and gratitude. "I love it," she said sincerely, her heart soaring as she looked into his eyes. "I love you. Thank you so much."

Sunshine rose onto her tippy toes, leaning in to place a tender kiss on his lips, savoring the moment. She turned around, lifting her hair and exposing the nape of her neck to him.

Tate's fingers grazed her skin as he reached around her. She felt the cool metal as he clasped it around her neck. Tate's hands lingered on her shoulders for a moment before trailing down her arms, sending shivers of warmth along her skin. She turned back to him and found him staring at her with a look of pure admiration.

"Beautiful," he murmured, though his gaze was fixed on her face, not the necklace.

Sunshine's fingers gripped the sharp edges of the sun's flames. She looked up at Tate, her heart full, the weight of her worries lightened in his presence.

As she reveled in the moment, her heart fluttered with the realization that she had something special for him too, something she had tucked away for this very occasion.

"I actually have something for you too," she said as she stepped back and moved towards her desk. She rummaged through a small drawer. An eager smile danced on her lips as she finally pulled out the vinyl.

With a flourish, she turned back to face Tate, holding the vinyl aloft like a precious treasure. The cover of Nirvana's Bleach gleamed under the soft light.

Tate's eyes widened in disbelief, and his mouth dropped open in a perfect O of surprise. "No way," he breathed, stepping closer to take a better look at the record.

"It's special edition," The anticipation in her chest swelled as she watched Tate's face light up, his expression shifting from surprise to pure delight. "I remembered you said it was your favorite album."

As he examined the vinyl, his fingers glided over the cover, tracing the intricate artwork with a tenderness that sent a thrill through her. The way he studied it, as if it were a priceless artifact, deepened the warmth of their connection.

"This is amazing, Sunny," Tate breathed, looking up at her with wide, shining eyes that sparkled with genuine appreciation. The light in his gaze made her feel seen, cherished in a way that wrapped around her like a comforting embrace.

"I know Violet doesn't have any of their albums," Sunshine explained. "But I figured she'd let you use her record player."

Tate's smile widened as he processed her words, the happiness in his eyes sending a rush of warmth through her. He carefully placed the vinyl on her desk. Then, without hesitation, he stepped forward and pulled her into a warm hug, wrapping his arms around her waist.

Sunshine melted into his embrace, feeling the steady beat of his heart against her chest. She inhaled the scent of him—something comforting and familiar.

Chapter 28

Sunshine leaned against the doorframe of Violet's room as she watched her sister sift through old photographs. "What's that?" she asked, breaking the silence.

Violet glanced up, briefly meeting Sunshine's eyes before looking back down at the scattered photos in her lap. "Some old pictures from the attic," she explained casually.

Sunshine moved from the doorway and settled beside her sister on the bed. Violet handed her a small stack of photographs, and Sunshine carefully sifted through them, her fingers brushing lightly against the faded edges.

There were old images of the house when it was first built and then a family portrait—formal and stiff.

"That's Nora," Sunshine whispered.

Violet leaned over her shoulder, squinting at the image. "How did you know?"

"She showed herself to me," Sunshine murmured. "She kept asking about her baby." A deep frown tugged at her lips, the encounter still fresh in her mind.

"Weird," Violet muttered under her breath.

"Can I come in?" Vivien's voice floated into the room, and both girls looked up to see her standing in the doorway, her hand resting on the gentle curve of her belly. Violet gave a nod, and their mother entered, closing the door softly behind her.

"So it looks like, uh... this guy's pretty serious about buying the house," Vivien began, her tone light but cautious. "I mean, we won't know officially until it's in escrow, but... I wanted to talk to you guys about it." She perched herself on the edge of the bed, her eyes flicking between her daughters.

Sunshine and Violet exchanged a worried glance. Violet couldn't leave, and they both knew it.

"What happens then?" Violet asked, her voice hesitant.

Vivien sighed. "Then I think... you, your sister, and I will go stay with your Aunt Jo until we find a place,"

Sunshine cringed inwardly at the thought. The last thing she wanted was to be pregnant and dealing with Aunt Jo.

"And what about Dad?" Violet asked.

"Well, Dad still has patients... I don't really know, sweetheart. We haven't figured it all out yet."

"So, this is really happening?" Sunshine asked, her voice quiet. "You guys are separating?"

"This wasn't the way it was supposed to go," Vivien admitted, her voice tinged with regret. "Your dad and I... we really loved each other."

"How'd you know you loved him when you first met?" Violet asked.

Vivien smiled softly, her eyes distant as if she were remembering a different time. "Well, he was... handsome and kind. But I don't know. The thing is, when you fall in love, it's kind of like you go crazy. Before you know it, the whole world looks different, and then you'll do anything for the other person."

Sunshine's mind drifted to Tate, her mother's words hitting too close to home. She couldn't bear the thought of leaving him behind, or her sister, for that matter. But could she really raise a baby in this house?

After a long pause, Vivien stood, smoothing down her shirt. "Well, goodnight, girls. I love you,"

"Love you." Sunshine whispered as her mother departed.

Violet let out a long sigh, slumping against the headboard of her bed. "What am I going to do?" she groaned. "I can't leave. I don't even know how they haven't found out about school yet."

Sunshine leaned back. "I may or may not have replaced my number with Mom's on the school contact sheet," she admitted with a sheepish grin. "As long as you keep turning in schoolwork, I figured they wouldn't come around... but they'll find out eventually if this offer is serious."

Violet's phone buzzed, breaking the momentary silence. She glanced at it before silencing the notification with a sigh.

"Who was that?" Sunshine asked, her brow furrowing.

"Leah," Violet admitted, her voice tinged with sadness. "She's been wondering where I've been."

Sunshine's heart ached for her sister. Leah would never set foot in this house again, and Violet would never see her outside of it.

"I'm sorry, Vi." Sunshine whispered, placing a comforting hand on Violet's leg.

Violet didn't say anything, just nodded, her gaze distant.

A sudden sensation rippled through Sunshine's stomach, startling her out of her thoughts. Her hand instinctively flew to her belly, her posture straightening as she gasped. "Whoa."

Violet's eyes widened in alarm, her body jerking upright. "What? What is it? Are you okay?"

A smile tugged at the corners of Sunshine's lips, the initial surprise giving way to wonder. She reached for Violet's hand, her fingers curling around her sister's as she guided it to her belly. "Feel."

Violet hesitated, her hand hovering just above her sister's stomach before she gently pressed her palm against it. A few seconds passed in silence, but then—there it was. A small, unmistakable movement beneath her hand, as if the baby was nudging back. Her eyes widened. "Holy shit," she whispered, staring at Sunshine in disbelief, her mouth slightly agape.

Sunshine nodded, her eyes sparkling as she glanced down at her stomach. Her hand rested protectively over where the baby had kicked.

There were no little hooves. No signs of anything unnatural. Maybe all her fears, all her anxiety about the baby being something other than human, were just that—fears.

Sunshine yawned, rubbing her eyes as she navigated the darkened hallways of the house. It was the middle of the night, and the overwhelming need to pee had pulled her from sleep. The house was quiet, the kind of silence that felt too thick, like the air itself was watching.

Halfway down the hall, a flicker of movement caught her eye—a small, red ball rolling toward her from the shadows. She froze as the ball bumped softly against her feet.

Sunshine flicked on the light switch, illuminating the hallway with a dim glow. There was nothing. No child, no one playing—just the ball at her feet. She placed a hand on her growing stomach as she bent down to pick it up.

The lights began to flicker wildly above her. Her panic mounting, she darted into the bathroom, slamming the door behind her. She flipped the light switch, the overhead light buzzing to life. Leaning against the door, Sunshine closed her eyes, taking slow breaths to steady her racing heart.

But when she finally opened her eyes, her heart dropped. There, sitting on the sink, was something she thought—no, hoped—she'd never see in her waking life.

Something black and glossy. A mask.

Her hand flew to her mouth, her fingers pressing against her lips as a cold wave of dread washed over her.

He wasn't real. He couldn't be real.

Her body trembled as she took a step forward, every fiber of her being screaming to run the other way, but her legs felt heavy, like they were moving through water.

Inching closer, she reached out with a shaky hand. The rubber felt cold and slick beneath her fingers, and the contact sent a sickening feeling through her body.

It wasn't a dream. It was never a dream.

She looked to the mirror, staring at her reflection, her eyes wide with the dawning horror. The truth she had buried, the truth she had denied for so long, had clawed its way to the surface.

She hadn't been touched by some biblical force. It wasn't God or the devil. It was him. He had taken something from her that she could never get back. And now, holding this mask, that truth became undeniable.

She clutched the mask tightly to her chest as memories surged forward—his cold, rubber-clad hands forcing her down, his body pressing against hers, the way he had silenced her screams.

Sunshine's tears spilled as she slowly backed away from the mirror, the mask still clutched in her chest. She stumbled out of the bathroom and back into the hallway, her vision blurred by tears. Her footsteps were slow, each step heavier than the last as she made her way back to her room.

Once inside, she closed the door behind her, her breath ragged as panic clawed at her chest. Her hands shook as she opened her dresser drawer, stuffing the mask inside with a sense of urgency, as if hiding it could make it disappear completely.

But the tears wouldn't stop. They flowed freely, her chest heaving with sobs that she couldn't control. Sunshine collapsed onto the floor, her legs giving out beneath her as the weight of everything came crashing down.

She fought to catch her breath, her hands gripping the floor, the panic swelling inside her until it felt like she couldn't breathe. She let out a desperate, anguished cry, feeling like her chest was caving in.

She felt hands on her shoulders, firm yet gentle. She jumped, falling backward, her tear-filled eyes snapping open. Tate was hunched over her, his face etched with concern.

"Sunshine, what's wrong?" Tate's voice was soft, but laced with worry as he knelt in front of her. He cupped her tear-streaked face in his hands, his thumbs brushing away the tears as he searched her eyes for answers.

But Sunshine couldn't speak. The words were stuck in her throat, choked by her sobs. Instead, she reached up for him, needing his comfort more than anything. Tate wrapped his arms around her, pulling her close as she buried her face in his chest.

He held her tightly, his hand rubbing soothing circles on her back, whispering soft reassurances into her hair. "It's okay, Sunshine. I've got you. I'm right here." His voice was calm, steady, the kind of voice that could ground her when everything else felt like it was spiraling out of control.

Sunshine's sobs gradually lessened, turning into exhausted sniffles and hiccups as she melted into Tate's embrace. Her face was blotchy and swollen, her eyes red and puffy, but she didn't care. She was just grateful to have him there with her. He didn't ask questions. He didn't push. He just held her, letting her cry until she had nothing left.

Chapter 29

Sunshine sat curled up on the floor of the bathtub as the steady stream of water cascaded over her. The hot spray did little to soothe her as she hugged her knees as tightly as her growing belly would allow, her tears blending with the water.

She hadn't slept in days, not really. Every time she closed her eyes, flashes of that night came flooding back.

Her hands moved to her belly, cradling the life growing inside her, but it brought her no comfort. Now it only served as a reminder of the horror she had endured, the violation that had changed everything. She felt trapped in her own body, suffocated by a reality she didn't want to accept.

She hadn't told anyone. Not Tate, not her family. She couldn't bring herself to say it out loud, because saying it would make it real. There was no going back, no fixing what had been done. She felt powerless, and the thought of burdening her family or Tate with the truth only made her chest tighten more.

They knew something was wrong, though. She could see it in the worried glances her mother shot her over dinner, in Violet's quiet questions about her mood, in Tate's searching eyes whenever he caught her staring blankly at nothing. But she refused to talk about it. She couldn't.

How could she tell Tate, the one person who had been her rock, that she had been raped by something... someone in this house. How could she admit that this baby she was carrying might not be what it seemed?

Tate had been her only comfort during these sleepless nights. He was always there, always offering a quiet presence when she felt like she was losing her mind. Somehow, when he was around, she could sleep — even if just for a little while.

Sunshine reached up and twisted the knob, the water sputtering to a stop. She sat there for a moment, staring at the porcelain as droplets fell from her skin. Slowly, she forced herself to stand, her limbs protesting as she climbed out of the tub.

Wrapping a towel around her body, her hair clung to her back. She stood in front of the mirror, her reflection hazy from the steam. Her blue eyes were hollow, ringed with dark circles, and her cheeks looked gaunt, drained of the vibrancy she once carried.

She moved a stray lock of hair from her face, as if fixing that one imperfection could somehow make everything feel more normal — could make her feel more like herself.

Her gaze drifted to the counter, where a orange pill bottle sat. It was the prescription the doctor had given her after her attempted abortion. She hadn't needed them then, at least not mentally. But now... now the storm of emotions crashing inside her was unbearable, and the idea of ▨▨▨▨numbing it all, of silencing the constant noise in her head, was too tempting to resist.

Her hand shot out, grabbing the hydrocodone bottle. There was no second thought as she twisted off the cap and dumped one of the small white pills into her palm.

She stared at it, the tiny pill holding all the promises of peace she so desperately craved. It wasn't enough to solve everything, but it could at least dull the edges—make the pain feel less sharp, less real.

Sunshine placed the pill on the counter. Grabbing her hairbrush, she slammed the end of the handle down on the pill, grinding it into powder with forceful, rhythmic hits. She didn't want to swallow it whole; she needed it to hit faster.

The powder scattered across the counter, and Sunshine stared down at it. She could already feel the shame creeping in, but it was quieter than the desperation. Right now, all she wanted was relief—just a moment where she didn't feel so heavy.

She used her finger to scrape the powder into a thin line. She lowered her head, closing one nostril with her finger, and hovered over the line. With one sharp inhale, she snorted half of it, the bitter burn creeping through her nose and dripping into the back of her throat.

Suddenly, a voice pierced through the haze. "Stop it!"

Sunshine's body jolted upright, and she turned to see Tate standing in the bathroom doorway, his eyes wide. He looked at her, then at the counter, piecing together the scene in an instant.

Before she could even react, Tate stormed over to the counter, blowing the remaining powder until it disappeared into the air.

"What the fuck, Tate?" she snapped.

Tate's face hardened, his expression darkening as he reached for the pill bottle. "Why are you doing this shit?" he demanded as he unscrewed the cap.

Without waiting for a response, he dumped the remaining pills into the toilet before flushing them away.

"You're pregnant, Sunshine!" he continued, his voice rising. "You shouldn't be putting this shit in your body!"

"Oh, bullshit," Sunshine shot back, her arms crossing defensively over her chest as she glared at him. "Don't pretend to give a shit about this baby when you can't even look at me."

He opened his mouth to speak, but no words came out.

"I know you try and you pretend to be okay with this," she said, her voice wavering as she fought to keep it steady. "But I know you're not."

Tate stood there, just staring at her. His silence was infuriating, as though her words had bounced right off him, making her feel invisible, like her fears and pain didn't even matter.

"Say something!" she demanded, her voice breaking as the vulnerability crept in. She hated how shaky it sounded, but she couldn't help it.

Sunshine's chest tightened as the silence stretched between them, suffocating her. Her anger flared in response to the deeper pain she couldn't let herself fully feel—not now.

"Do you even care?" Sunshine's voice was almost a whisper now, the anger giving way to the deep hurt she had been holding onto.

Tate's expression softened then, a flicker of something—guilt?—passing over his features, but it wasn't enough. He took a small step toward her, reaching out like he wanted to touch her, to comfort her, but she flinched, taking a step back, her body instinctively pulling away.

"Don't." Her voice trembled, but her eyes stayed locked on his. "Don't act like everything's fine. I know you're angry. I know you hate this, and I just—" She broke off, her voice faltering as the words stuck in her throat.

Tate stepped closer, wrapping his arms around her. His embrace was strong and grounding, and for a moment, Sunshine let herself lean into him, feeling the weight of her fears lessen, if only just a little.

"I'm sorry," he murmured into her hair, holding her tightly. "I'm so sorry."

She clung to him, the warmth of his arms soothing her even as her mind spun with confusion. Why did he look so guilty? What was he keeping from her?

For now, she pushed the questions away, burying her face in his chest as she allowed herself to break down. Tate stroked her back softly, as if trying to reassure her that everything would be alright, even though neither of them could know if it would be.

Sunshine sat before her mirror, her fingers lightly brushing the last bit of powder across her cheekbones. She leaned in closer, inspecting her reflection, trying to perfect the look. Dark circles beneath her eyes betrayed her exhaustion, but the makeup masked it well enough.

She needed this—something to make her feel like herself again, or at least something close to it. The past few weeks had left her spiraling but tonight she wanted to feel... good. She wanted to feel beautiful.

Despite everything she'd uncovered. She wanted to reclaim her body, her sense of self, and her sexual expression, something that had been tainted by trauma. Sunshine smoothed her hands over her hair, giving it one last glance before standing up, slowly.

Her dress hugged her figure in all the right places, flowing above her knees. She ran her hands down the fabric, straightening it, feeling a small sense of pride when she caught a glimpse of herself in the full-length mirror.

Her bump was more noticeable now, a subtle curve that announced the life growing inside her, but she didn't look as far along as most women at six months. That strange thought lingered in the back of her mind, a quiet reminder of the oddities surrounding her pregnancy. But she brushed it away, just for now. Tonight, she didn't want to think about that.

She turned sideways, her hand gently resting on her stomach as she studied her reflection. There was something surreal about seeing her body like this—changing in ways she never expected, in ways she didn't fully understand. A part of her was afraid, but another part of her felt stronger for it. This was her body. This was her baby.

Taking a deep breath, she let a small smile tug at her lips. It was fragile, but it was real.

Sunshine moved out of her room, the soft wood yielding beneath her feet as she made her way down the hallway. The house was quiet as she approached the basement door. Her tongue flicked out to wet her lips nervously before she pushed the door open and slipped down the narrow staircase.

Tate often sought refuge here, retreating into the shadows when he wasn't with her or Violet. She turned a couple of corners, peeking around them until she spotted him brooding in a chair, half-hidden in the muted light.

"Boo," Sunshine teased, making her presence known as she stepped fully into the space.

Tate glanced up, his expression reflecting indifference. He was leaning back casually in the chair, arms crossed over his chest, fingers idly picking at his nails. His feet rested on one of the old steel shelves.

"You still mad at me?" she asked, leaning against the archway, crossing her arms.

His gaze shifted to her, and she could see a flicker of irritation in his dark eyes. "You still doing pills?" Tate questioned.

"Don't you?" Sunshine retorted, recalling the way he had casually mentioned his past with drugs during late-night conversations.

"Not anymore," he replied as he turned his gaze back to the shelf.

Sunshine sighed. "I'm not going to buy anymore,"

Tate hummed noncommittally, his eyes still fixed on the shelf. Dropping her arms to her sides, she took a step closer, the distance between them shrinking as she approached.

When she reached him, she swung a leg over him, settling onto his lap. The warmth of his body enveloped her, and she felt the way he instinctively adjusted beneath her, forcing him to look up at her.

Sunshine gazed down into his eyes, which were shadowed by worry and something deeper—regret? Frustration? It was hard to tell, but it tugged at her heartstrings. She reached up, brushing away the tousled strands of hair that had fallen across his forehead, her fingertips grazing his skin.

"I promise," she began. "I want to be better. For you, for me, and for the baby," she continued, her hand finding his cheek.

Sunshine held his gaze. "I love you, Tate." She searched the depths of his eyes, willing him to see the sincerity in her soul, the promise embedded in her words. "Nothing will ever change that."

Tate's hands found their way to her waist, his fingers resting gently against her sides, anchoring her in place. He looked up at her, his expression earnest and raw.

"I love you," he whispered, the words tumbling from his lips.

Sunshine leaned down as she pressed a soft, lingering kiss against Tate's lips. Tate melted into the kiss, surrendering to the warmth and sweetness of the exchange.

Tate's hands drifted from her waist, gliding over her curves with a gentle reverence, finally resting on the tops of her thighs.

The kiss deepened, becoming more desperate as they lost themselves in each other. She reveled in the way his mouth moved against hers, the way he responded to her, drawing her closer as if he couldn't get enough of her.

Sunshine rolled her hips against him, her body instinctively seeking the warmth and closeness they both craved. Tate's fingers dug into the skin of her thighs, pulling her closer as if trying to meld their bodies into one.

Lost in the moment, Sunshine trailed kisses down his jawline, savoring the softness of his skin against her lips. She could feel the heat radiating from him, fueling her need. She paused for a moment, reveling in the sensation, before planting a soft kiss on the side of his neck. The taste of his skin was intoxicating, and she felt him shudder beneath her touch, a low, involuntary sound escaping his lips.

Tate's hands moved beneath her dress, fingers exploring the delicate curve of her body. He settled on her ass, squeezing gently. Tate drew her closer, urging her to grind against him. Sunshine's breath quickened, mingling with his as she lost herself in the sensation of his hands on her skin, and the intoxicating press of his erection on her heat.

Sunshine moved her hands down with calculated slowness as she worked on undoing his belt. Tate lifted his hips slightly, granting her access as his jeans slid down just enough to reveal his longing for her.

Her lips traveled back to his, biting down on Tate's bottom lip, perhaps a little too hard. The metallic taste of blood mixed with the sweetness of their kisses as it drew forth a sharp gasp from him. A wave of panic washed over her as she pulled back, concern flooding her eyes. Had she hurt him? But the look on his face told her otherwise; there was a glint of something primal in his gaze—something that wanted more.

Their kisses resumed, the initial surprise fading. The taste of blood lingered on their lips and with a surge of confidence, she wrapped her hand around his erection, slowly pumping.

A low, guttural moan escaped him, vibrating against her mouth, and Sunshine felt a rush of satisfaction at the sound. Each motion of her hand seemed to draw out more of those intoxicating sounds, fueling her desperation.

Sunshine lifted herself up slightly as she moved her underwear to the side. When she settled onto him, a soft gasp escaped her lips, her mouth forming a perfect 'O' at the feeling of him inside of her.

Tate let out a low, shaky breath as his hands found their place on her hips, guiding her movements as they began to synchronize. Sunshine could feel every inch of him, every pulse. Sunshine's eyes fluttered shut, nearly rolling back in her head as she rolled against him, her pleasure soaring with each movement.

Tate's hands roamed up her chest, fingers trailing along her skin like fire. He paused just below her collarbone, savoring the softness of her curves before wrapping his hand around her neck, his grip firm yet gentle. With a subtle tug, he drew her back down to his lips, their mouths colliding in a passionate kiss that deepened instantly.

Their breaths mingled, hot and frantic, as Tate's lips moved against hers. "Sunshine," Tate whispered as he felt himself growing closer and closer to the edge.

Sunshine's fingers tangled in his hair, pulling gently yet insistently. Their breaths grew heavier, more urgent, as she lost herself in the warmth of his body.

His hands gripped her waist firmly, pulling her closer as he let himself spill inside her, surrendering fully to the overwhelming pleasure that washed over him.

Chapter 30

Sunshine moved around her room, picking up discarded clothes and papers strewn across the floor. The clutter felt suffocating, and with a newfound surge of energy, she was determined to clear it all away.

She stepped over an old blanket, tossing it into the laundry pile, and moved toward the desk where notebooks, pens, and random items were scattered. Her eyes fell on her Juilliard application sitting on the corner, stopping her in her tracks.

She stood still, staring at the packet and the dream it once held. If she had submitted it, she might have been waiting for news about an audition by now. She reached out slowly, her fingers brushing the edge of the paper.

With a sigh, she picked it up, looking over the details of her own handwriting. She walked over to the trash bin and dropped the application inside. The paper crinkled as it fell, and for a split second, Sunshine felt the finality of that decision—a chapter closing, a different path unfolding before her.

Suddenly, the door to her room swung open, startling Sunshine. Her mother stood in the doorway gripping a duffel bag tightly in her hands. Behind her, Violet shuffled in, her eyes half-closed with sleep.

"Grab what you can. We're leaving," Vivien ordered, leaving no room for hesitation.

Sunshine blinked, caught off guard by the sudden demand. "What?" she asked as she looked between her mother and her sister.

"We're not staying in this house a second longer," she snapped. "Let's go, now!"

Sunshine and her family rushed out of the house, their bags full of anything they could grab in the short time they'd had. Vivien led the way toward the car before she popped open the trunk.

Sunshine shifted the strap of her duffle bag on her shoulder, glancing at Violet. Any minute now, Vivien would realize the truth—that Violet was already gone—and Sunshine wasn't ready to face that conversation.

Violet's gaze locked onto something behind them. Sunshine followed her sister's line of sight and froze, seeing Tate step out onto the front porch.

Her heart sank. She had known they wouldn't get far but the sight of him with tears in his eyes still took the wind out of her. Tate hopped over the porch railing as Vivien climbed into the driver's seat.

Sunshine tossed her bag into the back of the car, shutting the trunk with more force than she intended. "Let's get this over with," she muttered under her breath, glancing at Violet before sliding into the back seat.

"We don't have to be prisoners to this house anymore," Vivien said as she buckled her seatbelt, Violet moving to sit in the the passenger seat. The engine sputtered to life, but before they could move, Sunshine flinched at the sound of a voice right next to her.

"Excuse me, ma'am."

She jumped as two figures suddenly appeared on either side of her. Vivien and Violet both whipped around, startled.

"Oh, my God..." Vivien gasped.

"I'm hurt, and I need some help."

"I know you bitches."

Everything happened in a blur. Vivien let out a scream, and in a panicked rush, threw open her door, urging them all to get out.

Sunshine scrambled as fast as her body would allow, climbing into the front seat and practically falling out of the passenger door. Violet was already out, running toward the house with Vivien close behind her.

"Go, Vi! Go! Go!" Vivien screamed, turning back to make sure Sunshine was with them. Sunshine hurried, her breath coming out in frantic gasps as they ran back toward the safety of the house.

Vivien pushed her daughters inside, slamming the door behind them.

After the police had left, Sunshine shut the door to her bedroom, trying to block out the sound of her parents' argument that carried up the stairs. Her eyes fell on the bed where Tate had been sitting, watching him rise to his feet and cross the room.

Sunshine dropped her duffel bag to the floor, her legs feeling weak. She immediately sought comfort in his arms, burying herself in his chest. Tate instinctively wrapped his arms around her, pulling her close, and resting his chin on the crown of her head.

Her arms tightened around his waist, clinging to him, feeling the solidness of his body. In a house filled with restless spirits, Tate felt real— grounded. The other's seemed so lost, so stuck in their endless loops, repeating the same moments of pain over and over again. Though she had seen the invaders before, their cold lifeless eyes never made it any easier to handle.

Tate's hand moved to cradle the back of her head, providing her with the safety she desperately sought. Sunshine squeezed her eyes shut, feeling the rhythmic rise and fall of his chest. Just his presence alone was enough to ease the tension in her body.

"You killed them, didn't you?" she whispered, the sound muffled by his sweater.

Tate stiffened slightly. "What?"

Sunshine pulled away from him, her eyes searching for something she wasn't quite sure she was looking for. She wasn't naive. She might have been consumed by everything that had happened since then, but she hadn't forgotten.

"The people that tried to kill us," she reiterated. "Don't lie to me, Tate."

His eyes darkened with something she couldn't place. It wasn't anger— it was deeper than that, something that felt like shame. Tate looked down, avoiding her gaze, and Sunshine knew her suspicions were true.

He didn't deny it.

Tate exhaled slowly before meeting her eyes again. "I couldn't let them hurt you."

Sunshine felt her throat tighten. Deep down, she had known all along, but hearing him confirm it made it real. She knew who he was. What he had done in the past. Why would he be any different now?

"Why didn't you tell me?" she asked, her voice cracking.

"I didn't want you to be afraid of me,"

Was she afraid of him? She knew Tate was capable of darkness, but this– this was something else. He had taken lives for her. She knew if it wasn't for him then she would be rotting somewhere in a nurse uniform, but the thought unsettled her.

"They'll always be here... won't they?" Sunshine asked, her tongue wetting her bottom lip.

Tate stepped forward, taking her hand in his. His thumb massaged the back of her hand and just like that, any lingering fear had been wiped away. "They can't hurt us, Sunny. They're just trying to scare you."

"My mom doesn't feel that way," Sunshine blinked, shaking her head slightly. "I wish I could tell her. I wish I could tell her everything."

All she wanted was to run to her mother's arms, to tell her everything she had been going through. But she knew she would come off as crazy. Who would believe her if she said the Rubber Man from the attic raped her, haunted her? Sure, she had the evidence hidden away but her pregnancy had progressed so much that the timeline didn't add up.

Tate's expression shifted. "You can't," His eyes bore into her wild with fear. "If you tell anyone what we know, they'll say you're crazy. They'll lock you up, Sunshine. They'll lock you up, and they'll take you away from me. We would never see each other again."

The thought of being separated from him... pained her. But the reality was just as suffocating. "If I stay," she whispered, her tone resigned. "I'm going to die in this house."

It wasn't a guess; it was a truth she had felt when she stepped onto the property.

"Sunshine! Violet! Come downstairs, please!" Her father's voice reverberated, cutting through the tension.

Sunshine descended the stairs slowly, each step feeling heavier than the last. The sound of her parents' voices grew clearer, and when she finally entered the room, all eyes landed on her. Her mother stood there, her expression reflecting hurt and disbelief.

Ben was standing near her, arms crossed, a psychiatrist's patience etched into his features. "Violet said she didn't see anything," Ben began, maintaining a level tone. "So what did you see?"

Sunshine's gaze darted toward her mother whose eyes were desperate for someone to validate what she'd experienced.

Sunshine's mouth opened, but the words got stuck. She hesitated, her eyes flickering over to Violet, who was staring at her with a look that screamed— stick to the story.

"Go on, honey. It's okay," Ben coaxed, a slight nod as if he could pull the truth out of her.

Sunshine took a deep breath, turning back to her father and avoiding Vivien's gaze. "I didn't see anything." Her shoulders sunk under the weight of her decision.

Vivien's face fell, her hurt deepening. She looked at Sunshine as though the foundations of her sanity had been ripped out from beneath her feet.

"Sunshine..." Vivien choked.

"I'm sorry, Mom." Violet cut in, crossing her arms over her chest. "We don't know what you saw. You were upset, and... we got upset."

Ben seemed to accept the explanation. "Alight, you two can go."

Sunshine felt her heart throb with guilt as she turned away. They had been lying through their teeth and there was no taking it back. She walked out of the room with Violet, still feeling her mother's wounded gaze burning into her back.

Sunshine's eyes snapped open to the deafening sound of a gunshot reverberating through the house, shattering the silence. Her heart beat against her chest as she shot up in bed. Tate's arms were still around her, his own sleepy eyes fluttering open in confusion, his arms instinctively tightening their grip around her.

"What the hell was that?" Tate mumbled, his voice raspy with sleep.

Sunshine didn't waste time responding. She quickly moved his arms off her, tossing the blanket aside and leaping out of bed. She swung open her door, racing into the hallway.

She ran straight for her parents' room where the door was slightly ajar. She pushed it open, freezing when she saw her father doubled over in pain. His hands were pressed into the side of his stomach in an attempt to stop the blood.

"Daddy?" Sunshine's voice broke as she rushed to his side, her hands shaking as she placed them on his shoulders. His face was twisted in pain but he was still alert, still conscious.

Sunshine looked over to the bed to see her mother holding a gun limply in her hand. Her face was a mask of shock, pale and wide-eyed as if she couldn't believe what she had done.

"Oh my god." Vivien's voice cracked, dropping the gun onto the bed as if it burned her fingers. "I– I thought it was her," She cried, shaking her head. "I'm so sorry, Ben."

From the doorway, Violet appeared, frozen in the archway as she took in the scene.

"I thought it was her," Vivien repeated, her words dripping with guilt.

"It's okay," Ben grunted through his teeth, trying to remain calm for everyone's sake. "Just help me up."

Sunshine and Violet moved quickly, each taking an arm, helping their father stand. His breath was shallow from the pain but the injury didn't seem serious.

"Sunshine," Ben began, nodding toward the master bathroom. "There's some valium in the cabinet. Give one to your mom to help calm her down."

Sunshine nodded, her eyes darted toward her mother who looked utterly lost. She headed into the bathroom, quickly grabbing the bottle of Valium. Returning to her mother, she knelt beside her on the bed.

"I swear she was here," Vivien whispered, her eyes glassy with tears, but she took the pill from Sunshine's hand without protest. "I saw her, Sunshine. She was standing right there. She wants to take my baby."

"It's okay, Mama." Sunshine's voice was soft, filled with the kind of reassurance she didn't quite feel herself. Tears stung the corners of Sunshine's eyes but she forced herself to blink them away.

Chapter 31

Red and blue lights flickered across the front yard, sirens wailing in the background. Sunshine stood off to the side with Violet, watching as paramedics hovered over Ben, tending to the gunshot wound on his hip.

"You should see a doctor," one of the paramedics advised while securing a bandage.

Ben shook his head. "It's just a through-and-through. I'm fine."

The front door creaked open, and Luke Maxcy, the security guard assigned since the home invasion, stepped inside. His eyes scanned the paramedics and the bandages before locking on Ben. "What happened?" he asked, his tone edged with suspicion.

"We're fine," Ben replied, pulling his sleeves down. "As you can see, I'm in good hands."

Luke's gaze narrowed, unconvinced. "I need to speak to Mrs. Harmon."

"You can't," Ben snapped. "She's upset. I gave her a Valium to help her sleep."

Sunshine glanced at Luke, noticing how his jaw tightened. He turned to the officers nearby. "I'm with Heirloom Security. I got an emergency alert that—"

"You want an update, Luke?" Ben interrupted, his frustration rising. "Vivien thought someone was in the house. When I went to help her, she accidentally shot me. That's the whole story."

Violet, clearly fed up, quietly slipped out, leaving Sunshine awkwardly standing alone.

Luke crossed his arms, still not satisfied. "Did you guys talk to Mrs. Harmon?" he asked the officers.

One of them nodded. "We've got it under control."

Luke's frustration mounted as he gestured toward Ben. "Did he tell you he doesn't even live here? That they're separated? He told you that, right?"

Ben's glare was icy. "You son of a bitch."

Luke pressed on, his voice sharp. "Did he also tell you about his mistress with a criminal record? He mentioned that too, didn't he?"

Mistress? Sunshine's stomach dropped as the blood drained from her face. Was this the woman her mother kept claiming to see? She looked to Ben, silently begging for an explanation.

Ben's face flushed with anger as he turned to the officers. "I'm a licensed psychiatrist. My wife's having a psychotic break. She's a danger to herself and others."

Sunshine stood frozen, guilt seeping into her chest. If she had known her lies would put her mother in the hospital... But it was too late now. Her mother's instability was obvious to anyone.

Luke stepped closer. "So, what? You're shipping her off to a psych ward so you get the house, the kids, the mistress, and the dog? That the plan?"

Ben closed the distance between them, his voice low and menacing. "I don't know who you think you are to my wife, but this is my house." He jabbed a finger toward the door. "And you need to get the hell out."

Sunshine and Violet hesitated outside their parents' door, their mother's desperate wails echoing from inside. They exchanged a glance, uncertainty weighing heavy between them, before stepping into the room. All eyes immediately turned to them.

"They're ready for her," Violet said, her voice hollow as she crossed her arms.

A tense silence followed, thick with unspoken emotions, before two police officers stepped into the room.

Vivien's wide, tearful eyes darted between her daughters. "What's happening?" she whispered, her voice laced with hurt and confusion.

Ben stepped forward, his face a mask of forced composure as he approached his wife. "I had to, Vivien," he said softly. "You're unstable."

Vivien's expression crumbled, her lips trembling in disbelief. "No..."

Ben sighed heavily, his shoulders sagging. "You need to be evaluated," he continued, gently reaching for her. "These men are taking you to the hospital. I'm sorry, but it's the best option. I didn't want it to come to this, but you shot me. It's too dangerous now."

"But I wasn't shooting you," Vivien choked out, her voice breaking. "I was shooting her. Hayden... she's trying to take our baby." Her words were desperate, her eyes searching the faces of her family for understanding, for belief.

Sunshine's heart ached as tears welled in her eyes, her hand instinctively moving to her growing belly. She knew her mother truly believed what she was saying.

One of the officers pulled out a pair of handcuffs, but Ben quickly intervened. "That's not necessary."

Vivien, her spirit crushed, looked up at Ben. "Ben, can you get my coat?" Her attempt to remain composed was heartbreaking.

Ben nodded and quickly retrieved her coat, helping her slip into it. "Thank you," Vivien murmured, her voice barely audible.

As she reached for her purse, one of the officers gently stopped her. "You won't need that, ma'am."

Vivien nodded, her hand dropping as she turned toward the bedroom door. Luke stepped forward, placing a sympathetic hand on her shoulder. "I'm so sorry, Vivien."

"It's okay," she whispered. "At least I'll be out of this house." She glanced back at her daughters, her gaze lingering on them.

Sunshine's tears spilled over, her voice cracking. "I'm so sorry, Mama."

Vivien's expression softened, and despite everything, she managed a small, reassuring smile. "It's okay, baby," she whispered, gently rubbing Sunshine's arm before turning to leave.

The family followed her downstairs, their footsteps heavy with regret. The officers escorted Vivien outside, leaving Sunshine and Violet standing frozen, watching the aftermath of their choices.

"It's all my fault," Violet whispered, hugging herself tightly as she stared off in a daze.

Ben approached her, his voice soft but firm. "No, honey. It's not. You did the right thing by telling the truth." He pressed a gentle kiss to her forehead before turning to Sunshine, cupping her cheek briefly. Then, without another word, he left through the front door.

The distant hum of police cars faded, and the sisters stood side by side, paralyzed by guilt.

Tate appeared silently between them, wrapping an arm around each of them. He pulled Violet close, then turned to Sunshine, drawing her in as well. "It's okay," he whispered softly. "I'm here."

Neither sister responded, just resting their heads on his shoulders as they tried to process the weight of what had just happened.

Sunshine lay back in the warmth of the bath, her hand gliding through the soapy water. Her mind swirled with guilt, her eyes drifting toward her slightly protruding belly, just visible above the bubbles. Every day brought her closer to meeting her baby.

Despite everything, despite who had done this to her, she couldn't help but feel excited. She longed to hold him, care for him. The thought of her son was almost enough to make all the pain and heartache she'd endured feel worth it.

Her thoughts shifted to her mother trapped in a mental hospital against her will. Sunshine knew Vivien must be terrified, especially being pregnant. Yet, a part of her understood. At least she was far away from this house.

"Want some company?"

Sunshine jumped at the sound of Tate's voice, her heart skipping as she glanced over to see him standing in the doorway. "Christ, Tate! You're gonna kill me if you keep sneaking up like that." She sat up, the soap bubbles glistening on her skin.

"Sorry," Tate replied with a small smile, kicking off his Converse. Sunshine frowned, confused, as he stuck one foot into the water, still fully clothed.

"What are you doing?" she asked, both shocked and amused as he slid into the bath behind her, water spilling onto the tiles.

"Taking a bath. What are you doing?" Tate teased, completely unbothered by his soaked clothes sticking to him.

Sunshine laughed, shaking her head. "You're crazy."

"You're beautiful," Tate countered, wrapping his arms around her from behind. His chin rested on her shoulder, his hands gently settling over her swollen belly.

A soft smile spread across her face as she instinctively placed her hands on top of his. They hadn't shared many moments like this—it was as if he'd been afraid to touch her—but now, it felt perfect. She leaned back against him, his familiar scent calming her in a way nothing else could.

Tate's fingers moved lightly over her stomach, and then he whispered, almost too quietly, "I wonder what our baby will be like."

Sunshine froze for a moment, her heart swelling at his words. Our baby. It was the first time he had called it that—their baby. She turned her head slightly, her eyes searching his face, looking for any sign that he hadn't meant it.

"What?" Tate asked, feeling the sudden shift.

"You... you said 'our baby,'" she said softly, biting back a smile.

"Yeah. I mean, he's part of you, right? I want to take care of him. I want to take care of both of you."

A rush of warmth filled Sunshine's chest, happiness bubbling up. "Really?"

He smiled, brushing his nose against hers. "I mean it. I'll be here for both of you. Always."

Tears stung at her eyes, but this time they were from joy, feeling more at peace than she had in a long time.

Chapter 32

Sunshine descended the stairs slowly, exhausted from the endless homework and the looming responsibility of job searching. Her belly had grown, but she still hadn't done any shopping for the baby—partly because of her stubbornness. She'd be damned if she asked her father for money, not after everything. This was her choice, and she was determined to handle it on her own.

The sound of the basement door creaking shut jarred her from her thoughts, her hand pausing on the stair rail. She frowned, confused. Violet was upstairs doing homework with her, trying to catch up on missed schoolwork to avoid truancy officers, and their father was busy seeing patients.

A creeping unease settled over her. Sunshine moved toward the basement door, pulling it open just in time to hear muffled yelling rise from below.

"What is wrong with you, for God's sake? What is wrong with you?" Constance screamed, her voice breaking with each word.

"Mama!" Tate cried.

Sunshine rushed down the basement steps and as she reached the bottom, the violent sound of slaps echoed off the walls. She followed the voices to find Constance towering over Tate, who was crumpled against the wall, his face streaked with tears.

"Don't you realize what you've done?" Constance spat, her voice trembling with disgust as her hand prepared to strike again.

Sunshine's body moved before her mind could catch up. "Constance!" she yelled, fury bubbling under her skin as she stepped forward.

Constance's hand froze mid-air. Slowly, she turned to face Sunshine, her eyes glistening with tears of her own. The two women locked eyes—one consumed with raw rage, the other with pity.

Moving past Constance, Sunshine knelt beside Tate, wrapping her arms around him. He clung to her like a child, burying his face in her chest as sobs wracked his body. She ran her fingers gently through his hair, whispering soft words of comfort.

Constance stood there for a moment, watching them with an unreadable expression.

"I think you should go," Sunshine said firmly, her eyes never leaving Constance's face.

Constance's lips twitched into a sad, bitter smile as she wiped away the tears staining her cheeks. "You might be right," she muttered, composing herself. She adjusted her clothes, brushing away any trace of her earlier outburst.

Her gaze flickered down to Tate, still curled in Sunshine's arms, before locking eyes with her again. "Be careful with this one, sweet girl. You haven't the faintest idea of what he's capable of." And with that, Constance turned and walked up the stairs.

Tate clutched Sunshine even tighter, his sobs quieting. Sunshine kept stroking his hair, her voice soft and soothing. "Hey, it's okay," she whispered, pressing her cheek against the top of his head. "It's okay, baby."

But as she held him, a deep unease settled in her chest. Constance's warning lingered, making her wonder if she really knew Tate as well as she thought.

The house was unnervingly quiet as Sunshine moved through the hallway. The constant silence after her mother's departure weighed heavily on her mind. But something else gnawed at her—a need to know more.

Sunshine reached the door to her father's office, her hand hovering over the handle before pushing it open. Her eyes scanned the office before landing on the cabinet sitting against the far wall.

Sunshine walked over and her fingers grazed the cabinet, hesitating a moment before she opened the drawer. The patient files were neatly organized alphabetically. Her fingers dragged over them until stopping on a thin manila folder marked Langdon, Tate.

She slid the file out of the drawer and sat on the edge of the desk, pulling it open. The first thing she saw was a clinical diagnosis: Antisocial Personality Disorder. Her eyes scanned over the page.

Depression, violent ideation, lack of empathy. Lied about taking medication. Detached, erratic; often jokes about violence and death in an unsettling manner. Charming yet manipulative, able to steer conversations away from deeper topics.

Frequently describes dreams where he kills people he "likes." Shows no remorse when recounting these dreams, and often seems proud of his actions in them. Detailed description of a recurring dream where he violently attacks classmates and watches them die. I am no longer certain he is a safe presence in the home.

Her eyes darted to another note, dated a few weeks after the initial sessions.

Tate has begun taking prescribed medication, but I remain unsure if his progress is real or if it's part of his manipulative tendencies. Shows less volatility, but I question whether his compliance is genuine or if he is playing along.

Had he really changed? Was any of this progress real, or was Tate just pretending?

Tate claims to have "no more bad dreams." Appears more stable but expresses feelings of detachment from reality. Still not convinced his improvement is genuine.

Sunshine slammed the folder shut, her breathing ragged.

The creak of a floorboard outside the office made her jump, her heart nearly leaping out of her chest. She quickly shoved the file back into the drawer and slammed it shut. Sunshine wiped her sweaty palms on her shorts, hoping no one had seen her.

As she opened the door to leave, she found herself staring straight into Tate's eyes.

"What are you doing in here?" he asked softly, his gaze curious, maybe a little suspicious.

Sunshine swallowed hard. "Just... looking for something," she muttered, brushing past him quickly.

Sunshine tossed and turned in her sleep as his faceless black mask gleamed under the faintest light, the rubber creaking as he moved toward her. She tried to scream, but no sound came out. Her legs felt like lead, and refused to move. His rubber-clad hands reached out, pressing against her skin, holding her in place.

The familiar terror surged through her as he leaned closer. He weighed on her chest, stealing the air from her lungs. She could feel his cold fingers against her skin, his grip tightening as he pressed down, harder, unrelenting.

Sunshine jolted awake with a sharp gasp, her chest heaving as if she had truly been struggling for breath. She could still feel the ghost of his touch on her body. Tears welled up in her eyes, spilling down her cheeks as she fought to regain control of her breathing.

Beside her, Tate stirred, his hand instinctively reaching for her as he sensed her distress. He had been sleeping beside her, always watching over her, always protective. He sat up quickly, his voice soft but urgent. "Sunshine?" His hands found her shoulders, gently but firmly turning her toward him. "Hey, hey... what's wrong?"

She couldn't speak. The dream, the memories—it was all too much. Her tears came harder, uncontrollable. She buried her face in her hands, trying to stifle the sounds and push away the Rubber Man's lingering terror. But it wouldn't leave her.

"Shh, shh, it's okay," Tate whispered, pulling her into his arms, his hand smoothing over her tangled hair as she cried into his chest. "You're safe, I promise."

His words wrapped around her, slowly calming her erratic breaths. She could feel his heart beating steadily under her cheek, grounding her in the present, pulling her away from the nightmare. The sound of his voice, the comfort of his touch—it all helped to slowly push away the darkness.

Sunshine sniffled, her sobs subsiding as she lifted her head to meet his gaze. "I'm sorry," she whispered, her voice raw.

"Don't be sorry," Tate said softly, brushing a strand of hair away from her damp face. "I'm here, okay?" He tilted her chin up gently, forcing her to look at him. "I'll always be here."

She nodded slowly, her breath still shaky but more controlled now. She rested her head back against his chest, letting his presence soothe her.

Tate gently kissed the top of her head, his arms never loosening their protective grip. "Get some sleep, okay?" he whispered. "I'll be right here."

Chapter 33

"Sunshine, how are you feeling?" Dr. Novak asked as she entered the room, her expression serious yet calm.

Sunshine let out a deep, exhausted sigh. She shifted uncomfortably on the exam table, her fingers gently stroking the curve of her swollen belly. It felt like her body was moving at a pace she couldn't keep up with, a race against time she hadn't signed up for. "Honestly, I feel like shit,"

Dr. Novak pulled up a chair, her brows furrowed with concern as she sat down. "The nausea meds still aren't working?"

Sunshine shook her head.

"I'm sorry to hear that," Dr. Novak said softly before flipping open the chart in her lap. "The baby's development looks good, but..." She paused, glancing up at Sunshine with a look of concern. "The baby is developing much faster than we'd typically expect. I'm afraid it's becoming more likely that we'll need to perform an emergency c-section—and soon."

Sunshine's heart dropped, her mind spinning. "What?"

Dr. Novak offered a gentle, reassuring smile. "I know it's a lot to take in, but given how fast things are progressing, it's important to prepare. I will write you a note to excuse you from school for the rest of the pregnancy . Your priority now is rest—lots of bed rest, Sunshine. It's the best thing you can do for yourself and the baby right now."

The words felt too much to process at once. It had only been five months since she found out she was pregnant, and now she was nearly ready to give birth. The room spun slightly as she tired to steady her breath.

"I know it's overwhelming, and it's happening fast," Dr. Novak said softly, her voice warm with reassurance. "But everything is going to be okay. You're in good hands, Sunshine."

Sunshine sat at the kitchen island, a half-eaten bowl of oatmeal in front of her, the spoon resting limply in her hand. She stared at the bowl, absentmindedly stirring the oats, feeling as if eating had become a chore.

She sighed, setting the spoon down and resting her hands on her swollen belly. The excitement she'd once felt about becoming a mother had started to feel distant, overshadowed by how fast everything was moving.

A creak at the back door startled her, pulling her from her thoughts. Her head snapped up just in time to see Constance let herself in, a car seat—still wrapped in plastic—dangling from her arm.

"Constance," Sunshine greeted, straightening slightly in her chair. The tension between them still lingered but Sunshine had resolved to keep things civil, if only for the sake of her sanity.

"You know, I've been thinking about you," Constance said, her Southern drawl smooth. She set the car seat down, eyes sweeping the kitchen before landing on Sunshine. "Thinking about everything you've been through—and being pregnant on top of it all. Lord knows it's not easy. So, I did a little shopping for the baby."

Constance stepped closer, her heels clicking against the floor. "Thought it might help take a bit of stress off your shoulders."

Sunshine glanced at the car seat, forcing a polite smile. "Thank you, Constance. I really appreciate it."

Constance moved to the counter, resting her manicured hands on the back of a chair. "How's the baby?"

Sunshine exhaled deeply. "He's growing fast."

A brief silence stretched between them as Constance's eyes lingered on her. Then, her tone shifted, this time gentler. "I want you to know," she began, "that I intend to be here for you. Whatever help you need, Sunshine , I'm here. Babies, they're my thing. I have a special gift with them, and as a single mother... well, I know how we tell ourselves we don't need a man, that we can do it all on our own." She paused. "But the secret, darling? The secret is community. Sisterhood."

Sunshine blinked, caught off guard by the sudden warmth in Constance's words. It felt... genuine, and that alone made her suspicious. She nodded, unsure what to say or how to feel about the older woman's unexpected kindness.

Constance's gaze lingered on her for a moment longer before she spoke again, her voice quieter this time. "I don't mean to pry, but..." She hesitated as if already knowing the answer. "Has the father made any effort to...?"

"I don't know who he is," Sunshine interrupted, her voice tight. Her jaw flexed as emotions crashed over her, tears brimming in her eyes. She hadn't meant to open up, but the words came out before she could stop them. "I was raped."

A heavy silence followed. She stood there, her expression unreadable as Sunshine quickly wiped the tears from her cheeks.

"Please don't tell anyone," Sunshine added, her voice shaky. "Nobody else knows."

"Of course not," Constance said softly. "You poor thing. What you've been through... no one should have to endure that."

Sunshine forced a weak smile, faking a composure she didn't feel. "Thank you, Constance. For everything."

With a small, sad smile, Constance gave a curt nod and turned toward the door. "Take care of yourself, Sunshine," she said over her shoulder before slipping out.

As the door clicked shut behind her, Sunshine let out a long, weary breath, her hands falling to her lap.

Sunshine sat on the couch, her feet propped up on a pillow to ease the swelling. Violet was on the floor, sorting through a pile of DVDs, trying to decide what to watch. Since Sunshine was bedridden, she hadn't left the house in days and spent most of her time with Violet and Tate.

She sighed, leaning back into the cushions. Sleep had been elusive—her back constantly ached, and no position felt comfortable anymore.

Their father walked into the room. "Hey, so," he said his eyes flicked between his daughters. "I just got off the phone with the hospital. Your mom's being discharged tomorrow, and we've decided it would be best for all of us to head to Florida to stay with Aunt Jo for a while."

Sunshine froze, her hand instinctively resting on her stomach as her muscles tensed. Violet stopped what she was doing, looking up from the DVDs with wide eyes.

"Uh... Dad?" Sunshine began, pushing herself up slightly. "My doctor doesn't want me leaving the house, let alone getting on a plane right now. I'm way too far along. She said I could go into labor any minute."

Ben waved her concerns off, flashing a reassuring smile. "You'll be fine, Sunshine. It's only a four-hour flight. We'll be with you every step of the way."

Sunshine threw a look at Violet, who sat stiffly. They both knew there was no way Violet could leave the house—ever.

"Dad," Sunshine pressed, "I really don't think it's a good idea. I mean, what if something happens on the way? What if I go into labor mid-flight or before we even get to the airport? The doctor said I need bed rest."

Ben rubbed a hand over his face, clearly exasperated. "I get it, Sunshine. I know it's not ideal, but we're not staying here. It's not safe anymore. We're going to Aunt Jo's, and that's final." His voice took on a firmer tone, the kind that left no room for negotiation.

Sunshine exchanged a panicked look with Violet.

"Dad, please—" Sunshine began again, trying one last time, but he cut her off.

"Enough," Ben snapped, his voice stern but not unkind. "This isn't up for debate. We're leaving tomorrow morning after I pick up your mom, and that's the end of it. Pack what you need tonight."

With that, he gave them both a final, determined look and walked out of the room, leaving Sunshine and Violet in stunned silence.

Chapter 34

Violet and Sunshine stood side by side in Sunshine's room, gazing out the window as their father's car disappeared down the driveway. He was on his way to pick up their mom, and the thought of what would happen next was heavy on their minds.

Violet broke the silence first. "What's gonna happen when they get back? What do I say?"

Sunshine sighed, running her tongue over her bottom lip as she thought. "There's no keeping it a secret anymore, Vi."

Violet shook her head. "If they find out I killed myself, they'll lose it. For real this time. I can't let them know."

From the bed, Tate's voice cut in, casual but blunt. "You can't control it forever. I mean, it is what it is, Violet."

Violet slumped beside him on the bed, her hands settling in her lap. "It's not 'UTube' with a 'U,' it's 'YouTube.' Y-O-U," she corrected, glancing at the laptop where Tate had been typing.

"Oh," Tate muttered, retyping his mistake.

Violet's gaze drifted, her voice slipping into a bitter murmur. "One of these days, this computer will be obsolete. People will have microchips implanted in their brains or something. We won't be able to watch YouTube or anything. We'll be like all the others here; prisoners in a windowless cell."

Sunshine lowered herself onto the bed, sitting beside Tate. She rested a hand on her swollen stomach, her eyes distant. "I can't even imagine what that's like," she whispered. "Being stuck here... for eternity."

Tate shrugged, glancing over at her. "It's not all bad," he said with a smile. "You're here."

Sunshine smiled back, but it was sad, a flicker of something bittersweet crossing her face. "Not for long."

A chime of a baby's music box suddenly pulled them from their thoughts. All three of them turned their heads toward the hallway, the sound floating in from a nearby room.

"What the hell?" Violet muttered, already moving to investigate. Tate helped Sunshine up, her swollen belly slowing her down, and the three of them cautiously made their way down the hall. As they neared one of the spare rooms, muffled voices became clear. Violet reached out, pushing the door open.

Inside, Chad stood atop a ladder, adjusting decorations, while Patrick painted a dresser a bold shade of red.

"Who asked you to decorate the nursery?" Violet asked, crossing her arms as they stepped fully into the room. Tate's eyes flicked around, sizing up the changes, while Sunshine stared at the cribs.

Chad barely glanced over. "Let me break it down for you, sweetheart. This is our house, and we're having twins."

"Who's your surrogate? One of those nurses in my basement?" Violet shot back, her arms tightening against her chest.

Chad stepped down from the ladder with infuriating casualness. "No, no. A very, very human surrogate. Elvira—your lovely mother," he said, flicking his gaze toward Sunshine, "and your darling sister."

Sunshine's heart sank, her shoulders slumping. "Excuse me?"

"You think you're gonna steal those babies?" Tate stepped forward, crossing his arms defensively. His eyes darted between Chad and Patrick, clearly agitated. "You pathetic homos couldn't steal the shit out of your own ass!"

Chad and Patrick exchanged amused glances, laughing softly at Tate's outburst.

"Doesn't matter," Violet interrupted. "As soon as my parents get back, we're leaving. They're leaving. So, knock yourselves out." She looked to Sunshine, her lips pressing into a thin line before turning back to the couple.

Chad smirked, that knowing look in his eyes. "Honey, your parents aren't going anywhere, not as long as you're stuck here."

Patrick joined in. "And don't get snotty, little sister. You'll be begging to babysit soon enough. This place might be big, but it gets very, very lonely."

"Though, it could get ugly." Chad's eyes shifted toward Sunshine, his words nonchalant. "Were you a C-section? Is there an existing zipper we could use?"

"Fuck you," Sunshine spat, her face contorting with disgust.

Tate immediately stepped closer, fists clenched. "Watch it, you goddamn queen."

Chad feigned terror, placing a hand dramatically over his chest. "Oh, I'm quaking in my loafers. What are you gonna do, Tate? Murder me?" He tilted his head and Sunshine glanced at Tate, suspicion creeping into her eyes.

Sunshine waddled over to Constance's house, her fury simmering beneath the surface. She was exhausted—tired of being angry, tired of feeling sad, and tired of anything that wasn't peaceful or calm. Her emotions had been on a rollercoaster for weeks now, and it felt like she was losing control.

When she stormed through the back door, Constance was in the middle of the kitchen, slipping a dish into the oven. She straightened up, glancing over her at Sunshine's entrance. "Sunshine," she greeted. "What a lovely surprise."

Sunshine, already feeling winded from the short walk, sank into one of the dining chairs, her arms resting on the table. "I need help."

Constance's curiosity piqued, and she set her oven mitts aside, gracefully sauntering over. "What's this about, darling?"

"Do you remember those two guys that lived here before us?" Sunshine asked.

"Frick and Frack?" Constance let out a small laugh. "How could I ever forget?"

Sunshine's jaw clenched. "They're planning on taking my baby... and my brother."

A flicker of something dark passed through the older woman's features. "Let me assure you, that will never happen,"

"My mom's on her way back from the hospital today," Sunshine continued, anxiety gnawing at her as she rubbed her stomach. "And I'm supposed to be having this baby any day now. I just... I don't trust them."

"Don't worry," Constance muttered. "I'll take care of it."

Sunshine sat on the edge of her bed, her leg bouncing anxiously as she waited for Constance to show up. Her nerves were on edge, every minute that passed stretching her patience thinner and thinner.

Tate sat beside her, watching her closely. Sensing her distress, he reached over, gently taking her hands in his. "Hey, it's gonna be okay," he whispered, his thumb brushing over her knuckles in an attempt to soothe her. "I won't let them touch our baby."

Sunshine didn't respond right away, her eyes fixed on their intertwined hands. "They're never going to stop, Tate," she said quietly, shaking her head.

She sighed deeply, her chest tightening with the pressure of it all. "I really don't know how much more of this I can take." Her voice wavered as she spoke, the exhaustion creeping into every word. "I feel like I'm dangling from my last string of sanity, and it's fraying."

Tate squeezed her hands a little tighter. "You are… the strongest person I've ever met. I envy that about you. You'll push through, you always do."

Sunshine managed a weak smile. She wanted to believe him, but the constant fear and anxiety was wearing her down.

A soft knock at the door broke the silence, and Sunshine looked up to see Constance standing in the doorway. Her eyes flicked to Tate briefly before they settled on Sunshine.

"We're going to have to try another… alternative," Constance said, her voice tinged with regret as she stepped inside. "So, I called Billie Dean."

Sunshine frowned, her confusion clear. "What's she going to do?"

Constance sighed, folding her arms as she leaned against the doorframe. "I'm hoping she knows a way to get rid of them… for good."

"Do you really think she can help?"

"If anyone can deal with this... it's her."

Chapter 35

Billie hovered her hand in the air, feeling the very energy of the house. "So much pain here,"

Sunshine shifted her weight, and her swollen belly and aching back made it difficult for her to stand for long. Constance massaged her temples while Violet sat nervously in a chair in the living room, her eyes flicking between the others.

"So much longing and regret," Billie continued, her gaze sweeping across the room before landing on Sunshine. Her eyes dropped to her stomach. "Fear. Sadness. Guilt."

"And perversion," Constance interjected, moving behind Violet's chair, resting her hands on the back. "Now, can you ferret out the fairies for us? I mean, that's our main concern at the moment."

Billie didn't acknowledge Constance, her eyes fixed on Violet, watching her intently. "Targeting a particular spirit will be difficult. This house is... crowded."

Violet glanced uneasily at Billie, their silent exchange thick with unspoken understanding.

Constance rubbed her hands together. "So what can we do?"

Billie exhaled slowly. "Somehow, we have to try and dislodge them from the paramagnetic grip of this place."

Violet stood, frowning as she exchanged a confused look with Sunshine. "The what?"

"The evil," Billie clarified, guiding the women into the hallway. "It's a force, just like any other. Pure physics. Real and powerful. Created by events—events that unleash psychic energy into the environment, where it's absorbed."

They stopped in the dining room, and Billie turned to face them. "Like a battery stores energy. You see it all the time in places like prisons or asylums. Negative energy feeds on trauma and pain, drawing more to it."

Sunshine wrapped her arms around herself, feeling a chill crawl up her spine at Billie's words.

"The force in this house," Billie went on, "is larger than any individual trauma. It has a need. It wants to break through, to move in our world. It's using those trapped between this world and the next as conduits."

Constance, leaning casually against the archway, waved a hand dismissively. "That's all very interesting but what do we do about the gays? I mean, how do we get rid of them?"

"There might be a way, but I can't promise—" Billie suddenly stopped, her head tilting as if sensing a shift in the air. "He shouldn't be here."

Sunshine followed Billie's gaze over her shoulder. "Tate."

"That's my boy," Constance pointed. "That's Tate."

"I want to help," Tate said from the doorway.

Billie's eyes narrowed, her body tense. "You've helped enough."

Sunshine's attention snapped to Billie. What was it about Tate's energy that set her off so deeply? There was something Billie wasn't saying.

"Not now, Tate," Constance waved him off. "Go on."

Even after Tate left, Billie seemed visibly shaken, her hand steadying herself against the table.

"What was that about?" Violet asked, her brow furrowed, just as confused by Billie's reaction.

Constance let out a small, uneasy chuckle, though it lacked sincerity. She stepped up beside Billie. "It's just that, sometimes, when a medium meets a spirit so directly, it has a... powerful effect. That's all."

Sunshine frowned, sensing something off. If that were true, wouldn't Billie have reacted the same way to Violet? Before she could stop herself, the words slipped out. "You mean an evil spirit?"

Billie and Constance exchanged a quick, guarded look before Constance turned back to Sunshine. "It's nothing to concern yourself about."

The four women gathered around the dining table, a bottle of whiskey sitting between them. Billie took a long swallow from her glass, her eyes flicking up to Sunshine, who sat anxiously playing with her hands on the table.

"It's difficult to banish a spirit," Billie began, "but not impossible. The most successful attempt I know of happened when America was still known as the New World."

Violet scoffed, her head resting on her hand. "Are you kidding? That's, like, 500 years ago."

Billie turned her gaze to Violet. "Spirits don't follow our physical laws. Nor are they bound by time. The only thing they share with the living is their suffering—regret, pain, loneliness."

"In 1590, on the coast of what we now call North Carolina, the entire colony of Roanoke—117 men, women, and children—died mysteriously. It became known as the Ghost Colony because their spirits lingered, haunting the native tribes nearby, killing indiscriminately."

Billie slid her empty glass toward Constance, who wordlessly refilled it.

"The tribe's elder knew he had to act," Billie continued. "He cast a banishment curse. First, he gathered personal items belonging to the dead colonists and burned them. The ghosts appeared, drawn by their talismans. But before they could attack, the elder completed the curse that would banish them forever."

Sunshine leaned forward. "How?"

"By uttering a single word," Billie said, her voice dropping to a whisper. "The same word found carved into a post at the abandoned colony."

The room went silent as they waited for her to speak.

"Croatoan."

Sunshine and Violet entered the room, their faces drained, lost in thought. Tate, who had been anxiously pacing, stopped in his tracks and turned to them.

"What did she say?" he asked, hurrying over.

"We have to get something of his," Sunshine replied, her arms hanging limply by her sides. "Something important."

"If we have the talisman and do this ritual, he'll be gone," Violet added, trying to sound confident.

Tate scoffed, his expression darkening. "That sounds like bullshit." He turned away and resumed pacing.

"I know it sounds crazy, but what other choice do we have?" Sunshine sighed, rubbing her temples. "Billie Dean's a professional, and right now, she's all we've got."

Violet's brow furrowed in thought. "The bigger guy... he wears a ring. Like a wedding ring, but I can't remember which hand."

Tate bit his nails nervously, then abruptly stopped, his eyes narrowing. "I don't trust her!"

"Why'd she say all that stuff about me?" Tate's voice wavered as he crossed his arms, looking between the two sisters. "I did something bad, didn't I?"

Sunshine and Violet exchanged an uneasy glance before looking back at him.

Sunshine stepped closer, her hands gently resting on his arms, trying to calm him. "We need to try, Tate. For us. For the baby."

The tension in Tate's face softened at her touch. After a moment, he nodded, albeit reluctantly.

"I love you," Sunshine said softly, a small smile tugging at her lips as she raised her hand to caress his cheek.

Tate leaned into her hand, his eyes closing briefly as he placed his own hand over hers. "I love you," he whispered.

When Violet and Tate returned with the stolen objects—a ring and a Rolex watch—the two sisters descended into the basement. Sunshine approached the furnace, already burning with crackling wood, casting a nervous glance at Violet. Violet just shrugged, uncertain herself. Sunshine motioned for the items.

"Hand those to me?"

Violet placed the ring and watch into Sunshine's outstretched hands. Sunshine stared down at them as she inhaled deeply, hoping the ritual would work. She tossed the objects into the fire.

"What exactly do you think you're doing, young lady?"

Chad's voice pierced the silence, startling both sisters. They spun around, eyes wide as they saw him standing behind them, holding broken pieces of the red crib from upstairs.

"Is that my $12,000 watch you just threw into the furnace?" Chad asked incredulously, his eyes narrowing in disbelief.

Sunshine and Violet exchanged a quick look, gathering their courage, before turning back to him and shouting in unison, "Croatoan! Croatoan! Croatoan!"

For a moment, Chad's body convulsed violently as if the words had triggered some sort of exorcism. He dropped the crib pieces, his expression twisted in apparent agony. Then, to their horror, he started laughing. Straightening up, he flashed a smug grin.

"Just kidding."

"Son of a bitch," Sunshine muttered under her breath.

Chad bent down, picking up one of the wooden pieces and pointing it at them like a scolding teacher. "Let me guess, that little gem came from the press-on nail psychic who was here earlier? The Roanoke spell? Really?"

Sunshine and Violet stood frozen, realizing their plan had failed.

"Please, tell me you'll be slitting the throat of a chicken next, because I've always found that very dramatic." Chad continued with a smirk. "I also quite enjoy the burning of the sage to rid the house of spirits."

"It didn't work," Violet whispered, her voice shaky.

A part of Sunshine had expected that, but she'd still hoped. Anything was better than feeling this helpless.

"Of course, it didn't work," Chad scoffed, shaking his head. "It's bullshit. It's all bullshit. People make up these spells and chants in order to feel like they're in control. Well, guess what? They're not. Never have been."

Chad then snapped the wooden piece in half and tossed it into the furnace.

"What are you doing?" Sunshine asked, confused by his sudden change in demeanor.

"My own bullshit ritual," Chad replied casually, grabbing another piece of the crib. "There's not going to be any nursery," he sighed heavily, breaking another piece in half and throwing it into the fire. "We're not gonna be parents. Your and your mother's babies are safe. From us, at least. I'm doomed to spend eternity with a man who doesn't love me."

Sunshine felt the tension in her shoulders ease slightly, a quiet breath of relief escaping her lips.

Chad turned his gaze to Sunshine, eyes narrowing. "Of course, it could be worse. Your man does love you... but he'll always be a monster."

"You're wrong," Violet interjected, her arms crossed tightly across her chest. "Tate's changed. He doesn't even remember what he did."

"Oh?" Chad tilted his head toward her, mocking curiosity. "When did he change? When he murdered me? When he murdered my boyfriend?"

Sunshine's relief shattered instantly, dread creeping back into her veins.

Chad's smirk deepened as he turned his attention toward Sunshine. "Or did he change when he raped your sister?"

"What?" Sunshine's blood ran cold, her mind going blank as she blinked in shock. "He wouldn't do that... You don't know what you're talking about."

"Maybe not," Chad shrugged. "But I do know one thing." He stepped closer to her, his breath brushing against her cheek as he whispered, "He sure looks good in a rubber suit."

Chapter 36

"Sunshine!"

Her sister's voice barely registered as Sunshine bolted through the house, the world spinning and narrowing into tunnel vision. She couldn't breathe, couldn't stay in this godforsaken place for another second. The air felt like it was suffocating her.

Hot tears streamed down her cheeks, but she was too numb to notice. Her stomach twisted violently, a deep sickness that seemed to rise from her soul. Flashes of the Rubber Man interchanged with images of Tate, a horrifying montage playing in her mind. How had she been so blind? So desperate for his love that she hadn't seen the nightmare right in front of her?

"Sunshine, why would he say that?"

Her sister's voice was muffled by the storm of despair crashing through her mind. The thin thread of sanity she'd been clinging to had finally snapped. Everything was a lie. The one person she thought she could trust...

Sunshine stumbled into the kitchen and vomited into the sink. Her whole body convulsed as the bile forced its way out, but it was nothing compared to the agony in her chest. This pain—this crushing, suffocating ache—was worse than anything she'd ever felt. It radiated from her heart to her bones, wrapping around her neck and squeezing the air from her lungs.

"Sunshine, you're scaring me," Violet's voice trembled from behind her.

Sunshine shook uncontrollably, wiping the leftover bile from her lips with the back of her hand. She couldn't even look at her sister.

"Sun-"

"Shut up!" Sunshine snapped, her eyes flashing as they met Violet's. "I can't—I can't deal with this right now. I need to get out of this house."

She had to leave, before the house—before he—destroyed her completely.

Sunshine stumbled past her sister, shoving the front door open as she fled outside. Her legs carried her down the porch steps and into the lawn, but she barely made it a few steps before a sharp cramp tore through her abdomen, stopping her cold. Her hand flew to her stomach, panic rising in her chest.

Another, even more intense wave of pain hit her, forcing her to double over, a cry ripping from her throat. "Ah!"

"Sunshine!" Violet's voice was frantic as she rushed to her sister's side, catching her before she could collapse.

Sunshine's anguished cries filled the air, her entire body seized by a white-hot pain. She barely registered Constance running over to help hold her up, her vision blurring through tears.

"Oh, Sunshine, is-is the baby coming?" Constance asked but Sunshine couldn't formulate a response so she looked to Violet for help. "Help me get her inside!"

"No!" Sunshine screamed, her voice raw. "Please, no!"

"When a child's ready, there's no stopping it," Constance said her tone firm despite the situation. "Come on, we've got to get you inside."

Together, they half-carried, and half-dragged her back toward the house. Sunshine's breathing came in ragged gasps, and through the haze of pain, her eyes locked on Constance.

"You knew," Sunshine managed to spit out between agonizing breaths, her voice filled with betrayal. "Didn't you?"

Constance's eyes darted to her, but she said nothing, focusing instead on getting her inside. They eased her onto the loveseat in the music room, Constance quickly placing a pillow behind her head.

Another wave of pain hit, and Sunshine screamed, her body arching from the intensity. It radiated from her abdomen, spreading through her like fire.

"Take it easy, now," Constance instructed, her voice soothing but strained. "Don't forget to breathe. Breathe."

"I can't get any service!" Violet shouted in frustration, snapping her phone shut with a loud clack.

Ben rushed into the music room, his face a look of alarm. "What's going on?" he asked, his voice tight with concern.

"Dad, the baby's coming," Violet said quickly. Sunshine let out a strangled cry from the sofa, pulling his attention to her.

"Daddy, you gotta get me out of here," Sunshine sobbed, her voice shaking. Tears streamed down her face as she clutched her stomach. "Please, don't let me die in this house."

Ben was at her side in an instant, gently brushing the damp hair from her forehead. "Everything's going to be okay, sweetheart,"

"I tried calling an ambulance," Violet chimed in, still clutching her phone, "but there's no service."

"I'll try outside," Ben said, already moving, but Sunshine's trembling hand reached out, grabbing his wrist.

"No," she pleaded, her voice breaking. "Don't leave me here. Please, Dad. Don't leave me."

Ben's heart clenched, but he nodded, squeezing her hand. "I'm going to get you help, baby. I'll be right back." He forced himself to pull away, heading toward the door.

Sunshine's breath hitched, the pain intensifying as another wave hit. "I need to go to the hospital now!"

"It's too late for that," Constance cut in, casting a glance under Sunshine's dress. "You're already crowning."

Sunshine's sobs grew, her body wracked with uncontrollable shakes as the pain overtook her. It was too much, the pressure, the agony—everything was overwhelming.

"Breathe, Sunshine. Breathe," Constance coaxed, leaning over her, trying to keep her calm.

"Fuck!" Sunshine grit her teeth, seething through the excruciating pain. "It hurts so much."

"Well, of course, it does, honey," Constance said, her tone laced with a callousness that only deepened Sunshine's despair. "That's a woman's curse."

As if things couldn't get any worse, the house was suddenly swallowed in darkness as the power went out.

Sunshine's vision blurred in and out, barely registering the soft flicker of candlelight around her. Her eyes drifted down to see the ghost of Charles Montgomery preparing for her delivery. She blinked, trying to clear her sight, but whatever they'd given her for the pain made everything feel distant, muted. A sheet had been draped over her legs, granting her privacy.

"Nurse, bring me my doctor's bag," Dr. Montgomery instructed. "Find me the 12-gauge scalpel."

He continued barking orders, the sound of towels being spread beneath her barely registering.

"Sunshine."

Her mother's voice cut through the haze, pulling her from the darkness. Sunshine blinked, her eyes slowly focusing on Vivien, who hovered over her.

"Mommy?" Sunshine's voice was slurred, heavy with sedation. "I can't— I can't be here." Each word was a struggle, dripping with the weight of exhaustion and fear.

Vivien knelt beside her, gently stroking her hair. "The baby is coming, my love."

Sunshine's lip quivered, but that was all she could manage under the fog of the medication. Deep down, she knew. She wasn't going to survive this—not in this house. She felt like a pawn, trapped in a cruel game she never agreed to play.

Her eyes drifted to the nurses from the basement that surrounded her, attending to her as if this were any normal birth.

"What's happening?" she whispered, her voice barely audible.

"The house is trying to help," Constance said from a few feet away, arms crossed. "And right now, you're in no position to refuse."

One of the nurses leaned over the back of the loveseat, gently dabbing a washcloth across Sunshine's sweat-soaked forehead.

"Honey, you need to push, okay?" Vivien's voice sounded distant and blurry to Sunshine, her face hazy.

With trembling reluctance, Sunshine nodded, hot tears streaming down her cheeks. She took a deep breath, bracing herself as she pushed, her anguished cries echoing through the room. The pain intensified with each push, making it nearly unbearable.

"You're doing great, baby," Vivien soothed, wiping away her daughter's tears.

"You need to breathe, Sunny," Ben encouraged, kneeling beside Vivien.

Sunshine tried, but the agony was overwhelming, suffocating her attempts to take a breath.

"I need forceps, now," Dr. Montgomery demanded.

Ben's gaze darted to the doctor. "What's happening?"

"It's dystocia," Dr. Montgomery responded, gripping the forceps handed to him by a nurse. "I have to manipulate the baby through the pubic symphysis."

Ben and Vivien exchanged a panicked look before focusing back on Sunshine.

"I can't do this," Sunshine sobbed, shaking her head as tears spilled down her face. "I can't."

"You can," Ben said firmly, guiding her to look into his eyes. "I promise you, Sunshine, you can do this."

"Dr. Harmon, tell her to stop pushing until I say so," Dr. Montgomery ordered.

"You hear that, Sunshine?" Vivien's voice quivered but remained strong for her daughter. "You need to stop pushing until he tells you to."

Sunshine nodded weakly, holding her breath, trying desperately to resist the overwhelming urge to push. The pain surged through her, her body fighting against her will.

"It hurts," Sunshine whimpered.

"Just squeeze my hand as hard as you can," Ben said softly, gripping her hand tight and trying to anchor her.

She squeezed with everything she had, fighting against the primal urge to push.

"Get the gauze ready to stop the bleeding," Dr. Montgomery commanded, his voice cutting through the tension. He turned back toward them. "Now, Dr. Harmon."

"Push, Sunshine!" Ben urged, his voice filled with emotion.

Sunshine let out a strangled breath and pushed with all the strength she had left, a scream tearing from her throat.

"Push! Push!" The room buzzed around her, voices encouraging her, but the pain was all she could feel.

"Don't stop now, angel!" Constance's voice called from the side. "The end is near. I can see him!"

Sunshine's entire body trembled, her senses overwhelmed, screams ripping through her throat. She grabbed onto a nurse's uniform with her free hand, clutching with desperation.

And then, suddenly, relief.

A wave of calm swept over her, and a small, piercing cry filled the room. Sunshine gasped, her eyes snapping open to the sight of her baby.

"You did it, sweetheart," Vivien whispered, kissing her daughter's head gently. "You did so good."

But as the baby continued to wail, Sunshine's vision softened once more. Her body gave in to the deep exhaustion, the pain fading into a strange numbness. She felt herself drifting.

"Is everything all right?"

"She's bleeding," Dr. Montgomery muttered grimly. "I have to stop the bleeding."

The sound of blood trickling filled the room as Sunshine's vision wavered, the world around her darkening. She heard voices—faint, muffled—fading in and out like a dream she couldn't grasp.

"Nurse, apply pressure!"

"What's happening?" Vivien's panic broke through the haze.

"She's going into shock," Dr. Montgomery said, his voice tinged with urgency. "I can't stop the hemorrhaging."

"Sunshine, stay with me, baby." Vivien's voice cracked, her tears flowing freely as she watched her daughter slipping away.

"Sunny." The soft voice called from the edge of her awareness.

Sunshine's eyes flickered to the sound, her gaze drifting beyond her parents to see Violet standing there.

"Violet," she whispered.

Ben and Vivien glanced at each other, unable to see Violet.

"Listen to me," Ben urged, his voice pulling at Sunshine's fleeting focus. "Concentrate on my words."

But Violet's voice cut through the panic. "It's okay," she said softly, tears in her eyes. "If you're in pain, let go."

Sunshine's lips quivered, her mind numb, her body too weak to fight. "I don't think I have a choice,"

"Hold on, Sunshine," Ben pleaded, his tears falling. "Stay with me. Please, stay with me."

"Come to this side. Let go," Violet said through her tears. "You can be with me."

"Okay," Sunshine whispered, surrendering as the darkness consumed her. Her eyes fluttered closed, her body too tired to continue the fight. All Sunshine could hear through the enveloping darkness were the faint, distant murmurs of voices, echoes lost in the void.

"I'm sorry. She's gone."

"No..." Vivien's anguished cry pierced through the fog. "My baby... My baby!"

Ben's sobs broke through next, choked and raw, as he moved closer to his daughter's still body. Trembling, he placed a hand on her cold cheek, his voice cracking as he began to sing through his tears.

"You are my sunshine..."

"My only S-sunshine..." He hiccupped, but pressed on, his heart breaking with each word.

"You make me happy when skies are gray..."

Sunshine blinked, her eyes fluttering open, though she wasn't lying on the couch anymore. She was standing—standing beside Violet. Her heart clenched as she looked down at her lifeless body, seeing her parents shattered in grief. Tears fogged her vision as Violet's hand interlaced with hers, grounding her in this strange new reality.

She felt her sister lean her head against her shoulder, the weight of loss shared between them, both crying silently.

His voice faltered, shaking with emotion. "You'll never know, dear... how much I love you..."

He leaned down, pressing his forehead against hers.

"Please don't take... my Sunshine... away."

Chapter 37

Sunshine stepped into the kitchen, Violet following close behind. It felt strange—being dead. She experienced nothingness and then overwhelming emotions all at once. The details of her death and the moment she gave birth were hazy, yet the lingering memory of pain clung to her. Her gaze fell on Constance, who was cradling the baby and humming softly while gently bouncing him in her arms.

Constance looked up, her eyes meeting Sunshine's for a brief moment. A flicker of sadness crossed her features before looking back down at the bundle of joy in her arms. "He's beautiful," she said softly.

Sunshine managed a small smile, stepping closer to her. "Can I see him?"

After a moment of consideration, Constance nodded. "Of course."

Sunshine held out her arms as Constance carefully placed the baby into her arms. Cradling him close, she gazed down at his perfect little face, watching as he shifted slightly, his tiny lips pursing in response. With one arm securely supporting him, she gently traced his cheek with her free hand, marveling at the softness of his skin.

Violet moved closer, peering at her nephew. "Normally, babies are kind of ugly when they come out... but he's actually kind of cute."

Sunshine chuckled softly at her sister's comment, her heart swelling with love as she continued to stare down at her precious baby.

"What's his name?" Violet asked, glancing over with curiosity, a look mirrored on Constance's face as she watched them.

Sunshine's gaze flicked up, and she suddenly realized she hadn't even settled on a name. Sure, she had scoured baby name websites, but nothing had truly resonated with her. She paused, her mind drifting back to a German composer from the 17th century, someone who had played a part in the development of music.

"Michael," she finally replied, her heart warming as she said the name.

"Seriously?" Violet scrunched her eyebrows together in disbelief.

"I think that's a beautiful name," Constance chimed in, her hands resting gently on her upper arms.

Sunshine glanced between them. "Do you mind giving me a moment alone with him?"

Violet nodded and left the kitchen, her footsteps echoing softly as Constance hesitated for a moment before following suit.

Sunshine walked over to a nearby chair, settling down as she gazed at Michael. His eyes were open, their blue hue locking onto hers, and she felt a surge of warmth at the sight. He had her eyes—a detail that brought an involuntary smile to her lips. He was still too fresh to discern any other features, but he radiated an angelic aura that filled her heart with a sense of peace.

Her smile faded the longer she looked at him. Deep down, she knew she couldn't keep him here. She couldn't be the one to raise him, and the realization settled heavily in her chest. A profound ache filled her heart at the thought of missing out on everything: watching him take his first steps, hearing him call her "Mama," witnessing the little milestones that defined his childhood.

His life would unfold without her, and though she understood it was for the best, that knowledge shattered whatever remained of her fractured heart.

"I wish you could stay," Sunshine said as her bottom lip quivered. Tears stung her eyes, threatening to spill over. "And one day, you might think that I didn't want you..." She placed her free hand gently on his little chest, feeling the rise and fall beneath it. "But I do."

A couple of tears escaped as she noticed Michael gazing up at her, his tiny eyes wide and unblinking. "You're so loved, even if I can't be the one to hold you," she continued, her heart breaking with every word. "You deserve a better life than what I can give you." Leaning closer, she whispered, "Just know that I will always love you and you will always have a place in my heart."

Sunshine pressed a tender kiss to his forehead, her body shaking slightly from the tears and the grief that enveloped her. She closed her eyes, letting the moment linger, imprinting the memory of his innocence and the sweetness of their connection deep into her soul.

Sunshine hesitated before her bedroom door, acutely aware that Tate was on the other side. Taking a steadying breath, she wiped away the lingering tears that had fallen after she handed her son over to his paternal grandmother.

She reached for the doorknob, feeling it turn slowly under her touch. As she stepped inside, she kept her eyes fixed on the floor, shutting the door firmly behind her. The silence was heavy, her gaze glued to the ground as dread coiled in her stomach, afraid to confront the person who had brought her to this moment of distress.

Each heartbeat echoed in her ears as she flicked her gaze upward to find Tate lying on his side on her bed. Sunshine forced herself to step forward, crossing the space until she reached the foot of the bed. Tate seemed to sense her presence; he lifted himself up, a genuine smile spreading across his face at the sight of her.

Sunshine's eyes darted away from him as she flexed her jaw, struggling to piece together what she wanted to say. "I died."

"I'm so sorry." Tate reached out, about to make contact with her wrist, but she quickly pulled away.

"Don't." Sunshine closed her eyes, fighting to keep her composure. "Don't fucking touch me."

Tate looked down at the space where she had pulled back, confusion etching his features. She moved a few steps back, creating distance between them.

Swallowing hard, she continued, "My parents are downstairs, crying over my dead body."

Tate climbed over the foot of the bed, standing before her. "That makes me sad. I like your dad. He was nice to me."

"He has to be nice to his patients." Sunshine blinked, crossing her arms defensively as she met his gaze. Tears glossed over her eyes, but she refused to let him see her cry. "Even the ones that lie to him."

"What?" Tate acted confused, his brow furrowing.

"Cut the shit, Tate." Sunshine shook her head, desperation clawing at her for a shred of honesty. "You knew you were dead."

Tate seemed slightly taken aback. "Yeah. I knew."

"How did you die?"

"The cops shot me." He looked as if he were being lectured by his mother, his eyes flitting around the room. "Right here in this room."

"Do you know why they shot you?"

Tate shook his head. "I don't know."

"You remember those kids on Halloween?" Sunshine pressed, and he reluctantly nodded. "You killed them. You brought a gun to school and you shot them."

A tear traced its path down his cheek. "Why would I do that?"

"You tell me." Sunshine tilted her head slightly, rage simmering in her eyes.

"Why would I do that?" Tate's sobs began to heighten, each word a desperate plea. "Why would I do that? Why would I do that?"

Sunshine looked away for a moment, his tears tugging at her heart. Despite all the disgusting things he had done, she still loved him. "I don't know."

Her gaze flicked back to him. "Why'd you kill Chad and Patrick?"

Tate stood there looking defeated, hugging himself as he cried. Sunshine moved toward her dresser, stopping in front of it before pulling open the top drawer. Her fingers brushed against the black rubber mask, and she looked down at it for a moment before turning back to face him.

Tate blinked, tears streaming down his face as he stared at the mask she held out to him.

"Why did you rape me?"

"I'm sorry." His body shook with sobs as he looked at the mask. "I'm so sorry."

Sunshine huffed, disbelief flashing across her features as she tossed the mask aside. "You're sorry?" She stepped closer, narrowing her eyes. Grabbing his face with one hand, she forced him to meet her gaze. "I trusted you, Tate... you made me feel safe. But you..." She tore her hand away, her voice seething through gritted teeth. "You were the very thing I was scared of."

Sunshine stepped back, crossing her arms. "Look at you—the monster under my bed. The thing that turned my dreams into nightmares. My. Fucking. Hero."

"Sunshine, please," Tate pleaded, his voice cracking.

But she wasn't having any of it. "Why'd you do it?"

Tate looked away, avoiding her gaze.

"Tell me, Tate!" Sunshine raised her voice, frustration boiling over.

Tate closed his eyes for a brief moment, gathering himself before finally looking back at her. "I promised Nora a baby."

Sunshine let out a breath, disbelief washing over her.

Tate took a step closer, desperation etched on his face. "Sunshine, that was before I knew you."

"And that makes it any better? That makes it okay?"

Tate's shoulders slumped.

"I'm dead because of you." Sunshine stepped closer, her gaze locking onto his with pure vexation. "Our son doesn't have a mother... because of you."

Tate opened his mouth to speak, but no words emerged.

"The fact that you could stand there, watching me unravel throughout my pregnancy while knowing you were the father... Hold me after my nightmares, even though you're the one who caused them..."

Sunshine searched his eyes, her breath trembling as she spoke. "You're a fucking monster."

"Sunshine, please. I'm different now," he pleaded through his tears, yearning to reach for her but stopping himself. "You're the only light I've ever known. You've changed me, Sunny."

Sunshine swallowed hard, tears spilling down her cheeks despite her efforts to hold them back. "I want to believe that, Tate."

He dropped to his knees, desperation etched across his face. "Please... I love you. I'm so sorry."

She looked down at him, her heart aching, and knelt in front of him. Gently, she brushed his hair from his eyes, and he gazed up at her with hope. "I love you, too."

Her hands moved to cradle his face, her thumbs tracing the paths of his tears. "But I can't forgive you."

Tate's expression crumpled.

"You need to learn that there are consequences to your actions. .." Sunshine whispered, tilting her head and looking deeply into his eyes. "You've caused so much pain, baby." She opened her mouth to speak again, but the words caught in her throat. Standing tall, she looked down at him. "I can't be with you. I won't."

Tate shook his head, rising to his feet in disbelief. "What are you saying?"

"I'm saying go away."

"What?" Tate's voice trembled in disbelief, his eyes wide with panic. "No, no, don't do this."

"Go away, Tate." Sunshine's voice broke as more tears streamed down her cheeks.

"You're all I want! You're all I have!" he shouted, desperation lacing his cries.

"Go away!" She screamed, squeezing her eyes shut, wishing for this moment to end.

Silence enveloped the room, punctuated only by her cries. When she finally opened her eyes again, Tate was gone.

Her hand flew to her mouth as the sobs escaped uncontrollably. She instinctively clutched her now flattened stomach, as if the pressure could somehow alleviate the searing pain that gripped the space between her ribs. A gentle hand landed on her shoulder, and she turned to find Violet standing beside her.

"I'm so sorry, Sunshine," Violet said, her eyes brimming with unshed tears as she fought to stay strong for her sister. Sunshine's bottom lip quivered, and before she knew it, she had collapsed into Violet's arms, burying her face in the softness of her sister's hair. Violet wrapped her arms around her, holding her tightly as Sunshine unraveled.

Chapter 38

Sunshine sat on the kitchen counter, her feet swinging idly as Moira wiped down the surfaces. Violet sat at the island, both sisters wrapped in silence.

Moira glanced over at Sunshine, breaking the quiet. "I wonder, how is your adjustment going?"

Sunshine shrugged, her gaze dropping to her feet. "I'm...fine, considering. But I miss my family. I miss my baby."

Moira gave a somber nod. "Yes, well, it's always the living that make it hard."

Sunshine sighed, a hint of bitterness in her voice. "The dead don't make it any easier, either."

Moira looked at her knowingly. "I assume you're talking about Constance's son?"

Before Sunshine could answer, the front door was slammed, and she and Violet exchanged a quick glance. Ben walked in, carrying Michael's car seat, with Vivien following closely behind.

Sunshine slid off the counter and moved to where her father had set the baby down. Violet joined her, and together, the sisters leaned over to look at Michael, who gazed up at them with bright eyes before breaking into a tiny, heartwarming smile.

"Let's hurry up and get this over with. I don't want to be in this house any longer than necessary," Vivien said, her tone brisk as Ben prepared a bottle. He moved toward the microwave, only for Vivien to shake her head with a sharp, "Not the microwave, Ben."

"Right." He sighed, adjusting and running the bottle under warm water at the sink instead.

Sunshine leaned over the car seat, captivated. She let her thumb graze his soft cheek, marveling at his little face.

"He looks like he's staring right at us." Violet pointed out.

"Children are very sensitive to the spirit world. They sense more than we realize." Moira explained.

Sunshine absorbed this, her gaze still fixed on Michael. "Hmm," she murmured. Michael's tiny fingers curled around Sunshine's, and a soft smile spread across her face as she gazed at him. "I want to hold him so badly," she whispered, the ache in her voice unmistakable.

Violet placed a gentle hand on her sister's shoulder, offering silent comfort. "I know," she murmured.

Sunshine blinked back the tears threatening to fall, tracing her thumb lightly over his little hand. "It's like he knows who I am."

Moira watched them quietly, a touch of sorrow in her eyes. "Babies feel love in ways words can't touch. He'll carry that with him—your love, your memory. No matter where he is."

Violet gave her sister's shoulder a squeeze, both of them watching as Michael's eyes slowly began to close, his small fingers still holding tightly to hers, bridging two worlds that neither could fully leave behind.

Sunshine drifted through the house, absorbing each detail that would now be her eternal surroundings. The echoes of past lives filled every corner, and while she sensed countless presences brushing against her awareness, one felt closer than the others. She didn't need to look back to know who it was; his presence followed her, shadowing her every step, even when he remained unseen.

Pushing the weight of it aside, she steeled herself, putting on a brave face as she entered Violet's room.

She found Violet sitting cross-legged on the floor, organizing CDs, and Sunshine leaned casually against the doorframe, arms crossed. "We should probably start gathering up anything you want to keep."

Violet looked up, confused. "Why?"

"Mom and Dad are here to turn in the keys," Sunshine replied. "Someone else is bound to move in eventually."

Violet's shoulders slumped, her sigh filling the room. "Right."

Sunshine watched her for a long moment, recalling how Violet had also sent Tate away, severing ties that had once meant everything. A pang of guilt shot through her, knowing that her sister had lost her closest friend too. "I'm sorry, Vi. For... everything."

"Don't be stupid." Violet rolled her eyes as she stood up, brushing her hands off. "None of this is your fault."

Sunshine let out a deep breath, letting her arms fall to her sides. "I know... but still. I feel bad."

Violet gave her a reassuring shrug, stepping closer. "Don't. We might be dead, but at least we're dead together."

A small smile crept onto Sunshine's face as the weight in her chest eased just a little.

Sunshine stood alone in the music room, a strange heaviness on her shoulders. Though Moira had scrubbed the floors clean, the dark, faded stain of her blood still marred the loveseat. This had been the first room she'd fallen in love with, her haven within the house's twisted walls. Now it was also the place where her life had ended.

Her gaze fell on the grand piano, its polished surface catching glimmers of the light shining through the curtains. A bittersweet ache seeped through her, filling her bones. She hadn't played in what felt like an eternity. Sitting at that piano had once filled her with purpose, with dreams of a life she would never have.

Slowly, she moved to the bench, her heart tightening as she sat down. Her breath wavered, each inhale heavy with the gravity of all she had lost. Lifting the fallboard, she let her fingers drift over the keys, grazing them gently as if testing to see if she remembered the feeling.

She began to play the first notes of Asleep by The Smiths. Her fingers trembled at first, rusty from months of absence, but they moved with a grace that even death hadn't stolen from her.

Blinking away tears, she let herself get lost in the music, the chords wrapping around her heart and squeezing gently.

The room seemed to breathe with her music, each note drawing out memories she'd tried to bury. The longing, the grief, the lost dreams—all poured out through her fingertips, releasing a fraction of the ache she'd carried since the day she moved in.

As Sunshine continued to play, her surroundings seemed to blur, the world beyond the music fading as she immersed herself in the notes. Her fingers pressed down on each key with a deliberate softness. The mournful, lulling chords wrapped around her, filling the room with a melancholy warmth, almost as if the house itself were listening.

Her tears began to fall freely as she let the last note linger, the sound echoing and then fading into silence.

Quickly wiping away her tears, Sunshine stood up, the weight of sorrow still heavy in her chest. As she stepped away from the grand piano, a flicker of movement caught her eye, and she instinctively turned to see what it was.

Her heart raced as her gaze shot upward, locking onto the horrific above sight her. Her father hung limply from the chandelier, his body swaying gently like a marionette with its strings cut.

Her breath hitched, her hands instinctively covering her mouth.

"Sunshine."

She heard her father's voice drift beside her, and she turned to look up at him.

"Daddy, I'm so sorry," she whispered.

"It's okay, baby." Ben's soothing voice comforted her against the ache in her chest. He reached out to her, wrapping his arms around her, and for a moment, she melted against him, feeling safe and loved.

Sunshine pulled back slightly, her eyes wide with panic. "Where's Mom?"

After calling out for their mother, panic gripped them as the silence wrapped around the house. Sunshine, Violet, and Ben continued to shout her name, their voices echoing against the cold walls. The dread in their hearts grew heavier with each unanswered call until, at last, they stumbled upon the basement door, its hinges creaking in protest as they pushed it open.

Vivien lay sprawled on the cold floor. Her once vibrant figure now appeared frail, lifelessness seeping into her skin. Sunshine's heart sank as she took in the gruesome scene: Vivien's stomach had been violently cut open.

"Mom!" Violet cried, her voice cracking as she dropped to her knees beside her mother. Sunshine and Ben quickly followed suit, kneeling on either side of her, desperation painting their faces.

"Oh, Viv," Ben whispered, his voice thick with anguish.

"My babies," Vivien managed to whisper, her voice barely audible as her blurry gaze flickered between her daughters. The light in her eyes was dimming, the warmth that once radiated from her was now replaced by the icy grip of death.

"We need to get help," Sunshine insisted, shaking her head as a wave of desperation washed over her. She couldn't bear the thought of her mother being trapped in this horrific limbo like the rest of them.

"No," Vivien managed to say, her voice a strained whisper. "I want this. I want to be with you. All of you."

🗙🗙🗙🗙🗙🗙🗙🗙🗙

A/N: We still have the rest of afterbirth and then return to murder house before we wrap this bad boy up!

Chapter 39

A couple of months had passed since the Harmons' tragic deaths, and already there were new prospective buyers for the house. Sunshine had handed her son to his paternal grandmother to raise; as flawed as Constance was, Sunshine preferred her son to be close to her over anyone else—especially her sanctimonious Aunt Jo.

Sunshine was beginning to get the hang of her new reality, adjusting to the quirks of the afterlife. She and Violet were perched near the dining room as they watched Troy and Bryan toss pop-its at the new boy. He stumbled off his skateboard, wincing, and the girls broke into a fit laughter.

Sunshine strolled over to the skateboard, giving it a light kick with her foot. It rolled lazily back toward the teenage boy, who froze, staring at it as though it had a mind of its own. His eyes widened, a hint of fear creeping across his face as he glanced around, half-expecting to see someone—or something—nearby.

"He's kind of cute," Violet remarked.

"Oh? Did you have a change of heart, Vi?"

Violet scoffed, rolling her eyes. "Ew, no. I meant for you."

Sunshine watched as he exchanged a few words with his father, then turned and left the room. Her eyes lingered on the door he'd passed through.

She knew she wasn't ready to move on from her last relationship. And the thought of putting someone else at risk made her hesitate. Still, the idea of a distraction, something to break up the monotony of this place, was tempting.

"Violet, this is insane." Sunshine shifted nervously in what used to be her old bedroom as Violet rifled through the new boy's music collection—the boy they quickly learned was named Gabe.

"Calm down," Violet rolled her eyes.

Sunshine pressed her lips into a tight line just as Gabe walked in, a confused look crossing his face as he held his skateboard. "Who are you?" he asked, looking between the two sisters.

"You have awful taste in music," Violet remarked, barely glancing back at him. "Butthole Surfers?"

Gabe blinked, still trying to catch up. "Hello? Breaking and entering. Who are you?" His eyes darted between them, but Sunshine stayed quiet, watching her sister's bold introduction. It was good to see Violet trying to make friends, even if it hadn't ended well before.

"A ghost of my former self," Violet joked, holding out her hand. "Violet. We live in the neighborhood."

Gabe shook it, then turned his attention to Sunshine.

She waved awkwardly, managing a small smile. "Hi. I'm Sunshine."

He took a step forward, holding out his hand for her to shake. As she took it, he seemed to look her over curiously. "Your hand's cold," he remarked, though he didn't let go right away.

Sunshine laughed nervously, pulling her hand back gently. "Yeah."

"You know what they say. Cold hands, warm heart." Violet smirked, scooping up a box of CDs and dumping them onto his bed.

"Yo!" Gabe protested.

"Violet," Sunshine whispered, closing her eyes, embarrassed.

"Don't you have any Ramones? Like Animal Boy or Too Tough to Die?" Violet continued, ignoring him as she combed through the pile.

"Hey. Get out of my room." Gabe pointed toward the door.

Violet raised an eyebrow, ignoring his request. "Are you sure you want to be alone? They say this house is haunted."

Gabe shot them a bewildered look. "You two are kind of twisted, aren't you?"

Sunshine tilted her head slightly. "You don't know the half of it."

Sunshine sat up from her reclined position on the couch, a book she'd snagged from the mother of the house open in her lap. Suddenly, loud screams echoed through the house, drawing her attention. She quickly climbed the stairs, the sound growing louder as she approached her old bedroom.

"Please... don't kill me." She recognized Gabe's voice, trembling with fear.

"Oh, it's nothing personal," Tate's voice came through, unsteady. "She's all alone, and that's just not right!" There was a tense shuffle, then Tate's voice again, commanding and harsh. "Stand up! Stop that—turn around."

Sunshine rushed into the room to see Tate holding a knife to Gabe's throat, their backs turned toward her. She stepped forward, placing a steady hand on Tate's shoulder. "Tate... put it down... please."

He didn't turn, but his grip faltered slightly. "I can't. I'm doing this for you. I couldn't save you... it's my fault you're alone."

"Hey," Sunshine brushed his hair out of his face, trying to catch his gaze. "I'm fine. I have my family here."

"It's not enough," he whispered, voice shaking his pain. "You need someone."

"I don't want him," she murmured, desperation in her voice. "Please, Tate... stop."

Tate finally looked at her, eyes full of tears and pleading. "Then what do you want?"

"I want you, baby," she said softly, cupping his face in her hands.

A glimmer of hope lit up his expression as he melted into her touch, loosening his grip on Gabe just enough for him to break free and bolt from the room. But Tate barely noticed, captivated by her touch.

Sunshine blinked away her own tears. "If you can show me you've really changed... then one day, I'd reconsider being with you again, okay?"

He nodded, tears slipping down his cheeks. She wiped them away tenderly, her own heart breaking.

"Until then... goodbye." Her voice cracked as she swallowed back a sob, and she leaned in, pressing a desperate kiss to his tear-stained lips. When she pulled away, she vanished, leaving Tate alone in the room, holding onto the memory of her touch.

After the Ruivivars moved out, several months passed, and Christmas arrived once more. Sunshine moved around the tree, spreading out the branches with care, while Violet stood on a chair, fluffing the branches at the top.

Moira approached them, holding a dusty box of ornaments. "I found these in the attic," she said, offering a small smile.

Violet lifted one of the ornaments, examining it with a raised brow. "Wow. These ornaments are ancient."

Moira chuckled softly. "I suppose they are. In time, Violet, the word 'ancient' will lose all its meaning. When your existence becomes one endless today, age feels like nothing at all."

Sunshine's smile faltered. She'd never grow old, never have another child or marry. Her son, so close yet so far, lived just outside these walls. Every day she watched for him, catching only fleeting glimpses when Constance took him outside. She'd wave, and Constance would wave back, but that was all she could have—just a glimpse.

"Okay, everybody ready?" Ben's voice cut through her thoughts, and she looked up as he held the plug for the extension cord. With a smile, he plugged it in, and the tree lit up in a warm, golden glow. Sunshine's face softened, her smile returning.

"Look at that!" Ben said proudly, circling the tree. "Chopped it down myself. Have you ever seen anything so beautiful?"

"I have," Vivien's voice came from behind, and Sunshine turned to see her mother holding a tiny bundle in her arms. Vivien moved beside Ben, gazing down at the baby boy she carried. After her murder, they hadn't expected the child to attach to the home, but

Nora, overwhelmed with him, had handed him back to Vivien soon after his death.

"Look at him," Vivien cooed, glancing down. "He's amazing. The best temperament—hardly ever cries. Looks just like his daddy." She and Ben exchanged a loving smile before sharing a soft kiss.

Sunshine and Violet exchanged a glance, sharing a moment of wordless understanding. Despite everything, despite the tragedy that had led them here, they were a family again.

Epilogue

It had been three years—three years of reliving the same day, over and over again. Sunshine drifted through the house, dragging on a cigarette, its smoke curling around her. She had picked up her sister's habit in a desperate attempt to feel something, anything.

As she reached the living room, Sunshine's gaze landed on Constance sprawled out on the couch, the soft melodies from the record player filling the space. A drink dangled precariously from her fingers, threatening to crash at any moment. Just as Sunshine took a step closer, a flicker of movement caught her eye—the ghost of Constance appeared beside her urging her to turn her head.

Sunshine glanced at Constance when a voice rang out—a man's voice with a childlike edge calling for his grandmother.

Constance sighed deeply, locking eyes with Sunshine. "He's all yours." With that, she vanished, leaving Sunshine reeling.

A blonde boy, around her frozen age, entered the living room, his gaze landing on Constance's lifeless body.

Sunshine's shoulders slumped, the cigarette trembling between her fingers. This couldn't be happening. Michael would be three years old now, and yet, here he was, grown before her eyes. Shock gripped her as she noticed the unmistakable blue eyes reflecting her own and the tousled hair that must have come from her. He was the spitting image of her.

Swallowing hard, she stubbed out her cigarette in a nearby ashtray.

"No!" Michael cried, kneeling beside his grandmother, tears streaming down his cheeks. "No! Hey! Wake up! Please, wake up!"

"He looks just like you," she heard her father's voice beside her.

Sunshine blinked away her tears, acutely aware that there was a reason Constance had left him. The unnatural way he appeared grown only deepened her unease. The more she looked at him, the more she recognized the darkness that once lurked behind Tate's eyes.

She turned to her father. "You have to help him."

Ben had been having sessions with Michael for the past couple of weeks, and Sunshine watched from a distance. He really was trying to be better. Ben had convinced her that perhaps seeing his mother would help him, and so she stood there, her gaze fixed on him as he sat in the backyard, engrossed in whatever homework Ben had assigned.

Taking a deep breath, Sunshine steeled herself before making her presence known. She stepped onto the grass, the soft crunch of blades underfoot drawing Michael's attention. His head snapped toward her, eyes widening as he studied her.

"Mom?" Michael breathed.

Sunshine felt a smile break across her face, a warmth flooding her heart. She walked over to him, stopping just in front of where he sat on the brick ledge—the same one Violet used to sneak cigarettes on. "You know who I am?" she asked, tilting her head.

"I remember your face," Michael said, nodding eagerly. "I remember what you said to me."

Sunshine blinked as she fought to swallow back the tears threatening to spill over. It seemed impossible that he could hold onto those memories, yet here he was, standing before her as a young man, defying the passage of time.

Everything about her pregnancy and his birth had been confusing, and now, facing him, those questions felt irrelevant.

"Why'd you wait so long to talk to me?" Michael asked, his gaze searching hers for answers.

Sunshine's eyes drifted, her heart heavy as she searched for the right words. "I've always been here,"

"Are you going to stay?" he asked, hope shining in his eyes.

With a soft smile, Sunshine stepped forward and wrapped her arms around her son. He melted into her embrace, returning it with equal warmth. "Of course,"

"What are you doing? Stay away from my shit!"

"He was just exploring," Ben replied calmly.

"Exploring? He's messed up!"

Sunshine moved through the hallway as she followed the voices, wondering where Michael had gone.

"You stay away from my shit, you understand?"

She heard Tate's voice and peeked around the corner, spotting them in her old bedroom. Michael sat on the bed, clutching something in his hands, while Ben and Tate loomed over him.

"Well, I just want to be like you, Dad," Michael explained, his voice small.

"Who told you that?" Tate snapped.

"Other spirits. They whispered to me."

"You didn't spring from my nutsack, got it?" Tate stepped forward threateningly, but Ben blocked him. "Not even I could create something as monstrous, as evil, as you."

Sunshine stepped fully into the room as she caught Tate's gaze. "Tate."

"Sunshine," he whispered, his face falling at her tone.

Her eyes landed on what Michael was holding, and a cold ripple cascaded over her skin. She moved closer to him and gently grabbed the rubber mask from his hands. "Don't touch this ever again, do you understand me?"

Michael looked hurt, his eyes wide with confusion, but he nodded.

She turned back to Tate, handing him the mask. "Here. Just go, okay?"

Tate's gaze fell on the mask, guilt flickering in his eyes before he shifted them to Michael. "You stay away from me,"

All the progress Michael had made felt like it had been tossed down the drain after his father's rejection. In the wake of that pain, he began to spiral toward the dark side, experimenting with his troubling thoughts on the ghosts in the house for his own twisted amusement. As his behavior grew more erratic, both Ben and Sunshine started to lose hope.

When a new couple decided to move in, Sunshine leaned over the staircase, sharing a cigarette with Violet.

"I don't know what to do, Vi," Sunshine sighed, handing the cigarette to her sister and rubbing her exhausted eyes.

"You can't help someone who doesn't want to be saved, Sunny," Violet replied with a shrug, taking a drag. "I know you see it too. I used to think Tate was evil... but he... Michael is death."

Almost on cue, a shrill scream echoed from downstairs. Both girls exchanged worried glances before looking down, only to see their father dash into the next room.

"Stay here," Sunshine instructed, her voice more weary rather than fearful, before she took off down the steps.

As she ran into the room, the new owners lay stabbed to death, blood splattered across the walls. Sunshine's gaze slowly drifted up to see the Rubber Man standing before her. For a fleeting moment, she thought it was Tate, but he hadn't killed in three years—or so Ben had claimed.

Then, a hidden force sent Ben flying backward, slamming him against the hallway wall.

The Rubber Man slowly removed his mask, revealing Michael underneath. Tears stung Sunshine's eyes, and she struggled to hold them back. She backed against the wall, her chest tightening with despair.

"Let him go, Michael," she managed to plead.

Michael simply stared at her, his expression blank.

"Those were good people," Ben gasped, fighting against the invisible grip holding him. "They deserved a chance."

"They don't belong here," Michael finally replied, his voice devoid of emotion.

Sunshine instinctively covered her mouth, trying to suppress the sobs threatening to escape. There was no saving him; there was no saving her baby. She longed for this nightmare to mean something, but all it brought was an overwhelming sense of loss.

"Because of what you did, they'll be here forever,"

The ghosts of the new owners materialized, looking around in confusion. "What's happening? I don't feel right,"

"You didn't have to kill them," Sunshine cried, shaking her head in disbelief. "You don't have to be like this, Michael."

Michael's gaze locked onto hers for a moment. He dropped the mask and turned his attention to the new ghosts. Lifting his hands, he defied the laws of the world, fire sparking at their feet until their souls were reduced to ash.

Sunshine gasped as she forced herself to look away.

Michael collapsed to his knees, the toll of his powers draining him. Ben broke free from the magical hold that had confined him and rushed to Sunshine, wrapping his arms around her as she cried.

"I never could have helped you," Ben looked toward Michael. "It was foolish to think I could."

Sunshine didn't reveal herself to Michael again after that. His true calling had knocked on the door, and he left the house—just like that. Several months passed, and yet again, new buyers arrived. But this time, they weren't just any prospective owners; they were a witch and a warlock, curious and intent on uncovering the secrets of Michael Langdon.

After they spoke with Constance and her father, Sunshine knew deep down that she held the answers they truly needed.

Now, she sat across from the witch and warlock, perched in an old chair as they waited on the edge of the couch, impatient for her to speak.

Sunshine glanced down at her hands, hesitating as memories she'd long buried began to resurface. "Before I found out I was pregnant with Michael, I had a nightmare. I was on stage, playing piano, and then... I looked down and saw hooves scraping me from the inside."

The witch rolled her eyes, crossing one leg over the other with an annoyed sigh. "And what does this have to do with anything?"

"Just shut up," the warlock muttered, shooting her a glare.

Sunshine flicked her gaze between them and continued, undeterred. "After my abortion, I went to the hospital for abdominal pain. The doctor confirmed I was still pregnant, but she saw something... something that scared her so much that it made her faint."

The witch and warlock exchanged a glance, caught between disbelief and a gnawing sense that Sunshine might not be exaggerating.

"She told me I was carrying the Beast," Sunshine murmured. "I know it sounds insane, but given everything that's happened since... I can't deny it."

The witch leaned forward, eyes narrowing. "You're saying he's the fucking Antichrist?"

"Nothing about Michael was ever normal—not his birth, not his growth. He came into this world with a purpose." Sunshine's voice strained. "I distanced myself from him after what happened. But then strange things started happening. Every day, a murder of crows would circle the house. The temperature inside became unbearable. And then... they came."

The warlock leaned forward, his eyes fixed intently on Sunshine. "Who?"

"Satanists," she replied, voice lowering as she relived the moment. "They looked at Michael as if he were their lord and savior." She paused, watching the disbelief settle on their faces. "When they came, it was like they opened a door for him, one that showed him his true path."

"Why didn't you stop them?" Madison asked, now completely absorbed.

Sunshine let out a short, humorless laugh. "I thought it was some kind of sick joke," she admitted. "A part of me had always known… but I didn't want to believe it. Not until they kidnapped a woman, cut out her heart… and fed it to him."

She took a shaky breath, struggling to keep her composure. "It was then that I decided I had to kill him, that he couldn't go on like this. But… I barely got close enough before he tried to burn my soul." She allowed herself a small, bitter smile. "Tate saved me."

Sunshine sat at the bottom of the steps, tears consuming her afterlife. She couldn't process how everything had turned out like this. The world was going to end—and it certainly felt like it.

Madison appeared in the hallway, walking toward her, a flicker of sympathy in her eyes.

Sunshine quickly wiped away her tears. "I have nothing else to tell you, I'm sorry."

Madison crouched down to be eye level with her. "I think we've got enough on him anyway."

Sunshine slumped, her shoulders sagging. "Then what do you want?"

Madison forced a small smile, trying to connect. "Seems like you're having a hard time. You and that Tate guy have a real angsty thing going on."

Sunshine licked the inside of her cheek, looking defeated. "I can't be around him... He's a monster."

"He didn't seem like a monster to me."

Sunshine let out a bitter laugh. "You don't know him. You can't imagine what it's like to know all the horrible things he's done."

"And still be in love with him?" Madison tilted her head, seeing right through her.

Sunshine looked down at her hands. "I never stopped."

"I've done things I'm not proud of in my life and my second life. But those were my choices. I think what happened to Tate was different. He wasn't the real evil here."

Sunshine's gaze flickered with hope. "What?"

Madison held her gaze. "It's like this house used him as a vessel to create something way, way worse. Just like it's used you." She forced another small smile. "My guess? Any evil in Tate left with Michael."

Sunshine hated that she was making sense. "If only that were true."

Madison nodded knowingly. "Maybe you just need to see the truth for yourself." And with that, Madison blew a glittering powder in her face.

She blinked, her mind slowly untangling a realization that washed over her. When she looked at Tate—no, when she looked at the Rubber Man—she saw the darkness, that same malevolent shadow she had long associated with him. But now, she recognized it as something separate, something ancient. It had lurked within the walls of this house, an evil force biding its time, pulling strings from the shadows, using both of them as puppets to orchestrate Michael's birth.

A heavy breath escaped her, like she'd been holding it for years. A weight, buried deep in her chest, finally lifted.

It wasn't Tate. It had never been Tate.

Sunshine was so caught up in the rush of realization that she hadn't even noticed Madison had disappeared. Gathering herself, she rose from the steps, her voice wavering slightly as she called out, "Tate?"

Moments later, quick footsteps echoed down the staircase. Tate appeared, stopping on the last step.

He swallowed, struggling to find the words that could possibly be enough. "I'm so sorry for everything."

Sunshine's lip trembled as she reached out, her fingers lightly tracing his face. He stepped down to her level, leaning into her touch, almost afraid she might vanish. She wrapped her arms around his neck, pulling him close, and the familiar scent of him washed over her.

"I love you so much," she whispered, her voice breaking as tears slipped down her cheeks. Tate's arms tightened around her, and they stayed like that, holding each other.

"I love you, Sunshine," Tate whispered. He buried his face in her hair, and tears spilled down his cheeks as he clung to her, holding her so tightly he was almost afraid to let go.

Sunshine pulled back slightly, her gaze meeting his, taking in the familiar depths of his beautiful eyes. With a quiet breath, Tate leaned down, and their lips met in a kiss. Everything they went through faded into the background as they held each other, grateful to be in each other's arms once more. Forever.